An Anthology of East African Short Stories

EDITED BY

VALERIE KIBERA

Longman

In loving memory of my father Francis D'Cruz

Longman Group UK Limited,
Longman House, Burnt Mill, Harlow,
Essex CM20 2JE, England
and Associated Companies throughout the world

This edition © Longman Group UK Limited 1988
All rights reserved. No part of this publication
may be reproduced, stored in a retrieval system, or transmitted in any form
or by any means, electronic, mechanical, photocopying, recording, or
otherwise, without the prior written permission of the Publishers.

First published 1988
Second impression 1992

Set 10/12 pt Palatino
Printed in Kenya under licence for Longman Kenya Ltd., P.O.Box 18033, Nairobi.
by Acme Press (Kenya) Ltd., P.O.Box 40497, Nairobi, Kenya.

ISBN 0 582 89524 3

Contents

Preface	*v*
Acknowledgements	*vii*
Introduction	*1*
Karoki Jonathan Kariara	*21*
Who Am I? Bernard Mbui Wagacha	*31*
The Battle of the Sacred Tree Barbara Kimenye	*42*
It's a Dog's Share in Our Kinshasa Leonard Kibera	*55*
The Road to Mara Tom Chacha	*61*
The Return Ngugi wa Thiong'o	*70*
Kingi Sadrudin Kassam	*78*
Tekayo Grace Ogot	*85*
Departure at Dawn Samuel Kahiga	*99*
Moneyman Peter Nazareth	*116*
We Are Going Home Paul Ngige Njoroge	*122*
The Town Eneriko Seruma	*132*
Transition Peter John Bosco	*137*
A Mercedes Funeral Ngugi wa Thiong'o	*151*
Incident in the Park Meja Mwangi	*177*
Her Only Child T.S. Luzuka	*187*
A Kind of Fighting Jotham Mchombu	*192*
The Spider's Web Leonard Kibera	*199*
General Exercises	*211*
Further Reading	*214*

Preface

The stories in this collection come from a limited period, the decade between the mid-1960s and the mid-1970s. After that, for a variety of reasons, a 'literary drought' descended on East Africa and, with the demise of publications such as *Zuka*, *Ghala*, *Transition* and the university magazines, scarcely any substantial short stories have since appeared.

Individual East African authors have published collections of their short stories but we lack an anthology of the work of a variety of short-story writers from this region. This collection brings together stories by a number of our writers: some are by established writers like Ngugi wa Thiong'o, Leonard Kibera, Grace Ogot and Meja Mwangi; others, by less well-known writers, have been culled from periodicals which have long since ceased publication.

This anthology has been prepared especially for students studying literature in upper secondary schools, colleges and universities in East Africa. However, the editor hopes that it will not be confined to the classroom and lecture hall but will afford pleasure and interest to the general reader as well.

V.K.

Acknowledgements

We are grateful to the following copyright holders for permission to reproduce short stories:

East African Publishing House Ltd for 'Who Am I?' by Bernard Mbui Wagacha, 'Her Only Child' by T.S. Luzaka from *East Africa Journal* Jan. 1970, pp. 30–34, 11–12, 'Kingi' by Sadrudin Kassam from *East Africa Journal* Sept. 1966 pp. 3–5, 'It's a Dog's Share in our Kinshasa' and 'The Spider's Web' by Leonard Kibera, 'Departure at Dawn' by Samuel Kahiga all from *Potent Ash* (1968) pp. 16–20, 134–46, 80–99, 'Tekayo' by Grace Ogot from *Land Without Thunder* (1968) pp. 47–61, 'The Town' by Eneriko Seruma from *The Heart Seller* (1971) pp. 14–18; Heinemann Educational Books Ltd for 'The Return' and 'A Mercedes Funeral' by Ngugi wa Thiong'o from *Secret Lives* (1975); the Author, Mr. J. Kariara for his 'Karoki'; the Author, Professor Peter Nazareth for his 'Moneyman' originally published in *Zuka*; the Author, Paul Ngige Njoroge for his 'We are Going Home'.

We have unfortunately been unable to trace the copyright holders of 'Transition' by Peter John Bosco, 'A Kind of Fighting' by Jotham Mchombu, 'The Road to Mara' by Tom Chacha, 'The Battle of the Sacred Tree' by Barbara Kimenye and 'Incident in the Park' by Meja Mwangi and would appreciate any information that would enable us to do so.

Introduction

EAST AFRICAN LITERATURE:
A FRUITFUL DECADE

The stories in this collection represent some of the best work of a very productive time for creative writing in East Africa. It was during this period, which spanned the decade from the mid-1960s to the mid-1970s, that the work of our poets and short story writers first blossomed in national periodicals like *Zuka*, *Ghala* and *Transition* and in college magazines like *Darlite*, *Nexus* and *Penpoint*, later renamed *Umma*, *Busara* and *Dhana*. As one would expect, much mediocre work also emerged from this period of intense literary activity. Publishers were eager for anything 'African'; consequently a good deal of poor material, soon to be forgotten, was published.

However, amid the work produced was a quantity of good literature – stories, plays, poems and novels – which we now consider the beginnings of written East African literature in English. The novels included Ngugi wa Thiong'o's *Weep Not, Child* (1964), *The River Between* (1965) and *A Grain of Wheat* (1966); Robert Serumaga's *Return to the Shadows* (1969); Leonard Kibera's *Voices in the Dark* (1970); and Meja Mwangi's *Going Down River Road* (1976).

There was poetry by Okot p'Bitek (*Song of Lawino*, 1966; *Song of Ocol*, 1970; *Song of Prisoner* and *Song of Malaya*, 1971), Okello Oculi (*Orphan*, 1968), Jared Angira (*Juices*, 1970; *Soft Corals*, 1973) and Richard Ntiru (*Tensions*, 1971). There were anthologies of East African poetry (*Drum Beat* edited by Lennard Okola, 1967; *Poems from East Africa* edited by David Cook and David Rubadiri,

1971). A good deal of fine poetry was also featured in local literary magazines.

This was an exciting time for drama too. A cluster of interesting plays was published: Ibrahim Hussein's *Kinjekitile* (1970); Robert Serumaga's *A Play* (1967), *The Elephants* (1971) and *Majangwa* (1974); John Ruganda's *The Burdens* (1972); Kenneth Watene's *Dedan Kimathi* (1974); Ngugi wa Thiong'o and Micere Mugo's *The Trial of Dedan Kimathi* (1976); and Francis Imbuga's *Betrayal in the City* (1976). In addition, all through this period many unpublished plays in both English and Kiswahili were performed in schools, colleges, universities and at drama festivals.

This decade also gave birth to a rich collection of short stories. Among the earliest to be published were Barbara Kimenye's *Kalasanda* (1965) and *Kalasanda Revisited* (1966); Leonard Kibera and Samuel Kahiga's *Potent Ash* came out in the same year as Grace Ogot's *Land Without Thunder* (1968). Henry S. Kimbugwe, using the pen name Eneriko Seruma, published *The Heart Seller* (1971) and Ngugi wa Thiong'o published *Secret Lives* (1975). David Cook edited an anthology of student writing from Makerere (*Origin East Africa*, 1965) which included short stories, poems and short plays. Some of the stories in these collections first appeared in *Zuka, Ghala* or *Transition* and in the university magazines.

Another manifestation of the general interest in cultural and artistic matters were the debates engaged in by some of the liveliest minds in East Africa. They sought to answer questions like: What purpose does art serve? What should be the role of the East African writer in national life and development? Is there such a thing as 'African literature', or quite distinct national literatures from various countries in Africa? How can the artistic heritage of the African past be reclaimed and given living form in current imaginative literature? Should not Kiswahili be the region's sole national language? Can we validly talk of an African literature written in non-African (French, English, Portuguese) languages?

THE EMERGENCE OF WRITTEN EAST AFRICAN LITERATURE IN ENGLISH: HISTORICAL BACKGROUND

All the creative productivity mentioned above gained its initial impulse from the political changes then sweeping across East Africa and indeed the whole continent. At the beginning of the 1960s most of Africa was in the process of shedding its colonial yoke. The three East African territories, Kenya, Uganda and Tanzania, were poised on the brink of independence. Those were heady times characterized by mass participation in political activity of all kinds: strikes, demonstrations and constitutional conferences to decide on the process of handing over power to representative African governments. Most memorable were the mammoth rallies at which politicians gained the people's support by making inflated promises for the future, promises, which for the most part, they could not or would not ever fulfil.

'*Uhuru*! Freedom!' It was this expectation that set people's dreams and aspirations soaring and released the creative gifts of our literary artists.

Our writers, like most East Africans, were jubilant at the prospect of independence, but they responded cautiously and reflectively. They explored the past nostalgically, cast an ambivalent eye on the present and prophesied where the future seemed likely to lead. They found their societies riddled with problems that would have to be resolved if freedom was to be more than 'flag independence'. These problems hinged on the socio-economic, political and spiritual changes colonialism had brought about in our communities and in individual minds, and on the legacy of continued dependence colonialism was to leave to our new nations.

We can identify several thematic strands in East African writing which, like most modern African literature, started off in reaction to the colonial experience and its aftermath. Firstly, our writers were concerned with their past. The colonizers justified the imposition of their rule and social institutions by asserting that their new way of life was progressive and civilized. Contemptuously they dismissed local beliefs, customs and social organization as primitive and barbarous. Accordingly, our writers, historians, theologians and other scholars made it their first task to 'rehabilitate' their demeaned past, to recognize its particular flaws and strengths, to determine what was worthwhile in that traditional world and how it could be given a place and purpose in the present. They believed it was only possible to understand the present or plot the future by locating where, in the evocative words of an Ibo proverb, 'the rain began to beat us'.[1]

Much of the literary response was, understandably, sentimental and self-righteous. This is clearly seen in works like Okot's *Song of Lawino*, Kibera's 'Letter to the Haunting Past' (in *Potent Ash*) and in those sections dealing with Kenya's history in Ngugi's *Petals of Blood*. But elsewhere ('Tekayo' by Grace Ogot and Ngugi's *The River Between* are representative examples) writers were able to depict traditional life in a balanced, realistic manner.

A related theme in East African literature concerns the disruption caused to the old mode of existence by colonialism. Christianity, commerce, western education, technology, medicine: all these, for better or worse, led individuals up bewildering new paths. The violent meeting of the two cultures created tension not only between colonizer and colonized but also within and between individuals, families, clans and tribes. The old communitarian societies gradually declined, giving way, especially in the new urban centres, to a more aggressive, individualistic type of society. The result was a culture of transition, possessing few stable values and little continuity, which bred feelings of anxiety and rootlessness in the individual.

The loss of identity is a central theme in East African writing and for a good reason. During colonial times and later, most young, educated people experienced a split in their emotional lives. They had been born and reared in the rural areas where, despite the incursion of alien ways, traditional life still held sway. Then, at a tender age, the brightest (some would say the most impressionable) were sent to mission or government boarding schools and later to universities abroad. Within themselves these young men and women experienced a crisis of identity: *who* were they, these curious cultural hybrids who felt at home nowhere? The writers gave prominence to this issue precisely because they themselves were at the cutting edge of the dilemma caused by the clash of cultures.

This theme is of central importance in early East African writing: in non-fiction like Mugo Gatheru's aptly titled autobiography *A Child of Two Worlds*; and in fiction like Ngugi's *The River Between*, Kariara's 'Karoki', Wagacha's 'Who Am I?'. It is also a major theme of early East African poetry including, most forcefully, Okot's *Song of Lawino* and *Song of Ocol*.

A third thematic strand in East African writing deals with the freedom struggle. The fact that the struggle was most violent in Kenya with its large settler population is reflected in Kenyan writing. The Mau Mau rebellion of the early 1950s tore apart the Gikuyu people in suffering and bloodshed. Much of Ngugi's fiction and many of the stories in *Potent Ash* deal with this terrible period in Kenya's history.

The final major theme in East African writing concerns the post-colonial era in which we live. Again, it was writers who most eloquently voiced the disillusionment that descended on Africa's peoples. Despite some gains, it became generally recognized that the political-economic structures of colonial times had remained largely intact in independent Africa. East Africans, like their brothers and sisters all over the continent, suffered under a heavy burden of evils: civil war, military dictatorship, political repression, detention without trial, widespread corruption, poor economic planning, declining food production and an unhealthy dependence on the former colonial countries.

Our writers expressed the outrage, pessimism and betrayed hopes of their generation. Their subject matter encompasses the grim realities of present-day African experience: the monstrous gulf between a small monied élite and the vast majority, poor and powerless; the injustice, greed, ineptitude, indifference, hypocrisy and crass vulgarity of the *nouveaux riches*; the deprived, despairing lives of the urban and rural dispossessed; the sharp contrast between the glittering new cities with their plush hotels, boutiques, banks, hospitals and schools and, on the other hand, the hinterland squeezed dry of both its human and natural resources.

These depressing facts are tackled boldly in literary works such as Ngugi's later short stories, in his novels *Petals of Blood* and *Devil on the Cross*; in Kibera's *Voices in the Dark*; in Okot's *Song of Prisoner* and in some of the stories in the present collection.

This, then, is the general historical and socio-political background against which we need to read the literature that emerged from East Africa in the 1960s and 1970s, including the stories in this anthology.

THE SHORT STORY:
A POPULAR EAST AFRICAN LITERARY FORM

The short story features prominently in East African literature. Within its restricted compass it records, probes, assesses and comments on the issues besetting our societies. But why has this form been so popular with readers and writers in our region? There are several reasons.

First, the short-story writer has certain advantages over the novelist and playwright. He is able to communicate with the audience more readily and immediately than can the novelist. The briefer form of the short story allows the writer the opportunity to publish work in inexpensive, regularly-published magazines and journals which feature a variety of other reading matter and draw their readers from a wide literate public. In the 1960s and early 1970s short stories were accessible to this readership in the pages of stimulating publications such as *Transition, Zuka, East Africa Journal* and the university magazines.

Second, whereas reading a novel requires several sessions lasting days or even weeks, the majority of short stories can be taken in at a single sitting; in fact this can be regarded as a necessary feature of the short story. Unlike the staged play which demands one's presence at a particular time and place, one can read the short story anywhere and at one's own convenience.

A third compelling reason for the local popularity of the short story is that it is not a totally alien form in our region, as, for example, the novel is. The latter originated and developed in Europe in response to changing socio-economic conditions. Though it was readily accepted as a working form by our own writers, it lacks any real counterpart in pre-literate Africa. Not so the short story; like poetry and drama, the modern East African short story has links with our oral literature, the story-telling tradition being an important one in African communities for purposes of entertainment and education.

There is a major difference between the modern short story and the traditional folktale. The former, to qualify as such, must generally be realistic, anchored in what is actually possible in real life. Tales, despite their basis in human experience and behaviour, do usually have as important elements the fantastic and supernatural: animal characters, giants, ogres, etc.

The short story is the form many of our major writers chose to start with. Ngugi and Kibera, Seruma and Ogot began their literary careers in this more 'manageable' form before moving on to their first novels. It was as if they were testing their control and confidence, honing their skills within the more restricted scope of the short story before attempting more ambitious literary works.

It is interesting to note that some of the earlier short stories of a couple of these writers would later find a place in one or more of their novels. Ngugi's Joshua in 'The Village Priest' later re-appears as one of the leading characters in *The River Between*; the plight of Kamau in 'The Return' forcibly reminds us of Gikonyo's return from detention in *A Grain of Wheat*. Kibera's '1954' is echoed in sections of *Voices in the Dark*.

A GUIDE TO THE STUDY OF THE SHORT STORY

In order to appreciate fully a short story we need to know what it is, how it 'works', its characteristic features. The short story is not just a briefer novel; it calls for a certain set of skills from the writer no less than it requires a certain kind of response from the reader. So, in a general way, we shall now examine the short story as a literary form.

No brief definition can neatly encapsulate the short story. There is much diversity: in length, theme, style and structure. Short stories vary in length from as few as three pages to as many as thirty or more. Their themes are as various as life itself. Some are narrated in a straightforward style, others are thick with flashbacks. Most emphasize character and situation, a few are intent on creating mood and atmosphere.

Despite this variety, however, we can usefully distinguish some of the more common features of the short story.

CHARACTERISTICS OF THE SHORT STORY

Length

The most obvious feature of the short story is, of course, its brevity which to a large extent dictates its plot, time-span and the number of characters it can deal with.[2] The stories in this collection range from three pages ('Her Only Child') to twenty-one ('A Mercedes Funeral').

Characters

The short story presents a little drama of life. It highlights one small but significant part of a character's existence, a single incident or perception from which comes insight and revelation.

The writer has limited space and time in which he must create credible characters. The central characters are not shown to be developing and maturing which is what we expect in a novel. The cast of characters is limited in number; there are two or three and, most often, just one main character. Each detail or happening and all the other subsidiary characters are there for the sole purpose of bringing the central character into sharper focus, to reveal to the reader this person's thoughts, motives, feelings, experiences.

In 'Karoki', for example, the main emphasis is on a pathetic, middle-aged, mission-school teacher. The author explores Karoki's frustrated aspirations and in so doing helps explain his increasingly strange behaviour and tragic end. In 'The Road to Mara' we follow a young woman's hopeful journey from her country home to the town in search of her deceitful lover. 'A Mercedes Funeral' and 'Tekayo' each covers a longer period of time and sketches in a whole range of characters. Yet, even in these stories, it is the life and destiny of Wahinya and Tekayo which grasp the writer's and reader's interest.

Plot

This refers to the way the author selects and arranges the various happenings that form the basis of the story. Generally, the short story's scope is too brief to allow of too complex a plot or of more than a single major plot. The focus is upon a particular situation rather than on a chain of events.

> *Normally the story falls into a more or less recognizable shape. First comes the* exposition *or* opening situation *in which a basis is laid for the story as it affects the central character. The initial situation develops by means of* complications: *those events that have an effect upon the central character so as to make life more difficult for him. The train of difficulties eventually reaches a* crisis *or turning point in the story. In the crisis the central character can no longer escape from the pressure of events and has to face up to the problem, to come to some kind of decision about it. The decision made is important in the character's life, for by dealing with the problem the character undergoes an experience that changes his pattern of living. The new pattern is shown in the* dénouement.[3]

There are, of course, exceptions to every rule; not all stories are narrated in so linear a fashion. In this collection, for example, a story like 'Who Am I?' uses the flashback technique to intertwine past and present time.

In the passage quoted above regarding the usual 'pattern' of a story, we are given a clue to an important aspect of plot: to be of interest, the plot of a story (or novel or play) must contain *tension*, some conflict within the main character or between him and his environment, whether other individuals or the society at large. It is important that the events that occur and the perceptions of the central character should change him in some significant way; if there is no change, then it is not a short story but a sketch.

The chief character in 'Tekayo' or 'The Return', the mob in 'It's a Dog's Share in Our Kinshasa' undergo changes that are immediate and dramatic. In other stories in this collection, in 'Transition', 'Who Am I?' or 'We Are Going Home', the change that occurs is quieter, more understated but nevertheless as decisive in the lives of the characters concerned.

Background

Every human being inhabits a particular social environment which, to a greater or lesser degree, makes the person what he is. So background or setting are not just included for 'padding' but are important in helping us to understand and 'place' a character: the family, clan or village from which he comes, his status within these groups, his beliefs, economic or education level, etc.

The central character might be in harmony with his social setting but is more often uncomfortable within or in rebellion against it. In 'Transition', for example, the father rebels against the *ujamaa* policy taking hold in his village while his son supports it; this causes serious conflict between the father on the one hand and his son and the community on the other.

The background might not play a very crucial role in the story; it might just be sketchily described only in order for the reader to place the characters in their social setting. But the writer can use background to help *explain* a character's motives, actions and desires. In 'A Mercedes Funeral' we are made to appreciate Wahinya's aspirations and eventual fate very much in the context of present-day material values in Kenyan society.

Occasionally the background assumes the importance of a 'character' in the story as happens in Mwangi's 'Incident in the Park'. Here the setting is described in minute detail: the modern city, parliament and government buildings surround the park in which takes place the disastrous confrontation between city council *askaris* and the unlicensed fruit hawker. It is as though the author is implicating a whole society, its central institutions and dominating values, in the eventual destruction of the hawker.

Theme

The controlling idea of a story is its theme. A novel, because of its length, can tackle several main themes, but the brevity of the short story usually allows it to concentrate on just a single theme.

East African short stories are generally based on one of a cluster of themes which reflect our historical experience: the clash of cultures ('Who Am I?', 'Karoki'); the colonial period; the complex ways in which the freedom struggle shattered people's lives ('The Return', 'A Kind of Fighting', 'Departure at Dawn'); the post-colonial period characterized by various evils that maim and destroy human beings; for our writers, our growing cities and towns have become the epitome of heartlessness and oppression ('Incident in the Park', 'The Town', 'We Are Going Home', 'The Spider's Web').

Other stories in this collection have less of a social, more of an individually personal flavour; there is 'Kingi' in which a child from a 'respectable' home fantasizes about an eccentric, faintly disreputable old musician; 'Her Only Child' describes the ghastly tragedy that befalls the beloved child of a doting mother; 'Moneyman' is a comic account of a miser's experiences; the greed of the main character in 'Tekayo' transforms him in a chillingly bizarre way.

Time-span

The period of time covered in a short story is usually limited. This concentration allows the writer to create a dramatic impact within the circumscribed space and time allowed. The writer does not attempt to examine the whole lifetime of a character; rather, he focuses on one revealing moment of crisis in a character's life.

'Incident in the Park' is set in one particular lunch hour; 'Kingi', like 'It's a Dog's Share in Our Kinshasa', covers a few hours of one day; 'Who Am I?' stretches through a single night fusing together a man's present circumstances with his reflections and dreams of his past. Other stories span a longer stretch of time ('A Mercedes Funeral', 'Moneyman', 'We Are Going Home', 'The Spider's Web'). The past in these stories is recalled and summarized as a prelude to, or an explanation of, the characters' current predicament.

MAJOR STRUCTURAL AND STYLISTIC FEATURES OF THE SHORT STORY FORM

Thus far we have discussed *content* in the short story: the writer's subject matter, ideas and themes. There are two other crucial and closely-related components in all imaginative literature: *structure* and *style*.

Structure refers to the particular way a writer shapes his material into a story so that it will make a significant statement about human life. Style concerns each writer's distinctive handling of the resources of the language used to make his story meaningful and memorable. Content, structure and style all contribute to the creation of a satisfying work of prose fiction. It is through our appreciation of them that we are able to determine what is termed a writer's 'vision', that is his feelings and beliefs about human existence in his time and society. Our attention to both content and style alerts us to where the writer is directing our sympathy, to what or whom he is calling into question.

Structure

Because style and structure are an integral part of all literature, we need to be acquainted with some of their more important components. First we shall look at two elements of structure: *narrative* and *'point of view'*.

Ordinary life is fragmented, chaotic, a buzzing multitude of events; people and ideas clamour for our attention. Through narrative, the method chosen to tell a story, the writer *organizes* his material in a particular way. He creates order out of disharmony by selecting and arranging details so that they reveal to us something significant about human life.

As we have already remarked, a story usually has a pattern: a beginning, a middle and an end. The beginning indicates the situation the protagonist finds himself in. The middle section involves the working out of the character's hopes or the consequences of his actions. The ending or *dénouement* provides a solution, of one kind or another, to the character's dilemma; at this point the protagonist (and reader) arrive at a new level of understanding.

Not all stories have a well-defined beginning, middle and end. In some the writer plunges us dramatically into the middle of the action (as in 'The Spider's Web'); in others we have the intertwining of past and present time ('Who Am I?').

In a short story the writer has no time to waste; the reader must be drawn into the plot very quickly and presented with the problem that has to be confronted and solved. Accordingly, the opening paragraph, or even the very first sentence (as can be seen in many of the stories in this collection), whets our appetite for what is to follow besides offering an accurate clue as to how good and interesting the story is likely to be.

Similarly with endings: to create an impact and to force us to become alertly involved, the short story writer often uses shock tactics such as an unexpected ending or a surprising twist of plot; or he might leave us with no cut-and-dried solution to his protagonist's situation thus encouraging the reader to speculate on a possible conclusion based on what has gone before. What, for example, is the likely fate of Bena in 'The Road to Mara' or of Nalwoga in 'Her Only Child'?

A second vital element of structure relates to 'point of view' which concerns the particular *angle* from which the writer chooses to relate the story. He can select from several options.

One way is to tell the story in the first person singular (I, me, my, mine) as is done in 'It's a Dog's Share in Our Kinshasa' and 'Who Am I?' The first person narrator creates an intimate, plausible relationship between himself and the reader. We have, ostensibly, an individual relating a personal story, what happened, how he reacted and felt. Quite naturally, we identify with the narrator in the same way we would in real life with a friend telling us about something significant that has happened to him.

A less usual narrative method involves the writer recording what he has supposedly overheard or been told by someone who experienced the events being related. This narrative technique we term 'a story within a story'. We have an example in this collection in 'A Mercedes Funeral'; here the writer begins by explaining that he is merely setting down a story he heard told in a bar.

The most common narrative method involves using what is called 'the omniscient narrator'. Here the writer employs the third person mode (he, she, they) and is, like God, 'omniscient', aware of all that happens to his characters including their most intimate thoughts, their most secret fears and desires. The majority of stories in this book belong to this category of third person narration.

Style

Next we shall discuss some aspects of style. How a writer uses *language* is of central importance in literature. This is because language is the 'raw material' which the writer 'processes' (manipulates in his own unique fashion) to create an 'end product' (the finished work of literary art whether poem, play, short story or novel).

The competent and gifted writer devotes particular care to how he handles language, knowing that this will have a direct bearing on how fine the story is, how successfully it will communicate his ideas and feelings to the reader. The reader in turn, if he is to reap maximum benefit from his reading, needs to respond sensitively not just to what the writer says but to *how* it is being said.

We must ask questions about how and to what purpose the writer uses language. For example, do the characters 'ring true', that is do they speak and behave in a manner consistent with who they are (their age, social status, temperament, situation, etc)? Is the language the characters use, or the language used to describe them, appropriate? Notice how in 'Kingi' the short sentences reflect the child's naive, uncomplicated consciousness. In 'We Are Going Home', however, the more involved sentence structure accurately enacts the adult tussling with guilt and unsuccessfully trying to rationalize it away.

A story that consisted entirely or almost entirely of description and reported speech would make tedious reading. It is *dialogue*, direct verbal encounters between characters, which creates the drama that is at the heart of a good story. Through a character's words we are able to appraise his mood, the kind of person he is. Dialogue reveals the protagonist to us, acquaints us with the landscape of his inner life, allows us to understand him intimately. Dialogue also conveys the views of other characters in the story about the central character. In this way the latter is seen from several different points of view, which add up to a complex, many-sided portrait.

Another significant aspect of a writer's style has to do with his use of *image* and *symbol*. Our interpretation of a particular symbol depends on the *literary context* in which it is embedded. Symbols can have different meanings, even contradictory ones, in different contexts. Rain or blood or fire could be regarded as life-giving in one instance, life-threatening in another. The *cultural context* is equally important in deciding a symbol's meaning. For example, in one cultural group the colours white and red may denote death and mourning respectively, in another life and victory.

Why do writers use symbols? Because through them they are able to convey significance of desired kinds. The writer is spared having to *tell* us everything. Symbols have accumulated widely accepted meanings around themselves through the ages which means they have a certain generally understood significance. By using them the writer conveys meaning in a poetically economical form.

Symbols also bring a rich complexity to a piece of imaginative writing because they can be interpreted on several different levels at once. Take for instance the title symbol in Kibera's 'The Spider's Web'; this image works throughout the story to make us feel very strongly how the central character, Ngotho, himself feels: trapped, caught in a web of circumstances which limits his freedom. The other recurring images in the story – coffins, nightmares, knives, blood – are equally menacing and reinforce the central symbol. In this story the imagery itself tells us a lot about the destructive *social* situation in which Ngotho is caught up. But the web image *suggests* another latent possibility, one unrealized in the story itself with its class conflicts and social snobbery, but held out by the writer as an *alternative* social reality: we are reminded of the web of social interdependencies, bonds and human solidarity which Ngotho himself once dreamed of when political independence was imminent.

The road is another very common literary symbol. In different contexts it signals different meanings. It may stand for the freedom of 'the open road', or, as is the case in 'The Road to Mara', for a diminution of freedom: Bena leaves her rural home to follow to the city the man who has promised to marry her; only when she arrives at her destination does she discover he is a married man and that she is stranded.

Another opposed pair of symbols which feature prominently in this collection of stories is the town and the country. Usually the town stands for rootlessness, anonymity, a lack of human caring and oppression, as we see in stories like 'The Town', 'The Road to Mara' and 'Incident in the Park'. Conversely, the rural village connotes warm human relationships where each individual has an assigned place and worth. But we should not imagine that even these rather stereotyped symbols are watertight in what they signify. As Barbara Kimenye in 'The Battle of the Sacred Tree' humorously reveals, village life is not *all* sweetness and light.

Animal imagery is yet another common device used by writers when they wish to underscore the negative aspects of human beings: their 'beastly' qualities like ferocity, cunning, predatoriness. Mwangi in 'Incident in the Park' elaborately draws out the image of the big fish preying on the little ones in the park pond; this, as applied to its human characters, is very much the story's theme. In 'It's a Dog's Share in Our Kinshasa' Kibera, by using reiterated animal images, emphasizes the blood-lust of the snarling mob gathered to watch a public execution.

In everyday life we almost unconsciously try to gauge the temperament, mood and attitude of the person with whom we are engaged in conversation by watching his gestures, the expression in the eyes, the tone of voice, etc. Something similar is required of us in reading imaginative literature. To appreciate fully a short story, we must be able to 'identify' the writer's *tone*. We can do so by accurately assessing his verbal signals, that is by the way he uses words, images and allusions.

We have already discussed the use and purpose of symbols and imagery. Two other common devices used by writers are *irony* and *satire*. Though these terms are closely associated and though their effects are broadly similar, there is a subtle difference between them.

In irony a contrast is made between the real and the apparent, between what we expect in a situation and what actually happens. 'Tekayo' is a fine example of a story which is permeated by irony. We *expect* Tekayo the grandfather to protect his grandchildren; *in fact* he preys on them. As the savage craving gradually overwhelms his moral sense, Tekayo progressively cuts himself off from all human and social ties. Ironically he projects his own guilt on to his elderly first wife Lakech, as the following exchange shows:

> [Lakech] *therefore went and asked him, 'Man, what ails you?'*
> *Tekayo looked at Lakech, but he could not look into her eyes. He looked at her long neck, and instead of answering her question he asked her, 'Would you like to get free from those heavy brass rings around your neck?'*
> *'Why?' Lakech replied, surprised.*
> *'Because they look so tight.'* (p. 90)

It is Tekayo himself, of course, who feels a prisoner of the 'maddening craving that was tearing his body to pieces'. (p. 90)

Later, as he kills one child, then another, the irony becomes overt. His relations and clansmen wonder. 'Which animal can it be?' (p. 92) that is terrorizing their village. Tekayo's son even suggests his aged father might be in danger from this ferocious beast. When Tekayo is finally found out, he is treated like the animal he has become; he is locked in a 'windowless hut built for goats and sheep'. The villagers disown him before killing him: 'Kill him. He is not one of us. He is not one of us. He is an animal.' (p. 93, p. 95)

While irony works with subtlety, sharp and delicate, satire registers its point in a heartier manner. The satirist uses language and ideas to ridicule a person, idea, institution or system. He signals to the reader that the object of attack is to be regarded with amusement or contempt, anger or scorn.

In this collection, satire of varying degrees of intensity operates in 'The Battle of the Sacred Tree', 'Moneyman', 'The Mercedes Funeral' and in both the Kibera stories. In a story like Kimenye's or Nazareth's, the satirical humour is indulgent, almost affectionate; in Ngugi's or Kibera's stories the satire is scathing, intended to expose and ridicule the pretentious, the greedy, the unjust and the hypocritical. Satire is a wonderful weapon against the vices and folly of human beings and our writers have used it to marvellous effect especially in the short story.

In this Introduction we have made a basic survey of the short story in an East African context – the background from which it emerged and its thematic and stylistic features. The purpose of the guidelines provided, and of the exercises which follow each story, is to help make you more alert to various elements of theme and style, and to enable you to enjoy and understand the short story as a form generally and those in this collection more particularly.

These guidelines are not a checklist to tick off as you read a story. There is no magical formula which can be applied mechanically to your critical appreciation of all short stories. Studying a short story is not like a fishing expedition during which you will hook out examples of irony or symbolism or the writer's 'message'. The study of a short story merely for the purpose of dissection is a sterile exercise. Depending on the story and on the author's intentions, you will be expected to vary your own approach and the questions you ask. Your own preferences, values, experience and previous reading will all contribute to your enjoyment and interpretation of a given story.

Far too many students in schools, colleges and universities are very uncertain about their own evaluation of what they read, of their critical responses to literature. They lack confidence in expressing their views and feelings about the poems, novels and plays they study. They are over-dependent on teachers and lecturers, critics and study guides. Perhaps this is partly the result of uninspired teaching and an education system that overvalues passivity and examination grades. But no writer produces a poem or play or novel just to enable a student to pass an examination!

So, you may well ask, how can one 'tell' a good short story from an indifferent one? Gradually, the more you read, carefully and intelligently, the more discriminating you will become in your response to fiction. You will begin to distinguish between a fine story and a poor one. You will realize that most of the short stories in women's magazines, for example, are spurious. They are full of clichés and unlikely coincidences. Everything always comes out right in the end. The protagonist is superficially portrayed, from the outside. Characters change in sudden, implausible ways. The language, characters and plot are stereotyped, forced to work within a straitjacket of stock conventions. 'Popular' fiction of this kind is escapist, intended to lull the reader, to kill an hour on a dull Saturday afternoon.

The serious writer, on the other hand, attempts an honest explanation of his world. His work is intended not to reassure but to disturb us, to subvert the narrowness of our sympathies and cherished ideas. As Franz Kafka, a novelist and short story writer himself, once observed, literature should function like an axe to break the frozen sea inside us. Of central importance to good literature is how the writer 'stretches' language, uses it in new and surprising ways to explore and tussle with the problems of human existence.

It is therefore necessary for the discriminating reader to evaluate and judge, to ask questions like: Is this a good story, sensitive to the nuances of language and an honest exploration of life? Or does it falsify, distort and sentimentalize? Does the writer honour his characters' integrity, or does he demean or oversimplify their human complexity?

The exercises which follow each story in this anthology will help you look deeper into the story, to appreciate various aspects of its content and style. They will also help you develop your critical vocabulary, a necessity when you want to explain why one story might have left you cold while you consider another interesting, lively, and well-written.

There are no correct answers, in the way a mathematical solution can be either right or wrong. Different students will construct their answers differently. But two features *are* important. Firstly, that the answers should be your own *personal* response to the story in question and be backed up by evidence from the story. And, secondly, that your reactions be *shared*. The writing and reading of a literary work is an individual activity but our appraisal of it is, in the last analysis, a social one: do you see this situation, character or symbol as I see it? Do you agree with me this is an excellent (or mediocre or poor) short story and for these reasons? The resulting give-and-take is illuminating. It helps clarify our own ideas and evaluation of what we read.

NOTES

[1] *Quoted by the Nigerian novelist Chinua Achebe in his paper 'The Role of the Writer in a New Nation', in* African Writers on African Writing *ed. G.D. Killam (Heinemann, 1973) p. 8.*

[2] *We need to distinguish between 'a long short story' such as 'A Mercedes Funeral' and a novella, like Alex La Guma's* A Walk in the Night, *which is usually a good deal longer.*

[3] Tensions *Robert Millar (Heinemann, 1975) p. 21.*

Karoki

JONATHAN KARIARA
(KENYA)

HE WAS LOSING his teeth. His two front ones had grown alarmingly long of late, narrowing down almost to a point where they emerged from the pale gum. Now one had dropped off; the other, still standing, distorted the face slightly to the left. Looking at him you felt as if he had received a vicious slap across the left cheek, a terrible slap which had made him wince, contracting his facial muscles to one side; and that somehow the face had not relaxed from the blow.

In his forty-fifth year Karoki was growing old. He minded growing old, terribly. It wasn't that he was vain, no. But he needed his youth, his good looks, to protect him. In the mission school where he taught they kept a close eye on everyone. They whispered. They set themselves at vantage points, to watch. They waited to pounce.

He had come to the mission a young, proud boy. He had received his education 'standing,' as the villagers said. He had said their prayers, repeated their alphabet, worn their new clothes. But his eyes had stood above it all, proud and untamed.

A subtle battle of wills had developed between Karoki and the head of the teacher training college, Mr Bovitt. After his teacher training he had wanted to be posted at Karigiri school in his own village ten miles from Turu Mission, on the other side of the Thagana River. But the principal of the training college had refused, had insisted they wanted him at the demonstration school attached to the college. He had been teaching at the same school for the last twenty years, slowly getting out-dated in his methods. Why did the mission refuse to let him go to his home village? Of late the desire to get away from the mission, from this demonstration school, had gripped him tightly across his chest, waking or sleeping. But the mission still insisted he had to remain.

Then one day he had noticed his hair was thinning. The same day he sat down and wrote a letter of resignation, packed his things and went back to Karigiri. The mission had not responded in any way to this letter. They waited. After two months at home with his old mother Karoki grew tired of waiting to hear whether he had been sacked. He packed his suitcase and went back to Turu. He opened his front door, unpacked his things and reported to school as if nothing had happened. The principal's wife, who had taken over his class in his absence, had simply said when she saw him, 'We expected you back. Here are the keys.' She had walked out of the class. Did he see a sly smile on her face, as she turned to close the door behind her?

That was five years ago. This particular morning he walked towards his class slowly. He had lately developed the habit of missing morning assembly, which had set the whole school, both teachers and pupils, on the alert. He steadied himself at the door of his class, battling with the nausea which was welling up in his throat. He had been drinking for ten years now, in secret. But he enjoyed it. It was the one freedom he took at the mission, for he had been certain they would never catch him. Let them talk about it, but they could never point their fingers at him. He knew the signs they looked for. The slightly soiled collar of the shirt. The tie with a permanent knot, which was flung over the head each morning like a noose, and grew shiny where the knot rubbed the chin. The socks riddled with holes. The shoddy respectability of a small primary school teacher who has gone to seed. He knew the signs, and avoided them. In his dress he had changed very little from his teacher training days. His short-sleeved shirts were light blue, of a heavy cotton material. His khaki trousers were always freshly ironed and the black shoes shone in any weather. He hardly ever wore a coat, and his ties, dark blue cotton ones, still suggested the young trainee teacher.

He stood outside the door, wondering whether to go in. For once he was afraid of facing his class. He was particularly afraid of facing Wahome, a boy of fifteen who had recently transferred from another school to his class. Wahome was becoming a threat. The boy looked at Karoki as if he *knew* him. Normally he was a lively boy, but when he spoke to Karoki, he became subdued, and the way he talked to him suggested that they were speaking man to man. Sometimes Karoki would shout to call him from a group of playing boys, to see how the boy responded to his voice. He wanted to find out if this boy was making a pact with him, a pact of mutual understanding and sympathy, before he destroyed him.

Karoki started having nightmares. Sometimes Wahome would be standing over him, his young face made evil by a malicious grin, his finger pointing at the teacher's receding hair-line. On waking, the teacher fought a tearing desire to ask the boy why he laughed at him. It became a necessity in Karoki's life to keep checking on the boy, to hear his voice, almost to savour it on his tongue to identify that note of malice he suspected in it.

He came to loathe the boy's startled bright eyes, as the boy stood up for the thirtieth time in a morning to answer the questions the teacher constantly shot at him. Karoki wanted to break the boy's young proud face, which reminded him so vividly of what he himself had been. But this face would escape Karoki's fate, for now the boys didn't need to become teachers, as had been the case in his days. Now they dreamt of joining the Kenya Army, preferring the manly, open-necked life in the bush to the rat-hole existence of a primary school teacher.

Karoki opened the door and walked to his desk. He sat for a full minute, looking at the class, not trusting his beer-fuddled voice to call the names in the register. He would end by calling *that* name, he realized with irritation. His eyes felt like mere bubbles, so wracked were they by the dull, thudding pain at his temples. He ran his hand over his face and opened the attendance register. He felt better, almost himself, as soon as he started calling the names: Bacia, Cege, Gathoni, Githii, Karige, Komu, Mbatia, Njeri, Riitho . . . Wahome. He looked up to see Wahome rise quickly to answer to his name. The boy's voice, which was breaking, came booming at the teacher. It hit him like splintering glass. His head swam, and the boy's face blurred in his eyes, looming ever larger and nearer, menacingly coming down at him. Instinctively Karoki thrust out his hand to ward it off, but it was the table he banged, shouting in a demented voice, 'Wahome, come here!'

He did not see the frightened eyes of the other children but was painfully aware of the boy's firm movement as he walked slowly to the front of the class. He would tear with his cane those flexing muscles. The boy walked so confidently, but with the delicate grace of a young horse. When Wahome stood in front of him he could do nothing. There was no fear in the boy's eyes. There was no anger. Impossible to believe there was contempt, in the head thrown slightly back, the eyes looking at him coolly.

The boy had not offered sympathy to Karoki, had not tried to understand him. He had been strongly attracted by his new teacher, had deeply respected the quiet pride which preceded the teacher in anything he did. But now he was rejected. This caused him no bitterness, but suddenly the teacher had gone sliding down a steep slope in the boy's mind, and lay in a ridiculous heap in front of him.

Karoki felt the muscle of his stomach contract, go cold, as he looked at the boy. He couldn't be sure what he would do if he caught hold of him. He rose slowly, drunkenly, and walked towards the boy. Just as slowly the boy backed towards the door, his whole body concentrated on the face of the teacher, whom he had always suspected to be mad. He had always wondered why his teacher's eyes showed so much white when they turned to look, like the eyes of a frightened horse. He now knew, Karoki was slightly mad. The knowledge aroused him deeply, he felt he was embarking on his first adventure as a man. As Karoki pounced to grip him, his arms taut with the mania which was flooding his system, Wahome darted out of the class, slamming the door behind him. The older man caught the door as it went leaping to close, and hung on to it weakly, crying. Dry, rasping intakes of breath through clenched teeth of a man crying. The pupils, huddled in their seats, watched the crying man, and a shadow spread over the entire room so that they shivered. A tall, overgrown girl of fourteen snivelled shamelessly, wiping her nose on the sleeve of her dress.

When Wahome got outside he looked this way and that, expecting the playground to be full of madmen who were coming to get him. But the field was bare and forlorn, the beaten-down grass clung closely to the earth. He waited for the teacher to come out. His lively imagination created a ridiculous picture of what would happen, for he saw himself ducking this way and that, taking flying leaps, like a hen does when a cock runs to climb it.

He became suddenly depressed and ashamed and wondered what he was doing outside. He knocked at the door, asking to be let in. He felt calm, completely resigned to what the teacher would do to him. Yes, he felt, he was ready to be pummelled, thrashed by this teacher he loved (he now accepted the fact that he loved him), if it would make the older man feel better. Then he heard the crying.

When he was a boy of ten his mother had given him a large bone with lots of boiled beef on it, and he had sat outside the kitchen, gnawing and tugging. He was eagerly tearing at the meat, impatient to clean the bone. He had, ready at his side, a sharpened stick to get at the marrow with, and he was looking forward to it with indescribable happiness. Suddenly he felt a sharp sting on his cheek, and before he could turn the hawk was carrying his bone, in triumphal wave after wave of its large wings, towards the sky. A tearing pain was leaping from his cheek and clawing his guts. When he passed his hand over his face, the palm was covered in blood. He still carried a long faint scar on his left cheek which throbbed when he became excited.

He felt the same pain now when he listened to his teacher crying. He went away from the door feeling stunned, and walked across to the teacher training college, which was normally out of bounds to the school boys. He knocked at the principal's door, and when he entered the white man's office he started crying. Mr Bovitt looked up from the timetable he was drawing up, more surprised than irritated by this show of emotion. He had worked in this school for thirty years, and had more than once wondered at the way his students concealed their feelings from him. He had sometimes wondered if there were any feelings to conceal!

'My teacher is ill,' Wahome managed to say and burst out with fresh weeping at these words.

'*Mwalimu*[1] Karoki?'

The boy nodded. Wahome followed the white man out of the room.

25

Mr Bovitt felt excited as he walked to the primary school. He had always been intrigued by Karoki's manner. He was too separate, too lonely for someone who supposedly belonged to a clan, a tribe; a person who should not be wholly responsible for his life. He liked but distrusted him. He had kept him at the mission, hoping one day he would discover what made Karoki so separate. As soon as the schoolboy had said he was ill, Mr Bovitt's mind decided it wasn't malaria, or some such ordinary illness. It was something more significant.

Karoki met the white man outside the class. He had seen him coming. Mr Bovitt was shocked to see the teacher's face. Karoki had grown old. Why hadn't he ever noticed? He had not really looked at the man, had not wasted a thought on him for a long time. Karoki had become a part of the mission, like the keiapple hedges[2] which shut the mission off from the village and needed no attention unless they were overgrown. The teacher had lived just round the corner of the white man's busy mind.

Karoki stood outside the classroom as though guarding the young charges inside. He faced the Englishman as though he expected an explanation from him. Mr Bovitt became slightly uneasy and turned to the boy, Wahome, for an explanation. The boy looked down and said nothing. Karoki looked at the boy, and the Englishman was shocked at the intensity of feeling, of hate, or passion, in the eyes.

'Wahome,' the teacher said in a drugged voice, 'go inside.'

He shut his eyes slowly, as if to dismiss the boy from existence, and the Englishman noticed how thin the lids looked, almost transparent: such vulnerable guards for the large, slightly protruding eyes.

'What did the boy tell you?' he asked.

'He said you were ill.'

'He imagines things. It is very difficult to control him.' His voice sounded far off and tired, divorced from the body. He turned to enter the class, paused, and said to the Englishman.

'Leave him to me. I shall deal with him.'

He walked slowly and entered the classroom, the Englishman's puzzled eyes following the slightly stiff body, the head thrown imperceptibly back. For the first time in the thirty years he had been at Turu Mission, Mr Bovitt realized he had been dismissed from an interview. He walked back to his office wondering if the time had come for Karoki to leave. Should he tell him to go, now? Had he recognized a streak of something like madness in the ageing teacher? There might be a scandal if – if – his mind was flooded by all the things the African might do, and the shock of the things his imagination conjured up left him cold.

He scurried back to the school, expecting to find the man doing all sorts of obscene things in front of the class. But he didn't enter the room, for what he heard as he came to the door stopped him. A girl's beautiful voice was reading from *Mohoro ma Tene Tene*[3], a book of simplified Bible stories. She was reading the story of Abraham's sacrifice of his son Isaac, and sentence by sentence the picture built up, and even in this simplified version the blind faith of an early age, a faith in the unseen, which could be so cruel in its utter purity, came over. Somehow he began to feel reassured that all was well. 'And Abraham took the wood of the burnt offering, and laid it upon Isaac his son; and he took the fire in his hand, and a knife; and they went both of them together.'

Karoki had not seen him come and go. He was locked up in the same story. He felt sick with disgust at the old man Abraham. The Jew, the Jew, he kept murmuring under his breath. All the old man wanted was some fertile acres in some far off land, and he was ready to do in his son to get them. And then he wanted to laugh, when the girl came to the point where God reveals the ram, conveniently placed nearby. He had always felt terribly baulked by God's interference at this point. Something in him had cried for blood, human blood, when Abraham lifts the sword to strike his only son, a child of his old age. Then God shepherds in a fat ram, and all is tidied up! And then he realized he was really laughing at his own contradictions. The spell of the story had not worn off with years and he always came back to it when he was utterly miserable and confused. His blood knew sacrifice from his forefathers, and the drama of this story still appealed to him, still claimed his tormented mind.

The girl came to the end of the story and sat down. The teacher did not move; he sat as if he was straining to hear some retreating music, his head thrown back. A deep silence crept over the room and the children, torn with misery at the man's suffering, which was not theirs, started fidgeting. In one flash Karoki saw his life, and he knew he had been caught long ago. The day he asked his father to buy him a shirt and a pair of shorts, to go to school, he allowed himself to be caught. Why had he deceived himself all these years? He had walked, looking neither to his left nor right, thinking nothing could touch him, and all the time he had been a little primary school teacher, insignificant! Why had he not married and bred children and poverty as his schoolmates had done? He was a ridiculous little man, and Wahome, and the world, had a right to laugh at him. A fit of laughter caught him, his neck muscles welled up with laughter and he spluttered as he saw himself for what he was.

He walked out of the class, shaking with laughter. When he came to his house he took his new bicycle outside and started cleaning it. He washed and polished it until it shone. He stood outside his house, ready to get on the bicycle. He knew at a quarter past twelve the bell would ring, freeing the college for lunch. He also knew the engine noise of Mr Bovitt's ancient Ford, and could tell exactly where he changed gear as he drove up the sharp hill from the school to his house. With the sound of the bell he rode slowly towards the tiny post office building next to the church. Hidden by the keiapple hedge he waited for Mr Bovitt.

The sleeping mission station was woken up with a shock by a terrible screech of tyres. Wahome was among the first to get to the scene, and managed to see his teacher's torn body before the grown-ups came and drove the children away. Wahome did not join the army as he had dreamt. He left school and became a butcher's boy. He is becoming prosperous but quite often he has to be carried home in a drunken stupor. He sees eyes, eyes which show too much of the white part, drugged, glazed eyes from which the thread of life has been violently torn away.

NOTES

Mwalimu[1] – *(Kiswahili) Teacher.*

Keiapple hedge[2] – *Thorny shrub with sour yellow fruit widely used for hedging in Kenya.*

Mohoro ma Tene Tene[3] – *(Kikuyu) Tales of Long Ago.*

EXERCISES

1. 'Karoki' is the story of an ageing primary school teacher's physical and mental deterioration. Outline the stages of Karoki's decline, offering reasons for why he eventually destroys himself.

2. Re-read the story's opening paragraph. In what way is it preparing us for Karoki's predicament, for what we can expect to happen to him in the course of the story?

3. 'A subtle battle of wills had developed between Karoki and the head of the teacher training college, Mr Bovitt.' (p. 21)
   How true would it be to say that this 'battle' is one largely concerned with the ideas of freedom and control?

4. Read the following passages in the story:
   'When he was a boy of ten his mother had given him a large bone . . . He felt the same pain now when he listened to his teacher crying.' (p. 25)
   'A girl's beautiful voice was reading from *Mohoro ma Tene Tene* . . . and they went both of them together.' (p. 27)
   a) What do you suppose is the reason the writer introduces these episodes in the story?
   b) What are the parallels being drawn between these past experiences and their significance in the present lives of Wahome and Karoki respectively?

5. There are several instances of irony in 'Karoki'. Here are some. Read the passages and explain in detail why we can consider them 'ironical'.
   'The boy had not offered sympathy to Karoki, had not tried to understand him . . . preceded the teacher in anything he did.' (p. 24)
   'He [Bovitt] had always been intrigued by Karoki's manner . . . not be wholly responsible for his life.' (p. 26)
   'He [Bovitt] walked back to his office . . . Should he tell him to go, now?' (pp. 26–27)

6. 'Wahome was becoming a threat.' (p. 23)
   a) Why does Karoki in his clouded mind perceive Wahome as a threat? Why do his anger, envy and hatred fasten particularly on Wahome? Why does he wish to destroy the boy?
   b) Are his fears about Wahome justified?

7. The 'scapegoat theme' looms large in the story. How is it worked out in the analogies drawn between Karoki and Wahome, and in their relationship which is one of fear, loathing – and mutual attraction?

8. At the end Karoki commits suicide. Read the story's last three paragraphs and try to decide why:
   a) Karoki washed and polished his bicycle 'until it shone' since very soon it would be smashed up.
   b) In the context of the story, Karoki's method of killing himself is 'appropriate'.
   c) Wahome slowly destroyed himself, failing to realize the ambitions he once nurtured.

9. 'In one flash Karoki saw his life, and he knew he had been caught long ago.' (p. 27)
Explain this momentary 'illumination' of understanding about himself that Karoki experiences.

Who Am I?

BERNARD MBUI WAGACHA
(KENYA)

SPEAK UP YOU small monkey – my father says.

I limp back inevitably, increasing the distance between us. The pain from the thorns in my bare feet is intolerable. I keep turning my head to see there are no obstacles to my escape behind me, just in case he is not satisfied with my answer.

I insist. Before I go for my native beer across the river, I must know why the cows strayed, and about the sugarcane.

I keep limping back – stealthily . . .

I put on my pyjamas now. I have slept naked many years of my life. The electric fire we use in this spacious house heats the rooms well. In fact it is making the bedroom too hot just now.

It is late at night and I am feeling tired. I have had my night's share of beer and the hippy-hippy shake. I had no business trying to wriggle like a youth at the party tonight. Father, at the age of forty, would have been setting the rhythm of snoring in his large family – or singing native beer out of his head – or coaxing a young wife by careful thrashing to have the good sense to respect him the same way as all his other wives.

My wife, her waistline doubled these last twenty years since I married her, surprises me with her new energy for good living. She, too, tried to compete at the party with the young girls in mini-skirts. At drinking, she was better than most of them. Now she is in a hurry to sleep. She talks to me in a manner which she now accepts as the normal way to address me, her husband. If my father were to rise from the dead and hear her talking to me the way she does, he would bring his staff down on her back several times and then spit on her full in the face – turn to me and curse me for living with such a forward woman.

Are you going to keep the fire burning here all night?

No, I am going to sleep.

Then switch off that damned electric fire and the lights and come to bed.

I switch off the electric fire. I pull the curtains and switch off the lights, leaving only my reading light at the bedside. I slip into bed quietly. She has the illusion, of course, as she has had for a time now, that I am doing so like a weak male at her command. I have shown her my open hands many times. And she knows they are as large and strong as my father's. Knows too, I am unlikely to use them.

She is drunk again, like only two days ago when she hid the car keys and said I was not to go anywhere that night except to a party for which she had already planned. She rolls in bed and stretches out a hand across my chest, drawing her burning thighs closer to my body. She has forgotten her nightdress and she still has her earrings on. Their clinking as she rolls her head drunkenly is a most loathsome noise. She is as naked as when she was born.

Her clothing is lying in different places all over the room. High heels upside down, nylon stockings like two snakes on the floor.

She had been eager about tonight's party. She was dressed up and ready even before I had been home twenty minutes from work. And soon, she grabbed my hand in hers and led me towards the car. If you asked her, she would say she is pretty much running the show in this house, delegating authority over our younger children almost entirely to an *ayah*[1] whom she rules.

What can you have to be telling Gathu – she said at the party, calling me aside. Who could have invited him and his illiterate wife? She should be ashamed of herself, dressing down to her feet like a nun and hanging on to a glass of orange squash like an old maid. And she knows no dancing other than the circumcision dances she used to lead across the ridge in her youth.

She suppressed the ripples of laughter, almost spilling some beer on her dress.

Who invited you?

You shouldn't talk to them. It's silly for people to try stepping up into places where they do not belong.

Who belongs here?

You never understand. People cannot all flock to the same places. The Gathus don't belong here.

She went away for more beer. I went on talking to Gathu about our old times together. He is still a Grade Two teacher and we did our training together a long time back now. The Gathus have been family friends for a long time. My wife does not now encourage that friendship. I have recently returned to the country and I have a good job now. We have stepped up to a better life. And today Gathu is still a Grade Two teacher.

I pull up the bedding to cover myself. There is a book I have been trying to finish reading. It is under the pillow – a London crime mystery. This reading has little relevance to me here now or to my past. In any case, my doubts about reading it any further tonight are soon brought to an end. Her small hand makes a quick dash for the reading light across my chest. She flicks it out. There is darkness. I sleep.

Do you hear me? Did they or did they not stray to Kamau's garden? Did you steal sugarcane from his garden near the river? He enquires again, putting back the metal snuff box deep among his garments and wiping his nose.

They did not, Father. I took the cows nowhere near his garden today. It's a lie. And I never eat sugarcane.

There is a boy looking like an assassin, brown pointed teeth bared in a sneer. He is waiting down a path through the prickly thicket. Suddenly, he stands with his feet astride across the whole breadth of the path so that I cannot pass. I know now he wants to have a word with me before I go on. It is Gathu.

Uncircumcised dog, with whose permission do you walk down this path?

Why, is it yours?

You dare talk to me like that, you devil?

I see now the thick stick protruding from under the dirty shapeless cloth he wears. I have a stick myself, under the calico.[2] But this boy, Gathu, is bigger than myself, and it seems he wants to push this matter further than I would like to. No matter what comes I have to stand my ground. My grandmother has said I should banish all fear from my life.

Does this path belong to your mother? I ask.

Look here, you dog, if you want a fight, rub off this saliva.

He issues copious spittle on to the back of his hand, stretching it out towards me belligerently. I have grave doubts. Inside me, I fear that things are getting out of hand. But I hear those tremulous words again.

Don't fear to step on cow dung and the waste of sheep. If you fear, you will never be a free man. Fear of any kind destroys a man's spirit.

It is my grandmother, wrinkled and small with age. Her rings cling on to her ears loosely, adding no beauty now to her face. Her walking stick is at her side.

The sudden scream of a woman. It is my mother. She goes on screaming, painfully.

Say you didn't bring the creepers home to my sheep because you went to church. Since when did not my word serve as law in this house? Will you now bring the church to run my home for me?

My father bathes her face with an amazing amount of saliva, breathing heavily, his snuff-covered nostrils dilating and his deep-set eyes blazing. He goes on striking her.

I will send you back to your family, woman – get my cows back. I will send you back to the church to live there if ever again you disobey me. Is that clear? I am the man in this home. If you have any doubts, I'll sink the fact into your head now by sheer muscle.

If you beat me to death, I know I suffer for the Lord. And He will protect me. I shall obey you as I have always done because you are my husband. But now, I have known the new way of the Lord and you can no longer fill my life to the very breath in me. The Lord is supreme. Even you must accept Him and be saved.

Don't you dare say that to me woman! You fools have been cheated to close your eyes in prayer while all the Europeans outside the church are grabbing our best land. Had it not been for your folly in sitting at the feet of the hypocrites called missionaries, I would have helped with my *panga*[3] to cut them down. Then the land-thieves would have stayed their greedy hands in Britain. You who go to church are the root cause of all our present and future troubles.

There are fresh screams in the air now, of a young boy. It is me all right. A teacher is working on my back with a stick, smiling strangely.

You have failed your arithmetic, you did not bring your ashes with you this morning, lazy boy. Ever seen street sweepers in Nairobi? That's where you will end up, in black overalls, blaming me for not having coaxed you further into education.

It was raining, Sir. I fell into the river and lost the tin with the ashes and my books, even my lunch. I promise, Sir, I won't forget again.

It is an old lie. You told me that yesterday and the day before. A week has hardly gone since I punished you for setting on Gathu with a group of young savage rogues, lazy boy. I have passed by your home and seen your father beating his wives. I want to make a better man out of you. Before you are through with education, you will be dealing blows to the world only with your pen; your hands will be hanging at your sides like idle mallets. I want you to forget them the way a circus cheetah forgets its claws. You should see how tame circus cheetahs are.

He brings down the stick on my back and I yell again. My mother yells again from a new onslaught. We yell together in unison.

The scholarship is for three years. If you get into any difficulties before then, let me know. I can always come back to you and the family.

My young wife is flanked by our first two children at the airport, and she has one hand to her jaw sadly. I can see she still retains her simple ways and looks up to me during these early years of our marriage as the greatest living thing in all the world. Looks up to me the same way as any of my father's wives looked up to him.

Don't worry, dear. I'll go on teaching and try to manage with the children. And our friends the Gathus are always around. They are the kindest people I have ever known. I'll never forget them in all my life.

Gathu and his wife come in from out of nowhere.

Take your hand from your face. You will be all right with us around. It is Mrs Gathu talking to my wife.

You need not worry while I am here, Gathu says to me later as the announcement for departure comes over the loudspeakers.

I can't. I wish I could carry on for a few more years. I have a family out there you know. And my country needs me.

I am talking to another in the teaching profession who is not so interested in caning. It is in a strange far away land.

You don't rub the saliva eh! I'll rub it against your calabash-shaped stomach and it will mean the same thing. Do you hear? Rub it off you lily-livered dog. You are as cowardly as your mother.

The small voice comes again.

I've told it to you while you are young. In your time you may not carry the sword or spear to go and meet the tribe beyond yonder hills. You may not even wrestle with men for power. Education will be the new kind of spear and shield. But then as now, don't forget, fear of any kind destroys a man.

Those screams are louder now than any screams I have ever heard anywhere, mine and my mother's combined.

You take the Bible on Sunday and go to church and think you are fooling men. Which fool in all the world can't see through it? I have taken the path skirting the church. And after the morning service, I have seen you among women who stay behind in the churchyard, talking confidentially for long hours. While you stand there plotting against men, my sheep bleat hungrily, reminding me that my authority in this home is being flouted. You leave my children hungry and uncared for and that's no better than I have seen white women doing. Leaving their children to be looked after by nannies as if maternal love is transferable.

Ten more strokes remaining, lazy boy. You don't bring your hoe for digging the school garden. You don't bring your ashes or your books, or your lunch. How do you think your hungry brain can respond to learning while your stomach is in revolt? Next time, I will send you back home and run after you with a stick to the school fence to see you away.

He brings down the stick on my back repeatedly. I yell repeatedly. And the yelling from my mother is still in the air.

Who are you to divert my children from the ways of our tribe? You say our daughters should not be circumcised because the church says so. They will be, just as well as you in your time. And when their time comes, I may lean on my staff before them in the early morning to see the ceremony well done. You are a stupid woman to think I could even listen to the missionaries themselves, let alone to what they are supposed to have said.

I catch a glimmer in Father's eyes. Just in time too.

He spins his walking stick and propels it towards me angrily. I jump in the air and it whistles its way past under my feet. I see he has lost his temper quickly and my calico flies above me in the air as I take flight, limping with the intense pain from the thorns in my feet.

You small monkey. You dare call Kamau a liar? Do you know we squatted for circumcision on the same green? You are calling me a liar. Calling your father a liar. That's what it means.

I turn my head to see if he is following me. I see him issue angry spittle to the ground. He is standing arms akimbo with the ornaments in his slit ears swinging in the air as he shakes his head in anger. I keep limping on.

You should not go to those tribal dances my son, they are evil. The Lord wants you to change. Go and sing in the church and listen to his word.

But Mother, I have been doing these dances since I was on my feet.

I know that you have my son. But the Lord's way is the new way. These dances must stop because the preachers say they are of Satan.

Now to be compared to my mother in cowardice is a serious insult to me. I rush at that spittle and rub it off furiously – and thus throw down the gauntlet.

Even you are like your mother, filthy dog.

Me like my mother? And you rubbed off my spittle?

Yes, you are like your mother, or one of her daughters.

He connects a punch savagely to my neck and I stagger back. I am certain now he has been eating maize and beans longer than I. I rush at him and thrust two punches consecutively at his head. Strangely, they have little effect and he stays on his feet. And all the time I am watching that stick stuck beneath the sisal belt over the dirty stained piece of cloth which does not quite cover his body. I decide to take out my own stick. He sees it and takes out his own stick very fast.

As I swing mine in the air to smite him, he strikes it. I feel it leave my hand with a jerk, going up very high in the air. I am bewildered, dumbfounded, defenceless. I back away. He follows me up and brings down the stick on my shoulder several times. I fall inevitably to the ground and he lands astride on me, mumbling abuse at me all the time. He holds his stick at each end, pressing it on my neck. I fling out harmless hands and feet.

This brute on top of me is choking me, bringing my life and its joys to a fearful end. I am feeling weak. Don't fear cow dung or the waste of sheep. Fear of all kind destroys a man. But this is death. And my fear is so intense it grips my whole being. I cannot breathe now. I see death. I jump up with a jerk and fling the bedclothes to the floor. The reek of beer hits my nose. She continues to shake me from sleep.

She is up already ruling Amina, our *ayah*-cum-housegirl.

Amina, why is Kibunja crying? Stop him and dress them up all ready for school. Is breakfast ready, you lazy girl? Have you forgotten, my dear? It's Monday, you'll be late for work.

Feeling tired.

Pull yourself together my dear. You are still a young man at forty. And by the way, remind me to buy you something for your birthday next month.

As I dress to go to work, I hear her talking to Gathoni, my young daughter, at the door of the bedroom. She often talks to the children in English. Even the youngest of them has a smattering of the language now.

You've forgotten this morning. Say, Good morning, Mummy. How are you? Don't forget to wish Daddy good morning too. Amina! have you cleaned the car? Why is Kibunja still crying?

Amina is supposed to know Kibunja's moods better than this own mother does.

I have just been to see my native youth almost overshadowed now by the strong blend of the exotic grain in my living. And as I look at myself in the mirror, straightening my tie, I realize that my one half is of the calico-clad youth living in the smoky hut where father hectically questioned my mother's new attitude towards him, frequently bolting the door to apply corrective measures to her and assert his waning authority. My other half is here in this house where everything is as irrelevant to such a youth as could be.

My wife has the manner of an awkward woman, still steeped in the past unconsciously and yet so anxious to stride with the present, right up to *ayahs* and beer. She is as free as she ever wanted to be. She lives with me as if I were a beast tamed from the wild. As for me, pulled between my one half of the past and the other half of the present, I wonder who I am. And with Kibunja's crying still reaching me from the next room, I think about my children. Who will they be?

NOTES

Ayah[1] – *A word of Indian origin commonly used in East Africa to refer to a woman employed to look after children.*

Calico[2] – *A length of calico used in toga-like fashion or as a loincloth.*

Panga[3] – *(Kiswahili) A large machete-like knife.*

EXERCISES

This is an interesting short story which throws into imaginative form a problem that is very real for most of us in Africa today. No clear cut 'solution' is offered but it is an honest exploration of a current dilemma. The issue of identity is a pressing one for adolescents moving from childhood to adulthood. In our society it is crucial for everyone, regardless of age, because we are in a transitional stage, caught up in the move from the traditional Africa we have glimpses of to the modern one most of us recognize and inhabit.

1. 'Who Am I?' is a story of the narrator's quest for identity. He attempts to discover who he is by examining the pressures, strains and dilemmas he suffers, first as a child and later in adulthood. Notice how he describes his life largely in terms of threats, harsh words, beatings, physical violence and confrontations.
   Explain what conflicts and pain, past and present, the narrator is subjected to and how they affect him.

2. In the narrator's nightmare about his childhood, his mother's cries and his, in unison, are like a refrain punctuating the

second half of the story. Why do you think his and his mother's pain are linked in this way? (Here you will need to consider how the painful choices mother and son have to make affect their individual lives and their relationships.)

3. Examine the relationship between Gathu and the narrator. As youths they are rivals and Gathu, a circumcised boy, has the advantage. As adults the narrator has an edge over Gathu because he is armed with 'the shield and spear of learning'. What does this relationship reveal about the direction in which our society is moving?

4. 'I realize that my one half is of the calico-clad youth living in the smoky hut . . . My other half is here in this house where everything is as irrelevant to such a youth as could be.' (p. 38)
   a) Balanced against each other, how would you assess the satisfactions and disadvantages of each mode of life mentioned in the quotation above?
   b) In the context of the story, is the narrator being entirely honest and fair in his assessment of both 'halves' of himself?
   c) The narrator harks back nostalgically to the status of women in the old days. Examine the relevant passages in the story. What are your views about his attitude in this regard?

5. From his tone and observations, can you determine the kind of man the narrator is, his personality, attitude, etc? How have his experiences contributed towards making him the sort of person we are presented with in the story?

6. In 'Who Am I?' structure follows theme, i.e. form and theme are knit together in a significant way. Explain how this is so. In order to answer this question, you will have to consider the following points:
   a) The story itself: it comprises the narrator's thoughts and dreams which shift between his past life and his present situation. How does the mingling of past and present help the narrator in his attempt to answer the

title question? Why is the present tense used to describe past events and how is this effective in the story?
b) The title: notice the question form of the story's title. What kind of 'answer' or resolution does the story provide to the stark question 'Who Am I?'

7. 'As for me, pulled between my one half of the past and the other half of the present, I wonder who I am . . . *I think about my children. Who will they be*? (p. 39; emphasis added)

   Basing it on your own life and experiences, write an essay, story or poem attempting to explore the different elements of your own identity.

The Battle of the
Sacred Tree

BARBARA KIMENYE
(UGANDA)

THE SACRED TREE of Kalasanda is regarded more as a landmark than anything else these days, although where it stands is so far off any well-beaten track that it is mostly forgotten, and it probably would be completely so if only the Mothers' Union could desist from periodically waging war against it.

The last time the Tree received the full blast of their antagonistic attention was after the MU President, Mrs Lutaya, of 'wearing-shoes-in-the-house' fame, was out searching with her servant for a hen which had unaccountably strayed away from home, and she happened to catch a glimpse of a child from the primary school in the act of hanging a small banana-fibre parcel on one of the lower branches. Mrs Lutaya's squawk of protest sent the child scurrying in utter terror through the surrounding bush. Close inspection of the 'parcel' revealed it to contain a few coffee beans and a five-cent piece.

Mrs Lutaya, her wandering bird now quite forgotten, took this trophy, as if it were the head of John the Baptist, and made straight for the primary school and demanded to see the Headmaster, Mr Ssentongo, who was on the point of calling the children in from the mid-morning break.

He received her in the cubby-hole which was all he could call his office, and steeled himself against impending trouble as soon as he saw her baleful face. He wished that the interview was taking place in a spot not quite so confined, for although Mrs Lutaya could never be described as a large woman, anger or indignation appeared to inflate her, and, what with her brightly patterned *busuti*[1] . . . well, she gave the impression of filling the place, and Mr Ssentongo, even on his own stamping ground, now felt as insignificant as a fly on the wall.

However, determined to give the conversation a pleasant start, he beamed affably and said, 'Good morning, Madam! This is a pleasure!'

Mrs Lutaya returned the greeting as shortly as possible, and immediately rapped out, 'I know it's not my business, but one of your girls has just hung this,' – and here she dangled the half-opened parcel under his nose – 'on that disgusting tree over there! Now, if you teachers were doing your job properly, every child would know that pagan practices like this are wicked and sinful. It simply shows . . .'

Mr Ssentongo looked extremely serious, and interrupted with, 'Well, Madam, give me the name of the child and I shall certainly look into the matter.'

'How can you expect me to know her name?' Mrs Lutaya exclaimed. 'She ran away when I called her. She obviously knew she was doing wrong, but I recognized the school uniform.'

'Yes, she was doing wrong,' the Headmaster agreed. 'She had no business to leave the school compound during break.'

Mrs Lutaya was shocked. 'I think that what she was doing at the Tree is a much more serious matter. I must say, Sir, I expected you to be the first to recognize the danger. And I sincerely hope you are going to issue a strict warning that your children are not to go anywhere near that tree in future.'

'I shall, indeed, Madam. And thank you for taking the trouble to report this naughty child to me.' He glanced at his watch, rose from his chair and edged towards the door. 'Now, if you will excuse me, I have to ring the bell. Time is precious in the cause of knowledge!'

Mrs Lutaya's sniff of derision indicated that she was not entirely of the same opinion, but she went off home, smugly aware that she had once again done her duty.

The matter might have rested there, had she not, by dint of enquiry, discovered that the only action taken by the Headmaster was a threat of dire punishment for any child in his school who dared to step beyond the school boundaries during school hours. Not a word about the Sacred Tree or pagan practices, you'll notice. Mrs Lutaya was furious. She then and there made up her mind to rid Kalasanda of that sinful reminder of superstitious ages once and for all, regardless of the fact that the Rev. Musoke was no longer available to provide the backing of the Church.

The next meeting of the Mothers' Union gave her a favourable opportunity for broaching the subject.

Altogether there were only about six regular members of the Kalasanda MU including the President, Mrs Lutaya, the Secretary, Mrs Mulindwa and the Treasurer, Mrs Kizito, and the reason why they were so few in a village, which after all contained more than two hundred souls, was rather complicated, not to say mysterious, since the true facts are none too clear. One can only judge on the odds and ends of village gossip, liberally embroidered by Nantondo, but it is apparent that the Kalasanda MU is 'going it alone', having severed all connection with the national movement whose headquarters are in Kampala.

Of all the tales this has given rise to, the most feasible is that Mrs Lutaya and her cronies took it as a personal insult when the National Executive Committee decided that the MU branch at Gumbi was to be developed in such a way that it would also cater for two neighbouring villages, one of which is Kalasanda, and that a certain Mrs Kisekka was sure to be elected District President. Mrs Lutaya's set absolutely refused to accept this high-handed ruling, preferring to remain large fish in their own small pond, rather than compete with the big guns of Gumbi and Male villages for MU offices. In spite of the fact that two-thirds of their original members, rather thrilled at the thought of tripping off to Gumbi every week or so, where at least they would see a few different faces, gladly fell in with the plans of the National Executive, and that Miriamu Mukasa, of all people, joined the deserters, they carried on in a purely independent state.

However, to return to the business of the Sacred Tree. After Mrs Lutaya had related her story – everybody at the meeting had already heard several versions of it from other sources – the other members played up nicely by expressing themselves as completely horrified. One or two of them, notably those whose children had not been given very good end-of-term reports, went so far as to suggest a letter to the Minister of Education calling for the immediate dismissal of the Headmaster, but the others felt the removal of the Sacred Tree was more urgent.

'It should have been cut down when the school was being built, and it would have been, too, if that silly labourer hadn't told everybody that a leaf from it had cured an ulcer on his leg!' claimed Mrs Waswa.

'Oh, did it?' Mrs Kigonya was keen to hear details of the cure, and she was rather disappointed when somebody else broke in with a long list of grievances against both the Headmaster and the Tree.

Mrs Lutaya had heard most of what was being said on numerous other occasions, but she listened intently and quite forgot to refill the teacups until Mrs Kizito jogged her memory by rattling an empty cup suggestively in its saucer. When she judged that everybody had said all there was to say, she moved a solemn resolution that the Ggombolola[2] Chief be petitioned for the immediate destruction of the 'so-called Sacred Tree'. The resolution was, of course, carried unanimously, and all members promised to collect as many signatures as they could, to prove to Musisi that Kalasanda recognized its duty as a Christian village. The meeting broke up on this militant note, after an exceptionally soul-stirring rendering of 'Onward Christian Soldiers', and a Meeting Extraordinary was arranged for the following week.

The collection of signatures to boost the petition, or perhaps one should say the attempt at collecting signatures, sparked off the first signs of trouble. One would think that an easy-going community such as that of Kalasanda would think nothing of adding their names or, as in the majority of cases, their marks to a petition which, if successful, would rid them of something which seldom entered their thoughts from one day to another. It is therefore strange that the MU members on their door-to-door crusade met with scarcely anything other than blunt refusals.

At first, a few kindly people put them off with all kinds of stalling tactics and feigned indifference, but when the petitioners adopted a patronizingly bullying attitude, they received an uncompromising 'No', and, to their consternation, found several of the villagers goaded into an argument favouring the Sacred Tree. For instance, Saulo Bulega, usually so unassuming and a little shy, raised a cheer in the market, where he had been approached by Mrs Kizito ball pen and paper in hand, and was cornered neatly behind his vegetable stall, when he told her very plainly that neither he nor any member of his family would have anything to do with harming the Tree. The Tree, which, he said, once sheltered Kintu, the first Kabaka of Buganda, and was Kalasanda's main link with the Kingdom's history. He then added that he well remembered the time when Mrs Kizito herself, before her marriage, was seen loading its twisted branches with gifts.

The taunts of bystanders, 'So that's how you caught him,' caused Mrs Kizito to leave the market in undue haste.

And so, when the Mothers' Union met for their Meeting Extraordinary, there really was not much to show for their diligence. Twelve signatures, six their own, and four 'marks' obtained from immigrant labourers temporarily working on Yosefu Musoke's land was the sum total. They had not all been successful in persuading their husbands to add their names to the petition. The atmosphere was fraught with despondency as everybody related her own adventure in the pursuit of signatures, and some of the women were so genuinely upset that, though they sipped their tea, they simply could not bring themselves to touch a marie biscuit.

'Well, after all we have gone through, we are certainly not giving up now,' asserted Mrs Lutaya.

'No,' Mrs Mulindwa agreed. 'Some of the things we have heard make it all the more important that we force the Ggombolola Chief to take action.'

The other members contented themselves with a ladylike 'Hear! Hear!' and Mrs Lutaya suggested that they get down to the proper wording of the petition. This, she stressed, was of the utmost importance, since a strong appeal to straightforward logic would go a long way to rectify any adverse impressions created by a deficiency in signatures. The final draft, composed after much argument, read:

'Sir, We the people of Kalasanda, fully represented by the Kalasanda Mothers' Union, strongly protest against the tree behind the primary school and consider it a temptation in the ways of paganism. We consider that you, Sir, as our Ggombolola Chief, will be failing in your duty if you refuse to have the tree destroyed immediately, and urge you, Sir, to do the same immediately.'

The members of the MU felt a great deal better as soon as this imposing piece of authorship was concluded, and most of their former enthusiasm returned when Mrs Lutaya said she would have it typewritten. It was arranged that they should meet again three days later and proceed to the Ggombolola Headquarters where the petition would be formally presented.

However, the village grapevine kept Musisi adequately informed of what was going on in Kalasanda, and, as soon as he learnt that the Mothers' Union was after him, he prudently arranged for his work to take him daily to the farthest outposts of his Ggombolola. After a week of this, the Mothers' Union grew tired of dressing up to the nines, merely to spend unfruitful hours in the sombre offices of the Headquarters and, in the end, they were moved to hand the precious document over to a clerk who was compelled to swear that he would hand it to the Chief as soon as he returned.

Whether the clerk adhered to his vow is a matter for conjecture, but a week later, just as the patience of the Mothers' Union was stretched to its limit and threatening to snap, Mrs Lutaya received a brief, ambiguous note from the Chief, to the effect that the matter was receiving attention. Another seven days went by without anything more happening, and the members of the MU, according to Nantondo who was, needless to say, widely reporting every move in the game, were on the point of exploding. It was as plain as a nose on a face that Musisi intended to let things slide into obscurity. But the Mothers' Union were equally determined that this time their efforts would not be in vain.

They now began bombarding him with slightly hysterical letters, and, finally, when the one-way stream of correspondence had been going on for a fortnight, they lay in wait for him as he came back from a very busy day spent in Mmengo.

Six self-righteous women were the last thing Musisi would have wished for at the end of an afternoon which had comprised a series of frustrations familiar only to a conscientious civil servant. Though he led the ladies with charming politeness into his office, his baser instincts were at the same time urging him to boot the whole lot of them down the steps.

He heard them out with as much patience as he could muster, all the time fingering the file, marked in ominous black letters 'MU', which, besides the petition for the destruction of the Sacred Tree, contained a sheaf of similar documents: complaints against the Happy Bar, against the nomadic Bahima who, knowing no land boundaries and caring even less, drive their cattle through anybody's compound, as well as complaints against Musisi himself, which his immediate superior, the Ssaza Chief, had received and passed back to him with cryptic little notes written in the margin.

When the MU had obviously neared the end of its unified recital of recriminations, he could not resist the temptation to be just a little malicious, and said, 'Well, ladies, your motives are no doubt excellent, but I really do wish you would find somebody else to do your typing, we are badly under-staffed here, and how can a clerk do my typing when he spends so much time doing yours?'

He was pleased to see them look more than a trifle uncomfortable, knowing there could be no denial when a certain disfigurement of the letters 'k' and 'd' in the petition was a sure indication that the Headquarters' typewriter had been at work.

Musisi then went on, 'But about your petition. These signatures can hardly be representative of the people of Kalasanda, and, from what I hear, there would probably be real trouble here if that tree were wilfully harmed. It would be wrong for Government to interfere in such a domestic affair, and, although I quite realize how strongly you feel about it, I really must advise you to . . .'

'You mean you won't do anything?' It was Mrs Lutaya. 'You mean you will allow that tree to stay there and corrupt our children?' She was so angry that she launched into a lurid description of the little girl from the primary school hanging a present on the Sacred Tree, making it sound for all the world as if the child has been discovered in the act of selling her soul to the devil.

'Nonsense! All children do that sort of thing!' Musisi expostulated. 'Believing in magic is part of childhood!'

'I was brought up to believe in Almighty God!' Mrs Mulindwa put in, piously, and was decidedly shattered when Musisi retorted, 'Well, isn't God the greatest magician of all?'

An official interview between the Ggombolola Chief and the Mothers' Union was fast turning into a theological argument, with voices raised to such an extent that Nantondo, eavesdropping outside the window, could hear every word as plainly as if she had been sitting with them in the room.

Musisi was gesticulating in the way he always did when he got excited, and grew so hot that he automatically unfastened the tiny button at the neck of his *kanzu*,[3] revealing, to the general astonishment of the MU, that he had neither shirt nor vest beneath it. His eyes, behind the thick lenses of his spectacles, were flashing wildly as he continued to hammer home the point, in answer to the Union's constant assertion that the Old Testament gives all the authority necessary for cutting down the Sacred Tree, that the Almighty was at liberty to take what action he considered fit, but that the Kabaka's Government was not going to upset its taxpayers by pretending to act in His name.

At last, the ladies got up to go, their dignity very much ruffled, and they sailed out of the Headquarters with great flouncing of *busutis* and clicking of tongues, loudly asking each other what the Kingdom of Buganda was coming to. Musisi, no less ruffled, followed them out, called for an office messenger to lock the place, and crossed the compound to his house where he made short work of a bottle of beer.

Of course, the whole of Kalasanda knew about the interview early the following day, if they had not heard of it that same evening, and everybody was sure that this time the Mothers' Union had been put in its place once and for all, quite forgetting the many previous occasions on which they had thought the same thing. For the Kalasanda Mothers' Union was a very resilient body of women. They might have their faults, but one thing had to be acknowledged: no matter what setbacks they encountered they never entirely gave up and would be back to make another onslaught as soon as they recovered their energies.

In the case of the Sacred Tree, Musisi's downright refusal to be of any assistance in the matter caused them for a brief while to give way to despair, but later, when they gathered, for a change, at Mrs Mulindwa's, they were considerably calmer and generally prepared to bring the crusade to a fitting conclusion. Only a woman called Mrs Kigozi appeared to have doubts. She was a timid sort, anyway, who would actually have liked to have gone over to the bigger Union at Gumbi where they did all sorts of exciting things, like taking trips to the National Assembly in Kampala and being given tea by their Member of Parliament, not to mention buffet suppers with a bishop's wife as Guest of Honour. But somehow Mrs Kigozi had been taken up by the ruling set of the Kalasanda MU, and, rather flattered by the social implications of the relationship, she had remained reluctantly in tow when her less favoured friends went off happily to savour the delights of the Gumbi branch. While she often felt the urge to be bold and join them, the mere thought of being conspicuous as a solitary deserter held her back. She had never been at all happy about the business of the Sacred Tree, and even her half-hearted attempt at collecting signatures for the petition had left her shattered. Now she summoned every bit of courage at her disposal to say, 'Wouldn't it be better to keep quiet for a time? I mean, the Ggombolola Chief did tell us there may be trouble in the village if we, well, if we . . .'

Her words trailed away into mid-air for she was always too shy to finish a full sentence, particularly if other people gave her their attention.

'Trouble? What sort of trouble? Young Musisi always talks of trouble if he wants to get out of doing anything,' Mrs Mulindwa retorted. 'No! That terrible tree must go, if we have to chop it down ourselves.'

These words were undoubtedly fighting words, but Mrs Mulindwa thought she could afford to be slightly reckless or revolutionary within her own home. Nevertheless, she was much taken aback, as were the others, when Mrs Lutaya cried, 'That's it! Why ever didn't we think of it before? Yes, we'll chop that tree down ourselves!'

'Well, really, I only meant if nobody else would do it.' Mrs Mulindwa's explanation sounded extremely lame.

'And who else in Kalasanda is likely to do it?' Mrs Lutaya demanded to know. 'No! I repeat, we shall have to do it ourselves.'

'But when?' Mrs Kigonya asked, in a voice that was almost a wail.

'The sooner the better, and I suggest tonight!'

Nobody really knew what to say to this, and Mrs Mulindwa could have kicked herself for making the suggestion in the first place. However, they were all so used to bowing to the dominating personality of their President that immediately after their initial hesitation they were as keen as she herself on the idea, or at least they pretended to be.

They planned their attack on the Tree for about eight o'clock that night, choosing a time when the market, through which they would pass, would be more or less empty, except for a few late stallholders, and when the whole village could be expected to be at home and eating supper. By then the moon would be high enough to make it unnecessary for them to carry lanterns or electric torches.

The expedition was to start off from Mrs Lutaya's house, since Mrs Mulindwa, now that her scheme was being hatched, had no further desire to figure in it prominently.

But the enthusiasm which Mrs Lutaya had so quickly aroused in the breasts of the MU members was not slow to evaporate once the women reached home and had difficulty in explaining to their respective husbands why they would be going out again before the evening meal. It was with a good deal of reluctance that four of them arrived at the Lutaya's house. Mrs Kigozi was not among them. A young boy came instead with a note saying that she was suffering from a sudden fever.

As the gallant five set out for the Sacred Tree, anybody meeting them on the way might at first have thought they were returning from a burial. Their *busutis* were mostly hidden by shabby *shukas*;[4] three, Mrs Lutaya amongst them, wore shapeless cardigans, and all had kerchiefs wound tightly round their heads. The only really odd thing about their appearance was that they carried *pangas*.

Not one of them spoke a word until they reached the primary school, which stood silent and lifeless in the moonlight, and then Mrs Kigonya whispered querulously, 'O-o-oh! I do wish we had brought a light of some sort!'

'What do we need a light for?' snapped Mrs Lutaya. 'It's as clear as anything. I can see quite plainly.'

Still, she was glad when they all moved closer to each other, and crept in a huddle round the school and towards the thick scrub beyond. They paused, a little breathlessly, on its fringe. Was it imagination, or were they really being followed? That odd rustling noise in the undergrowth: a small animal or stealthy, human footsteps? Whatever it was, the ladies became paralysed with fear as the noise grew louder with every passing second. Then, abruptly, it stopped, and all that could be heard was the twittering of bats in a nearby mango tree and the tinkling music of night insects.

'It must have been a rabbit, or perhaps a fox,' breathed Mrs Lutaya.

The other nodded dumbly, and followed her once again as she stepped tentatively through the bushes.

The Sacred Tree stands in a small clearing of coarse and tufty grass. By day there is nothing disturbing about its appearance; it simply looks what it is: a misshapen stumpy tree with gnarled branches bearing scarcely any foliage. But in the ghostliness of the moonlight, it seemed to increase in size until it towered menacingly above the women. The shadows cast by the Tree's stunted branches distorted themselves into watchful snakes lying in wait for unsuspecting prey. Here, in the clearing, the night noises unaccountably ceased, giving way to an oppressive but expectant quiet.

The five members of the Mothers' Union stood motionless, staring at the Tree as if they expected it to glide in their direction, and feeling that should it do so they would be incapable of moving.

'Come. We must get on with the job. It's no use standing here.' Mrs Lutaya made a visible effort to shake off the trance-like state which was speedily overtaking them, but the others either could not, or would not, move another inch.

'Come on.' She nudged Mrs Kigonya, who shuddered, took a step backwards and moaned, 'Oh, I don't think we should.'

These words helped to dispel some of the terror which had gripped them and released the tension. Everybody started talking in loud whispers.

'Doesn't it look different by moonlight?'
'Suppose somebody hears us chopping it down?'
'I must say, I shall be glad when it is all over.'
'Well, come on, then. Let's get on with it!'

This time they meekly followed Mrs Lutaya, and gathered around the Tree's trunk, looking for its most vulnerable spot. The Tree was so old and brittle that they did not think for a minute that they would have any serious difficulty.

'Right. I'll start here,' Mrs Lutaya considered that she, as President of the Mothers' Union, was entitled to strike the first blow, and raised her *panga* accordingly.

As she did so, a searing pain shot through her arm, to be quickly followed by another on the inside of her thigh, then in her armpit and then . . . well, in a matter of seconds, Madame President had lost track of all the little red-hot needles which seemed to be boring into her. She dropped the *panga* as though that, too, was red hot, and began jigging about and tearing at her *shuka*.

'Safari ants!' she squealed. But there was no need to explain, because her companions were only too well aware of the fact. They were also being bitten in extremely embarrassing places, and were busy trying to discard their clothing, which was the only way to rid themselves of those large, shiny, black insects whose jaws clamp into flesh and hang on until forcibly removed.

The ground where the ladies were prancing with unconventional abandon was literally seething with ants. After the first few moments of blind panic, the five frantic women tore, half-naked, out of the clearing, and very nearly bumped into Nantondo who had been avidly taking in the interesting spectacle from behind a bush.

'Well, well,' she cackled, 'Who would have thought it of you? Bold girls!' But there was no time to bandy words. Scarcely glancing at her, the members of the Mothers' Union fled on.

The rest of the Kalasandans found it edifying next day to visit the Tree and examine the pieces of discarded clothing and *pangas* strewn at the base of its trunk. Nor could they hear Nantondo's sensational story often enough.

'Dancing naked you say? Incredible!'

'Are you telling us they took all, really all, their clothes off?'

They turned to look at the Sacred Tree with new respect, for it had proved beyond any doubt that it was a fit match for the Mothers' Union. 'Can you imagine the craftiness of that funny old piece of wood, allowing its enemies close enough to strike and then turning them mad to the extent that they danced stark naked? Oh yes, it can look after itself all right.'

Understandably, the members of the Mothers' Union found it expedient to stay indoors as much as possible during the ensuing few days, until the scandal had had time to quieten down. It had not been easy to give a satisfactory explanation for their state of *deshabillé* upon reaching home that night, and once their husbands got hold of the story Nantondo was spreading, life for the women was intolerable.

A very subdued gathering of members assembled for the next meeting of the Mothers' Union. Mrs Kigozi had sent word that her husband insisted upon her resigning from the Kalasanda MU and taking out membership at Gumbi branch, and, it goes without saying, the Sacred Tree was conspicuously absent from the agenda.

NOTES

Busuti[1] – *(Luganda) Traditional dress worn by Baganda women.*

Ggombolola[2] – *(Luganda) Territorial administrative unit in Uganda.*

Kanzu[3] – *(Kiswahili) A white ankle-length long-sleeved cotton garment used by men in certain East African communities.*

Shuka[4] – *(Kiswahili) A length of calico worn toga-like or as a loincloth.*

EXERCISES

1. Read the section on satire in the Introduction. Then answer the following questions:
   a) What ideas and which kind of people are the objects of Barbara Kimenye's satire in this story?
   b) *How* does she satirize them?
   c) Do you think that her satiric treatment of these ideas and people is justified?

2. Do you, from your own experience, find that the characters and situations portrayed in 'The Battle of the Sacred Tree' are typical of small town or village life? Explain how.

It's a Dog's Share in Our Kinshasa

LEONARD KIBERA
(KENYA)

I ALWAYS THOUGHT until that Saturday morning that I was not a sadistic man. I admit that I would have preferred a cup of hot coffee in bed to the sight of blood. But that morning I woke up earlier than usual. Everybody woke up earlier than usual. The whole town woke up earlier than usual.

There must have been something strange in the air that urged everyone to go and have their grisly worth of this very public affair at the unearthly hour of half-past six. The dawn sun crept its claws through my bedroom curtains and a sinister warmth seemed to beckon me outside. Much as I admit I am partial to the morning sun, I felt a strong urge to bury my ignorance – of what I might perhaps be capable of – in the dark comfort of the white bedsheets; and not to expose what might turn out to be self-revelation, self-betrayal. I would hate to enjoy it all.

But, come to think of it, what was wrong with following the mob? What was wrong with joining in the spirit of the State? Did not the damned man deserve death?

I dressed up and hurried outside.

As I approached the execution spot a mile away, I could not help detecting a heaviness in the air. Once or twice I caught myself heaving my shoulders, like a ridiculous elephant, as if to relax.

'Traitor! Traitor!' yelled the mob.

The morning was clear; the issue was clear. Everything seemed – yes, seemed – in order, organized, academic. There was hardly a speck of cloud to mar the light-hearted heavens. All around was the spirited cry in chorus, *'Traitor! Traitor!'*

Only the air hung heavy.

Here and there were mixed faces. Black, white, brown humanity breakfasting in unison and all pushing forward, necks craned with a strange passion. Sleepy soldiers kept us at bay. We clung to the circumference of the semi-circular rope, our limit, so that, to the heavens looking down upon us, we must have appeared like a ridiculous half-moon of mad passion yawning its wide mouth, dying to send a man to his death. I remembered that to our forefathers – very superstitious, I hear – a certain shape of the moon spelt lunacy on earth.

'Great sight, eh! Hang all traitors!' said the jubilant man beside me, stretching an elastic snarl to reveal yellow teeth. Twisting his face, he scratched at the night's growth of beard. 'Ever seen such a large crowd before? Funny thing is . . . hey, what's the matter with you? Friend of yours?'

No, I said, no friend of mine. I apologized for not being a great talker in the morning. But my new friend, obviously disappointed in me, muttered something like 'sentimental idiot' and turned the other way. I heard him growl and snarl what must have been the same piece of thirsty information to the man behind him. The latter, on grinning back a rusty row of molars, gripped his new friend by the shoulder and, barking at the top of his voice, agreed it was a spectacular sight.

'Traitor! Traitor!' roared the crowd, as if in echo. A peculiar oneness.

Over the raised ground, I could just make out the features of the damned man tied to a pole. Although the raised ground was little higher than our vantage point (our half-moon of greed being to his east), the condemned man braved the rising sun and played down at us a contemptuous grin. The smile disarmed and annoyed me. It was as if he would break loose at any moment, spring upon us like a master on his dog, and I wished I was back in bed. But as I accidentally caught sight of my unshaven companion I could have sworn he bared his teeth right back at the prisoner and I felt a strange assurance that, if that contemptible man should break upon us, I was well protected. I hated that playfulness of smile because it belittled me. Did he not realize his condition? Must he look down upon us as if we were a breed of hounds?

It was now well past eight o'clock and we began to wonder.

The firing squad was not yet here. Only the policemen and soldiers, who had now united forces with a rare friendliness, saw to it that we kept to the right side of the tantalizing rope. As the sun rose higher and higher we began to sweat; tempers rose, cries of *'Traitor! Traitor!'* became more violent, and hunger stung in our bellies. The condemned man seemed to smile with contemptuous satisfaction more than ever. Perhaps the firing squad aimed to work us into this heat so that when it arrived everything would be a climax, the town gossip for weeks on end.

A clear African sunrise is no guarantee of a cloudless day. This was true of that Saturday morning. Here and there were now formed strips of clouds. But they were no shield against this sun which acted like a catalyst of anger, a curious inspiration. Paradoxically, it was as if we did not need any clouds at all. They seemed to disturb the orderly geometry of the heavens. Occasionally we would be questioned with a silent shadow of doubt as a cloud, on its way to the anticlimax in the west, hovered above us, obscuring the sun.

But it had now become an angry affair. Reason as to why the man was dying had fled us in our thirst for blood and we gave ourselves to the benefit of this doubt.

'Traitor! Traitor!' cried the mob in singsong.

'Icecream!' cried a vendor.

'Coca Cola!' cried another.

Business and pickpocketing flourished.

My unshaven neighbour, who now seemed to change his opinion of me for the better, swept his paw across his face to wipe off the sweat and belched a guffaw – more like a choke on a bone. He and I shared an icecream.

At last, about midday, the policemen and soldiers fell upon us with a physical request to make way, and I now counted the firing squad of twelve cutting its way sharply into our mad crescent.

'Attention!' yelped the officer in charge. Blood rose.

For about ten minutes we seemed to be deliberately tantalized. We were the anxious spectators pressed together for the climax, or was it comfort?

Then, somewhere, in our midst, a little girl cried. Diving under the rope, she ran towards the officer with a bunch of flowers. A soldier intercepted her. But the officer noticed and said, with stiff posture, sword up, that the girl could come to him – or something like that, I was too far to hear. After a still minute or so, the little girl hesitated her way to the doomed man and at last stood looking up at his heroic face. He did not so much as look down. He had, it appeared, worked himself into a trance. When he did finally notice the girl – the flowers – his contemptuous smile vanished. He was, apparently, moved. It seemed to us that he asked the little girl to put the flowers at his feet. For the first time he had dropped his head and, although I was too far to see clearly, I had no doubt that the smile had been but a veneer, a screen against our hardness of heart; and he wept. With gratitude? Grief? I don't know. All I can say is that as the little girl wept her way back again, a knowledge of something sacred betrayed to public emotion seemed to have touched our hearts and weighed there heavily, like the day of judgement.

Women drew out their handkerchiefs. We, the brave men, seemed to drop our heads down in chorus and pressed together. With shame? Even that I cannot tell. But I found myself moving away – backing out? – towards home, tail between my legs.

Behind me, I saw the unshaven man; he, too, bent on all fours, beaten. He made an attempt to address me but suspecting, rightly, that I would not answer him, scratched at his itchy beard and thought the better of it. The whole thing was itchy. Maybe he too could not wait for the climax. Maybe he too had been touched at a very soft spot. But we had not far to escape. We heard the report of shots and turned in time to take our due share of the violent anticlimax. The next we knew we had clutched at each other.

This is what we had come for: smoke at one end, blood and dust at the other.

We disengaged ourselves, rather ridiculously I must say, and he went a different way; for a strengthening lunch, no doubt.

NOTES

Kinshasa (Title) – This is a reference to a spate of politically motivated public executions in the mid-1960s in Kinshasa, the capital of the Congo (now Zaire).

EXERCISES

1. In this story we see the mob mentality, the herd instinct, at work. This kind of grim 'event' has the power to bring together very different people in an unholy alliance and temporary comradeship.
   a) In what different ways is this shown in the story?
   b) What comment is Kibera making about this kind of human 'solidarity'?
   c) How does this kind of solidarity differ from that which the little girl shows with the condemned man?

2. '... the condemned man braved the rising sun and played down at us a contemptuous grin. The smile disarmed and annoyed me.' (p. 56)
   a) What reasons does the narrator offer for the condemned man's 'contemptuous grin' and for his own irritated reaction to it?
   b) Can you think of other reasons for the man's contemptuous smile and for the annoyance it creates in the narrator?

3. The girl's compassionate gesture softens both the 'traitor' and the mob gathered to watch him executed.
   a) *How* and *why* do the man and the mob react to her gesture in the way they do?
   b) Do you notice there is a change in the narrator's tone after the girl's gesture? How does the tone change?

4. 'In this story the action of the state in organizing a public execution and that of the mob in coming to gloat over a fellow human being's legalized murder is questioned in different ways: by the very tone of the narrator; by the mob's false camaraderie; by nature itself; and, finally, by the little girl's action.' Discuss.

5. 'But, come to think of it, what was wrong with following the mob? What was wrong with joining in the spirit of the State? Did not the damned man deserve death?' (p. 55)
   Does the story provide 'answers' to these questions of the narrator?

6. Examine the extensive use made of animal imagery in the story.
   a) Single out the images and explain what precise purpose they serve in relation to the story's theme.
   b) Is it perhaps unfair to the animal world when the negative qualities of human beings are described in 'beastly' terms?

7. In fiction the narrator's tone and theme generally complement each other; that is, he chooses a tone appropriate to the subject matter. This is not the case in 'It's a Dog's Share in Our Kinshasa'. A sombre story is told in a flippant manner. As a result, there is a lack of harmony between the story's subject matter and the tone in which it is narrated.
   a) How did you react to the narrator's tone when you read the story?
   b) 'It is precisely this lack of harmony between subject matter and tone which makes this story so effective in its sharp impact on our hearts and minds.' Discuss.

8. Do you think that the story's ending is too sentimental? To answer this question consider the following questions:
   a) Is the change that comes over the condemned man and the mob as a result of the girl's gesture too sudden and implausible?
   b) Why does the narrator describe the condemned man's face as 'heroic'? (p. 58)

9. Examine the narrator's *focus* in the story. It can be compared to the way a TV cameraman might render a public event. The narrator gives us 'crowd shots' of the mob milling around, the vendors and pickpockets, etc. He also zooms in for 'close-up shots' of particular individuals at the scene: the unshaven man, the 'traitor', the girl, etc.

   Why is this an effective way of telling this particular story?

The Road to Mara

TOM CHACHA
(TANZANIA)

THE DAY WAS hot and humid. The air had the stillness of death. Somewhere in the distance a bell seemed to toll forlornly. The girl paused to listen. But the rustle of wind in the corn, the drone of cicadas and the faint, happy cries of playing children swallowed any trace of the ringing's echoes. Even so, she knew it must be four o'clock.

She walked on slowly, almost reluctantly, the snug, sleepy village receding ever farther behind her, but she shook off the weight of her feelings and tried to step out more briskly. Her left arm relieved the right one of the small bundle she was carrying. She smiled wryly at the picture she must present: the bundle securely tucked under her left arm was all the property she owned in the world, everything she could now call her own – apart from Gatimu . . . She thought of him fondly for several minutes, until she was forced to notice her limp. The murram[1] road was hard and hot through the thin soles of her shoes. She stopped to ease her feet and looked back the way she had come. The village was already out of sight beyond the bend, but while she watched she saw the little red cloud of dust appear that meant the bus at last was coming. She waited impatiently. She heard it before it came into sight, groaning as if in great pain as it negotiated the gradient near the village. Presently it rounded the bend, an old green bus, smoking and shuddering, boxes and bicycles piled precariously on the roof-rack. She waved to it to stop.

'Mara?' shouted the driver above the racket from the engine.

She nodded, climbing aboard, and went to sit in a vacant seat near the front. She sat up rather stiffly and looked about. On her right were seated three other passengers: an old man in a stained old coat, a woman of indeterminate age and a young man. The woman smiled. The young girl, feeling rather embarrassed, returned her smile. No word passed between them.

The young man's eyes shone with speculation. He leaned over and whispered, 'This must be the girl we heard about, Father – Bena.' His tone was excited.

'Can't you keep your eyes off these girls?' the old man whispered back, in strong reproof. He eyed Bena covertly, frowned and bit his lower lip. He could not imagine how a young girl like Bena could travel alone without an elderly companion. The old man's eyes caught those of his wife; in that moment, when their eyes met, he knew that she was thinking the same thing as himself.

'This is one of the modern spoiled girls,' the old man seemed to be saying, in grim disapproval. 'She is probably going to be a common prostitute in the town.'

The woman, sensing the old man's thoughts, looked at Bena again. Her lips parted, but not in a smile this time – in mixed sympathy and embarrassment. To the wife, Bena was a symbol of shame to all respectable women. She seemed to her somehow outcast, without roots or bearings, having selected the state herself and carrying a vacancy within. Bena wore no tribal markings on her face. She did not wear the iron rings on her neck. Instead she sported some imitation pearls. On her wrist the tribal multicoloured beads were replaced by a small nickel-plated watch.

'The towns are spoiling our girls,' the wife murmured to her husband.

'It is so,' the old man sighed, nodding his head.

'Soon the villages will be empty.'

The old man nodded again, unhappily.

It was only the young man who looked at Bena with admiration and excitement. He had watched her wiggling into the bus in her tight-fitting frock, holding his breath as he gazed. Bena was lithe and young and beautiful, her beauty somehow racier and more emphatic in its non-tribal presentation. Her hair was soft and coal black, her eyes warm and tender, her lips tempting . . . and her breasts and hips were softly curved and feminine in the tight frock. The young man winked and grinned at Bena, but the grin didn't come off. He cleared his throat confusedly, shifted his position in his seat, bit his fingernail, lit a cigarette, then looked at her again directly. He seemed to transmit a message through his eyes: 'I am with you. I am on your side. The tribe and all the old-fashioned ways are behind us.' But his face remained as inscrutable as everyone else's: only his eyes gleamed.

The rattling old bus carrying her so wearily onwards seemed to Bena the only thing with either meaning or purpose. The black wheels kept turning beneath her. The seat kept rocking her. And the passengers kept harassing her with their stares. Outside, the rolling hills inched past, the trees, the streams, the neat cultivated fields. And soon signs of approaching civilization began to appear: a store with a lurid advertizing hoarding, rusty tin shacks, a petrol station, abandoned junk, idlers. A sign 'Welcome to Mara' loomed and disappeared. The traffic increased. Bena took fresh heart and sat up in her seat. The chipped welcome sign encouraged her, as if Gatimu himself had spoken, giving her confidence and hope about the fabled new world.

They reached the outskirts of the little town, slowed to avoid the cyclists and pedestrians, and shook and grumbled down the narrow crowded main street. The bus stopped in front of the Mara Blue Bar and Restaurant. The passengers got out, the old man and his family standing for a second or two in silence; in the faces of the old couple pity, disapproval and embarassment moved like troubled shadows. But the young man winked at Bena and gave her a broad smile. His farewell was well meant. He was on her side.

Bena stood expectantly on the pavement, looking impatiently from right to left. She tucked the bundle under her arm, waiting, as the last of the bus passengers trickled away. Her eyes moved ceaselessly over the drab, untidy town: across the rows of ramshackle *dukas*[2], the hotel front, the cafés; across the jostling people with their shut faces and restless urgency. She waited for quite a while, the expectation and excitement only slowly fading from her face. She cast one more look about her, then transferred the bundle to her other arm. Nervously, she walked down the length of the main street, then up the other side again, bumped and jostled by the impatient townsfolk. She hung grimly on to her bundle, trying to thread a safe passage through the crowds and ignoring the remarks of the brassy young men. She looked in the face of every man who passed by, silently rebuffing the advances her interest provoked. But she did not see Gatimu.

The crowds suffocated her and the uncouth young men made her nervous. She was tired after the journey and increasingly alarmed about Gatimu's non-appearance. The shrill cries of the playing children, running in the gutters and scuttling down the refuse-scattered alleys, added to her heaviness. They reminded her of other children playing happily in the long grass and by the river's side. She found herself momentarily envying these children: the town was their playground, as familiar to them as the village and the fields had been to her. Here she was, a stranger in a lonely town – and Gatimu had not been there to meet her.

The jukebox in the Blue Bar and Restaurant was thumping out the strains of some raucous hit-parade record. The music was brash and confident, forthrightly announcing the vigour and competence of youth, and their impatience to take over a world peculiarly their own. Loudly and unsubtly it invited her, spoke to her hesitations and uncertainties and dispelled them. She went in. Flushed faces turned towards her as she stepped inside. She held her bundle more tightly. Her eye were fixed on the floor.

'There's a seat behind you,' the waiter said in an offhand manner.

She sat down.

'Yes?' he asked negligently.

She hesitated. Her fingers found the table-cloth and she began playing with it. After a time she looked up. The waiter was surlily waiting for an answer.

Reluctantly she said, 'I . . . I . . . wanted to see somebody.'

'Who?'

'I was expecting him to meet me at the bus stop,' she said softly.

'Well?'

'I am a stranger here,' she said innocently, without looking at the waiter, 'but he works in the railways,' she added.

'Then go to the railway headquarters and ask for him there,' the man said curtly. 'The place is near. Turn left outside and go straight on.'

Bena rose. She collected her bundle and tucked it under her

left arm. For the first time, she registered the noise in the café. Chatter, shouts, hard laughter, music. The incongruity of it all struck her. She threw a glance at the waiter and said politely, 'Thank you, sir.' She went out, almost running. The waiter stood looking after her until she disappeared. He shook his head scornfully, then turned back to watching the dancers.

Bena followed the waiter's directions, a train of images passing through her mind as she threaded her way down the pavement. The crowd that bumped and pushed around her, without any apologies, ceased for the moment to exist. She felt bitter at heart. Beads of sweat that had collected on her forehead trickled down her brow like tears, and her own eyes began to fill as her loneliness, frustration and misery welled in her heart. She let the tears flow unheeded, as if tears alone could heal the ache in her heart. And anger began to burn within her breast. Was it her fault that she had not liked Bako? Her father had chosen him for her because Bako came from a well-to-do family. But how could he be her husband? A coward. A man who had wept at his initiation ceremony. A man who could not stand up to any challenge. The other women would taunt her at having married such a girl of a man. 'Bako a husband indeed!' she sniffed to herself, and dismissed him from her mind.

She was wondering whether she would find Gatimu in the railway headquarters when she was startled by a hand touching her shoulder. Without looking back to see who had touched her, she cried out with joy, 'Gatimu, my love!' and spun round with suddenly shining eyes. But the person standing there, smiling ironically, was not Gatimu. It was a young woman in tight slacks that flattered her feminine curves.

'Sarah,' Bena said dully.

'Bena.' And the young woman took Bena's hand affectionately. 'What brings *you* to Mara?' she asked mockingly.

'Oh, I've just come.' Bena tried to smile. They used to be friendly, but Sarah, as she now called herself, had left the village more than a year ago.

'This *is* a surprise,' said Sarah warmly. 'You must have come to look for something very special, Bena,' she went on archly.

At this Bena looked down shyly, wiped her cheeks with her free hand, then changed her bundle to her other arm.

'But come,' Sarah said briskly. 'You must be exhausted, and

thirsty too. We shall go to the New Paradise – it's where the crowd hangs out.'

Bena followed obediently.

'What will you have?' Sarah asked, when they had found a table and settled down.

'Only something soft.'

They were brought two Fantas and some dry cakes.

'How is everyone at home?' Sarah asked, pouring herself the drink.

'Well,' Bena said, and then: 'Sarah, I came to this town to look for –' She stopped, picked up her drink, but put it down again; then took up a cake, but, when she was about to bite it, put it down too.

'Don't tell me you're looking for a job,' Sarah said teasingly. 'Not our docile and domestic Bena!'

Bena tried to force a smile and managed with an effort. She looked up, and there was a desperation in her eyes as she asked, pleadingly, 'Please tell me where Gatimu is.'

'Surely you didn't make the whole journey just to ask that,' Sarah answered. Bena waited tensely. Hope, desire, embarrassment fought in her breast.

'Where is he?'

'Oh, around.'

'You mean in town? Here?' Her excitement was mounting.

'Oh no, he left with his wife a week or two ago for Tabora.'

The glass Bena was holding fell, and broke into pieces. She stared at Sarah blindly. Her fingers were trembling. She stood up to pick up the pieces of broken glass, but Sarah told her brusquely to leave it to the waiter. She sat down again, still in a daze; then she covered her face with her hands.

'I . . .' A sob caught in her throat. 'I . . . was to marry him . . . soon.'

Sarah stared at her in confusion.

'Oh, I see,' she said, lamely.

The waiter came and Sarah paid, glad to bury her head in her purse. She took Bena's hand awkwardly.

'Come home with me,' she said. 'Rest. Don't make this the end of the world.'

They left the café and Sarah hailed a taxi in the street. She was carrying Bena's bundle and holding her gently by the arm.

'Nyamongo quarters,' she told the driver, and helped Bena into the car.

In the taxi, Bena felt the stabbing in her heart again, dispelling the daze into which she had fallen. Her blood ran cold along her veins. She could not convince herself that she was not going to Gatimu's home, the little bungalow he had so often spoken of and enthusiastically described. She remembered the day Gatimu had told her, 'I am yours and you are mine. Nothing can ever change that, Nancy.' He had grown fond of calling her Nancy. And with the memory of the sound of his voice she remembered too the words he had spoken that night under the clear moon. She could see Gatimu and herself leaning against a tree, Gatimu holding her tenderly and close to him, her head on his wide shoulder, his voice sounding like distant music to her ears. The voice became louder and more real:

> *Nancy, Nancy, are you the angel of my dreams,*
> *Are you the beauty I see in the empty skies,*
> *The lass I see on the face of the moon?*
> *At night I sit and stare at the empty skies,*
> *The moon comes and the stars dance around her.*
> *The glow-worms sparkle her way,*
> *As the nightingales sing in her praise.*
> *And yet I am all alone.*
> *Nancy, Nancy, be the moon of my world,*
> *I'll be the nightingale to sing your praise,*
> *The glow-worm to sparkle your paths*
> *And the star to dance around you.*

Slowly, the gruff music of his voice died away. She strained hard to hear it, but it trailed off into silence. In that moment of darkness and loneliness, the words of her mother came mockingly back to her. 'Bena, the city people are no good. You belong in the village. Only the hard ones can be happy there.'

Did this mean that Bako was to marry her after all? No. Impossible! No one, nothing could shut her away from Gatimu forever. There must be some hope. She must go to him. She must. She loved him.

'Sarah . . .' she began after some minutes, her voice barely audible. 'Sarah, do you think he will love me . . . will he want me and need me . . . while he has another woman?'

Sarah did not answer at once. She looked out of the window.

'Men are strange. Very strange,' she said eventually, in a whisper. Almost to herself.

Before them, the moon floated pale and lonely in the empty evening sky.

NOTES

Murram[1] – *A lateritic red soil used for untarred but levelled roads in East Africa.*

Duka[2] – *(Kiswahili) A small shop or general store.*

EXERCISES

1. There is a marked contrast in the attitude shown to Bena by the old couple in the bus and that shown by their son.
   a) How and why do they react differently to her?
   b) What are your own feelings of the attitude of the three individuals to Bena?

2. We can speculate on the likely fate of Bena in the story. What do you think eventually happens to her? Give reasons, based on clues in the story, for your answer.

3. " 'Men are strange, Very strange,' [Sarah] said eventually, in a whisper. Almost to herself." (p. 68)
   A Ngugi story, 'Minutes of Glory' (in the collection *Secret Lives*), ends in a similar way. Read that story and compare the relationship in it between Beatrice and Nyaguthii to that of Bena and Sarah in 'The Road to Mara'.

4. The main aim of this story is to contrast the life and values of the country with those of the town. In what different ways does the author indicate this contrast? (In answering this question you need to go beyond the bare

outline of the plot and make a close study of the author's choice of details to describe both village and town life.)

5. Explain the significance of the following images in 'The Road to Mara':
   a) the road;
   b) Bena's glass which falls and is shattered to pieces. (p. 66)

The Return

NGUGI WA THIONG'O

(KENYA)

THE ROAD WAS long. Whenever he took a step forward, little clouds of dust rose, whirled angrily behind him, and then slowly settled again. But a thin train of dust was left in the air, moving like smoke. He walked on, however, unmindful of the dust and ground under his feet. Yet with every step he seemed more and more conscious of the hardness and apparent animosity of the road. Not that he looked down; on the contrary, he looked straight ahead as if he would, any time now, see a familiar object that would hail him as a friend and tell him that he was near home. But the road stretched on.

He made quick, springing steps, his left hand dangling freely by the side of his once white coat, now torn and worn out. His right hand, bent at the elbow, held on to a string tied to a small bundle on his slightly drooping back. The bundle, well wrapped with a cotton cloth that had once been covered with printed red flowers now faded out, swung from side to side in harmony with the rhythm of his steps. The bundle held the bitterness and hardships of the years spent in detention camps. Now and then he looked at the sun on its homeward journey. Sometimes he darted quick side-glances at the small hedged strips of land which, with their sickly-looking crops, maize, beans and peas, appeared much as everything else did – unfriendly. The whole country was dull and seemed weary. To Kamau, this was nothing new. He remembered that, even before the Mau Mau emergency,[1] the over-tilled Gikuyu holdings wore haggard looks, in contrast to the sprawling green fields in the settled area.[2]

A path branched to the left. He hesitated for a moment and then made up his mind. For the first time, his eyes brightened a little as he went along the path that would take him down the valley and then to the village. At last home was near and, with that realization, that far-away look of the weary traveller seemed to desert him for a while.

The valley and the vegetation along it were in deep contrast to the surrounding country. For here, green bush and trees thrived. This could only mean one thing: Honia River still flowed. He quickened his steps as if he could scarcely believe this to be true till he had actually set his eyes on the river. It was there; it still flowed. Honia, where so often he had bathed, plunging stark naked into its cool living water, warmed his heart as he watched its serpentine movement round the rocks and heard its slight murmurs. A painful exhilaration passed through him, and for a moment he longed for those days. He sighed. Perhaps the river would not recognize in his hardened features that same boy to whom the riverside world had meant everything. Yet as he approached Honia, he felt more akin to it than he had felt to anything else since his release.

A group of women were drawing water. He was excited, for he could recognize one or two from his ridge. There was the middle-aged Wanjiku, whose deaf son had been killed by the Security Forces just before he himself was arrested. She had always been a darling of the village, having a smile for everyone and food for all. Would they receive him? Would they give him a hero's welcome? He thought so. Had he not always been a favourite all along the Ridge? And had he not fought for the land? He wanted to run and shout: 'Here I am. I have come back to you.' But he desisted. He was a man.

'Is it well with you?' A few voices responded.

The other women, with tired and worn features, looked at him mutely as if his greeting was of no consequence. Why! Had he been so long in the camp? His spirits were dampened as he feebly asked: 'Do you not remember me?' Again they looked at him. They stared at him with cold, hard looks; like everything else, they seemed to be deliberately refusing to know or own him.

It was Wanjiku who at last recognized him. But there was neither warmth nor enthusiasm in her voice as she said, 'Oh, is it you, Kamau? We thought you –' She did not continue. Only now he noticed something else – surprise? fear? He could not tell. He saw their quick glances dart at him and he knew for certain that a secret, from which he was excluded, bound them together.

'Perhaps I am no longer one of them!' he bitterly reflected. But they told him of the new village. The old village of scattered huts spread thinly over the Ridge was no more.

He left them, feeling embittered and cheated. The old village had not even waited for him. And suddenly he felt a strong nostalgia for his old home, friends and surroundings. He thought of his father, mother and – and – he dared not think about her. But for all that, Muthoni, just as she had been in the old days, came back to his mind. His heart beat faster. He felt desire, and a warmth thrilled through him. He quickened his step. He forgot the village women as he remembered his wife. He had stayed with her for a mere two weeks; then he had been swept away by the Colonial Forces. Like many others, he had been hurriedly screened and then taken to detention without trial. And all that time he had thought of nothing but the village and his beautiful woman.

The others had been like him. They had talked of nothing but their homes. One day he was working next to another detainee from Muranga. Suddenly the detainee, Njoroge, stopped breaking stones. He sighed heavily. His worn-out eyes had a far-away look.

'What's wrong, man? What's the matter with you?' Kamau asked.

'It is my wife. I left her expecting a baby. I have no idea what has happened to her.'

Another detainee put in: 'As for me, I left my woman with a baby. She had just been delivered. We were all happy. But on the same day I was arrested . . .'

And so they went on. All of them longed for one day – the day of their return home. Then life would begin anew.

Kamau himself had left his wife without a child. He had not even finished paying the bride-price. But now he would go, seek work in Nairobi, and pay off the remainder to Muthoni's parents. Life would indeed begin anew. They would have a son and bring him up in their own home. With these prospects before his eyes, he quickened his steps. He wanted to run – no, fly to hasten his return. He was now nearing the top of the hill. He wished he could suddenly meet his brothers and sisters. Would they ask him questions? He would, at any rate, not tell them everything that had happened: the beating, the screening and the work on the roads and in quarries with an *askari*[3] always nearby ready to kick him if he relaxed. Yes. He had suffered many humiliations, and he had not resisted. Was there any need? But his soul and all the vigour of his manhood had rebelled and bled with rage and bitterness.

One day these *wazungu*[4] would go!

One day his people would be free! Then, then – he did not know what he would do. However, he bitterly assured himself, no one would ever flout his manhood again.

He mounted the hill and then stopped. The whole plain lay below. The new village was before him – rows and rows of compact mud huts, crouching on the plain under the fast-vanishing sun. Dark blue smoke curled upwards from various huts, to form a dark mist that hovered over the village. Beyond, the deep, blood-red sinking sun sent out finger-like streaks of light that thinned outwards and mingled with the grey mist shrouding the distant hills.

In the village, he moved from street to street, meeting new faces. He inquired. He found his home. He stopped at the entrance to the yard and breathed hard and full. This was the moment of his return home. His father sat huddled up on a three-legged stool. He was now very aged and Kamau pitied the old man. But he had been spared – yes, spared to see his son's return.

'Father!'

The old man did not answer. He just looked at Kamau with strange vacant eyes. Kamau was impatient. He felt annoyed and irritated. Did he not see him? Would he behave like the women Kamau had met at the river?

In the street, naked and half-naked children were playing, throwing dust at one another. The sun had already set and it looked as if there would be moonlight.

'Father, don't you remember me?' Hope was shrinking in him. He felt tired. Then he saw his father suddenly start and tremble like a leaf. He saw him stare with unbelieving eyes. Fear was discernible in those eyes. His mother came, and his brothers too.

They crowded around him. His aged mother clung to him and sobbed hard.

'I knew my son would come. I knew he was not dead.'

'Why, who told you I was dead?'

'That Karanja, son of Njogu.'

And then Kamau understood. He understood his trembling father. He understood the women at the river. But one thing puzzled him: he had never been in the same detention camp with Karanja. Anyway he had come back. He wanted now to see Muthoni. Why had she not come out? He wanted to shout, 'I have come, Muthoni; I am here.' He looked around. His mother understood him. She quickly darted a glance at her man and then simply said: 'Muthoni went away.'

Kamau felt something cold settle in his stomach. He looked at the village huts and the dullness of the land. He wanted to ask many questions but he dared not. He could not yet believe that Muthoni had gone. But he knew by the look of the women at the river, by the look of his parents, that she was gone.

'She was a good daughter to us,' his mother was explaining. 'She waited for you and patiently bore all the ills of the land. Then Karanja came and said that you were dead. Your father believed him. She believed him too and mourned for a month. Karanja constantly paid us visits. He was of your *rika*[5], you know. Then she got a child. We could have kept her. But where is the land? Where is the food? With land consolidation[6], our last security was taken away. We let Karanja go with her. Other women have done worse – gone to town. Only the infirm and the old have remained here.'

He was not listening; the coldness in this stomach slowly changed to bitterness. He felt bitter against all, all the people including his father and mother. They had betrayed him. They had leagued against him, and Karanja had always been his rival. Five years admittedly was not a short time. But why did she go? Why did they allow her to go? He wanted to speak. Yes, speak and denounce everything – the women at the river, the village and the people who dwelt there. But he could not. This bitter thing was choking him.

'You – you gave my own away?' he whispered.

'Listen, child, child . . .'

The big yellow moon dominated the horizon. He hurried away

bitter and blind, and only stopped when he came to the Honia River.

And standing on the bank, he saw not the river, but instead his hopes dashed to the ground. The river moved swiftly, making ceaseless monotonous murmurs. In the forest the crickets and other insects kept up an incessant buzz. And above, the moon shone bright. He tried to remove his coat, and the small bundle he had held on to so firmly fell. It rolled down the bank and, before Kamau knew what was happening, it was floating swiftly down the river. For a time he was shocked and wanted to retrieve it. What would he show his – Oh, had he forgotten so soon? His wife had gone. And the little things that had so strangely reminded him of her, and that he had guarded all those years, had gone! He did not know why, but somehow he felt relieved. Thoughts of drowning himself dispersed. He began to put on his coat, murmuring to himself, 'Why should she have waited for me? Why should all the changes have waited for my return?'

NOTES

Mau Mau emergency[1] – *Mau Mau was the name given to the Kikuyu guerilla war waged in the 1950s against British colonial rule and to regain land alienated by the white settlers.*

When the new governor, Sir Evelyn Baring, arrived in Kenya in September 1952, he found the security situation in the country, especially in Central Province, rapidly deteriorating. On 20th October, 1952 he signed a proclamation declaring that 'a public emergency has arisen which makes it necessary to confer special powers on the Government and its officials for the purpose of maintaining law and order'. The emergency officially ended on 12th January, 1960.

Settled area[2] – *The 'White Highlands' reserved for European settlers in colonial Kenya.*

Askari[3] – *(Kiswahili) Policeman, soldier, guard.*

Wazungu[4] – *(Kiswahili) Europeans.*

Rika[5] – *(Kikuyu) Age-group.*

Land consolidation[6] – *A process which began in Kenya's Central*

Province in the 1950s. *Various scattered pieces of land owned by an individual were 'consolidated' into one farm. Land consolidation and freehold land titles reduced the traditional rights of Kikuyu tenants on the new farms and many were left landless.*

EXERCISES

1. Critics have observed that an important theme in Ngugi's fiction is his characters' 'returns' and 'homecomings', and their subsequent disillusionment.
   a) In what important ways is Kamau in 'The Return' disillusioned with his homecoming?
   b) Considering the situation in the story, and the fact that people and circumstances change, is Kamau not being naive and unrealistic in expecting to find things the same as when he had left five years before?

2. In 'The Return' Ngugi tries to suggest the trauma suffered during the Emergency by the Gikuyu people, both as individuals and on a communal level. How successful would you say he is in the task he set himself in this story?

3. After Kamau learns he has lost his wife to Karanja, he reacts in the following way: 'He felt bitter against all, all the people including his father and mother. They had betrayed him.' (p. 74)
   Imagine that you lived in Kamau's community at the time. You have been assigned the task of trying to soothe his hurt feelings, of 'explaining' matters to him. How would you go about it?

4. 'The bundle held the bitterness and hardship of the years spent in detention camps.' (p. 70)
   a) What is the *symbolic* significance of this bundle to Kamau?
   b) And of its accidentally falling into the river and floating away?

5. In the Introduction it was mentioned how sometimes a writer incorporates a character or an episode from one of his

short stories into a longer work. Ngugi has done this often. Joshua in 'The Village Priest' later reappears in *The River Between*; the English couple who feature in 'Goodbye Africa' become the Thompsons in *A Grain of Wheat*; Kamau in 'The Return' is the 'prototype' for Gikonyo in *A Grain of Wheat*.

Work on this project: read *A Grain of Wheat* and explain how Ngugi went on to develop the character Gikonyo in greater depth and complexity than his original model Kamau in 'The Return'.

Kingi

SADRUDIN KASSAM
(KENYA)

HE WAS CALLED Kingi Bald. Glistening black and plump with cheeks blown out like big bubblegum balloons, he was a familiar sight in the village doing the rounds of the houses riding a high, rickety donkey-cart sagging under *debes*[1] of spilling water.

Daily he would come rattling down to the villages ringing a bicycle bell nailed to his cart, greeting women, frightening children, or just booming a song.

On Sunday afternoon, however, he was 'off'. Then he would put on a kilt[2], a small balmoral cap[3] and a crumpled white shirt, and, with a big whitewashed bagpipe[4] slung tightly across his chest, march down the tarmac road blowing his instrument. The skirl[5], loud, wild, abandoned, yet tuneful, could be heard far and wide over the village.

A child would appear, then another, and another, and soon there would be a crowd of little boys and girls straggling behind him beating tins and singing and whistling and dancing. When he came to our house he stopped, and began to sing. The song was 'Have I told you lately that I love you . . .?' But Kingi knew only that much, so he made up for the rest of the tune by adding the words 'I love you, love you, love you'. Now and then he would squint towards our window where Nargis and I would be watching him. Sometimes he would stop in the middle and try the tune on his pipe but, failing, would quickly revert to his singing, his huge, resonant voice swirling out all about the place. After a few moments, squinting at us for the last time, he would walk on, singing, until he thought he was out of hearing. Then the pipe would begin again and as he walked away the skirl would grow fainter until, a long time afterwards, it could be heard no more.

The village proper consisted of only a dozen or so *dukas* and 'hotels' standing along the main road. But there were many huts scattered about in the surrounding *shambas*[6]. It was somewhere across this maze on a high cliff that Kingi lived.

We were the only Indian family in the village and I suspect this was the reason Kingi changed to singing when he approached our house. I think he wanted to show us that he could sing in English. And Nargis and I were awed by his song and yet enjoyed it.

Unfortunately we were not allowed to follow him like the other children. Mother said if we did he would carry us away to his hut and bewitch us so that we would become his obedient slaves and would never want to return to our parents. But I knew she as cheating us for he never harmed the other children whom I saw daily playing around the village. And, in any case, who would not want to serve Kingi? Sometimes I cried before Mother and said I was not being allowed to go out anywhere; I only wanted to follow Kingi to the last *duka* and then I would come running back.

One day I decided to risk it by stealing out while Father and Mother were asleep. As a precaution I would carry my cub's penknife and a whistle hidden in my pockets. I promised Nargis that if nothing happened, the following Sunday we would go out together.

The first Sunday came. We sat at the window waiting for the piper. Nargis seemed sad and concerned and kept admonishing me as if she were Mother and I were going away to England or some such far-away place for further studies.

Then the shrill tunes came from far off in the distance. I could see him in my mind, walking with big steps . . . amid those children. My heart began to beat faster. Kingi was coming. At Nargis's reminder I checked my penknife and whistle. But I was impatient, excited, yearning to meet him.

I would do it very carefully, without hurrying. I would be well behind him at first, but, if he didn't do anything, I would begin to walk faster until I was quite near him. Then I would be able to find out if the chequered cloth reaching to his knees was actually a skirt or shorts and whether he was wearing anything under it. I also wanted to touch his pipe and, if he would allow me, even to blow it. I could do it, it was quite easy.

He must be near now, just round the bend.

And then . . . There he was . . . *Kingi*! And, oh, blowing so hard on the pipe I feared his smooth round cheeks would burst. He was swaying gaily, his fingers rising and falling on the chanter[7] in a kind of drumming movement.

As he approached our window his music slowed down and then he stopped. He took out a dirty handkerchief and mopped his glistening forehead and cheeks, as if there should be no sweat without music.

Then he sang, but only for a few seconds standing there, and began to walk on again.

Wishing Nargis bye-bye I slipped out through the back door.

Kingi saw me join his procession and he put more energy into his flagging voice. And now, how it boomed: deep, powerful, resonant, encompassing all the surrounding land. And how erect he walked.

Soon many more children joined in, while some people came out to watch us. Today Kingi sang longer. And, I knew it, it was for me, and I inwardly thanked him for it. He stopped at an Arab *duka* for a cigarette then, coming out, he began his pipe again. I was quite near him now. Now and then he would smile or wink at me, which thrilled me tremendously. Why was he doing that? Was he going to adopt me, or make me his pupil and teach me to play his pipe? I wouldn't mind if he did so. I wanted to learn to play the pipe. And slowly, as I stood there watching him intently I imagined myself dressed in similar clothes and the big pipe slung across my chest, going from house to house, delighting people, earning their applause (and also some money). He is the youngest bagpipe player in the world, someone would exclaim.

A large crowd had gathered now. The piper stopped and majesticaly looked round, and then at me

Extending his left hand he asked me with a big smile, 'How are you?'

'Very well, thank you,' I replied.

'You are very well?' he asked again.

'Yes.'

'Very good, very good,' he said patting me on the shoulder. It was really a giant's hand, yet so gentle. I felt elated.

He went into the shop again and came out with sweets. He offered me one which I accepted with a big bowing thank you. It impressed him so much he quickly offered me another. But now [7], of course, declined. I asked him if he would let me try the pipe.

'You want to play this?' he asked, pointing. 'Come,' he said, offering a finger. 'Come, let us go. I will teach you how to play the pipe like an expert.'

There was no time to think.

I took the finger and we began to walk away. My dream was coming true. Soon I would be offering my finger to the village children, even to the grown-ups. He's the greatest bagpipe player in the world, everyone would say.

He didn't walk military-style now, but he began to sing. On the way he asked me if I liked the song.

'It's a song on a big gramophone record,' he added reflectively.

I said I liked it very much and wished I could sing like him.

We turned left to a path zigzagging through coconut *shambas*.

His hut stood before a cluster of pawpaw trees. From the tip of its *makuti*[8] roof flew a black rag: his flag, he explained. His donkey, 'Kingi Junior', was tied to a coconut tree nearby.

The hut was small, dark, uncemented and round, furnished with only a narrow wooden bed and a small cupboard filled with bottles and kitchen utensils. The room smelt heavily of copra and *tembo*[9].

He lighted a rusty lantern on the cupboard and seated me on his bed. Then he offered me a *mahamri*[10] and some *mbarazi*[11] on a dirty plate, and sat down beside me, without his pipe. When I had finished he picked up the pipe and slung it across my chest.

'There you are!' he said.

I didn't know what to say or do. And the pipe was so heavy.

'I'll just change, and then teach you my pipe,' he said.

And soon he was smiling in front of me, stark naked (he didn't wear anything under the kilt). I was terrified, though only for a moment.

He went to the cupboard and began to rummage through a bundle of clothes. He found a *kanga*[12], tied it round his waist and came up and sat down beside me again. Taking back the pipe he started to teach me.

I asked him what tune it was. He thought for a moment and said slowly that it was the Portuguese version of the song 'I love you, love you'. It reminded me of the Fort Jesus[13] in the days of Portuguese rule and I fancied their soldiers lounging near the entrance and humming the tune or playing it on huge bagpipes of brass or beautifully carved wood. I thought Kingi must have fought in those wars in his childhood or youth, otherwise how else could he have learnt it?

'I must now teach you to sing,' he said. 'Singing is very important if you want to become a good piper.'

And so he launched into his song. But now he depressed me. His voice was hoarse and forced. If only I had something to offer him to drink!

Soon we got up and, holding each other's hands, began dancing and singing and doing a Digo *ngoma*[14]. Now and then his *kanga* would loosen and slip down and he would be naked again. But I was no longer frightened. I liked his strong body and wished I was as big and muscular as he was.

When we were tired we returned to the bed, and he began to tell me a story he had read, as he said, in a big African book of adventures.

Once upon a time there was a great Sultan ruling over Zanzibar and the coast, he began. I sat there beside him, rapt, fascinated, abstracted, my mind closed to everything but the Sultan's story.

There was a knock at the door.

I perceived it only vaguely, like a grain of sand dropped in a deep bowl of water. I looked towards the door, still only dimly aware of any intrusion.

The piper broke off and got up.

Then a thrill ran through my blood. I stared after him, trembling with wide open eyes.

Father! As the door swung open, I screamed and looked round, but there was nowhere to run. My heart beat heavily. I knew what would happen to me: I would be whipped, whipped like a slave till I bled. There would be no mercy upon me, nothing but lashes.

He was accompanied by an *askari*.

'You satan!' he thundered at me.

I burst out crying and screaming and pleading for forgiveness. He dragged me away from the bed, tweaking my ear and warning me of the worst that would befall me at home.

'You rascal! You wait, you'll never forget this night,' he growled, as we emerged from the hut.

We walked to our old boxbody by the main road and drove away. I was sobbing, and now more frightened as I thought of the prison cell and the drunkards and robbers with whom I would have to sleep and eat nothing but boiled beans and *ugali*[15].

Mother and Nargis were waiting at the door of our house. As the car stopped I ran in past them and locked myself in my room. I heard Father shouting and arguing with Mother and scolding Nargis.

But soon I was asleep.

NOTES

Kingi (Title) – From 'King'. Name given to the leaders of competing musical troupes which, till before independence, used to perform in public processions in Mombasa and Malindi.

Debe[1] – (Kiswahili) Four-gallon tin used for carrying water.

Kilt[2] – A skirt of tartan cloth reaching from waist to knee; part of Scottish male dress.

Balmoral cap[3] – Scottish cap.

Bagpipe[4] – A Scottish musical instrument with a bag (which holds air), and melody and fixed-note pipes.

Skirl[5] – The characteristic sound of bagpipes.

Shamba[6] – (Kiswahili) Farm.

Chanter[7] – A bagpipe's melody-pipe.

Makuti[8] – (Kiswahili) Dried coconut palm-frond thatching.

Tembo[9] – (Kiswahili) Palm wine, the fermented sap of the coconut tree.

Mahamri[10] – *(Kiswahili) A kind of doughnut spiced with cinnamon or cardamom.*

Mbarazi[11] – *(Kiswahili) Pigeon peas.*

Kanga[12] – *(Kiswahili) A brightly-coloured length of patterned cloth worn by women as a long skirt or shawl.*

Fort Jesus[13] – *A stronghold built by the Portuguese in the years 1593–96 at Mombasa in order to control the East African coast. Captured by the Omani Arabs in 1698. During British times it was used as a prison for sixty years until 1958 when it was declared a national monument.*

Ngoma[14] – *(Kiswahili) Dance.*

Ugali[15] – *(Kiswahili) Cooked maize meal.*

EXERCISES

1. 'Kingi' is told from the point of view of a child narrator. Make a study of the different methods the writer uses to reflect this fact. Consider the following points:
   a) The language and narrative method used.
   b) The child's hero-worshipping of Kingi. Why does he (and the other village children) find Kingi such a fascinating figure?
   c) The child's reasoning, his strong imagination, his curiosity, love of stories and propensity towards fantasy.
   d) The narrator is, as children tend to be, clearly perceptive. He records his intense admiration of his idol but he also notes his idol's shortcomings.
   e) How does the last sentence of the story reveal a child's attitude to experience, fear, adventure and life?

2. Are the boy's parents justified in disapproving of their son's going off with Kingi? Give an explanation for your answer.

Tekayo

GRACE OGOT
(KENYA)

THE PERIOD OF short rains was just starting in a semi-arid part of the Sudan. The early morning mist had cleared, and faint blue smoke rose from the ground as the hot sun touched the surface of the wet earth.

'People in the underworld are cooking. People in the underworld are cooking!' The children shouted as they pelted one another with wet sand.

'Come on Opija,' Tekayo shouted to his son. 'Give me a hand. I must get the cows to the river before it is too hot.'

Opija hit his younger brother with his last handful of sand, and then ran to help his father. The cows were soon out of the village and Tekayo picked up the leather pouch containing his lunch and followed them.

They had not gone far from home when Tekayo saw an eagle flying above his head with a large piece of meat in its claws. The eagle was flying low searching for a suitable spot to have its meal. Tekayo promptly threw his stick at the bird. He hit the meat and it dropped to the ground. It was a large piece of liver, and fresh blood was still oozing from it. Tekayo nearly threw the meat away, but he changed his mind. What was the use of robbing the eagle of its food only to throw it away? The meat looked good: it would supplement his vegetable lunch wonderfully. He wrapped the meat in a leaf and pushed it into his pouch.

They reached a place where there was plenty of grass. Tekayo allowed the cows to graze while he sat under an *ober* tree[1] watching the sky. It was not yet lunch time, but Tekayo could not wait. The desire to taste that meat was burning within him. He took out the meat and roasted it on a log fire under the *ober* tree. When the meat was cooked he ate it greedily with millet bread which his wife had made the previous night.

'My! What delicious meat,' Tekayo exclaimed. He licked the fat juice that stained his fingers and longed for a little more. He threw away the bitter herbs that were the rest of his lunch. The meat was so good, and the herbs would merely spoil its taste.

The sun was getting very hot but the cows showed no desire to go to the river to drink. One by one they lay down in the shade, chewing the cud. Tekayo also became overpowered by the afternoon heat. He rested against the trunk and slept.

While asleep, Tekayo had a dream. He was sitting before a log fire roasting a large piece of liver like the one he had eaten earlier. His mouth watered as he watched rich fat from the roasting meat dropping into the fire. He could not wait and, although the meat was not completely done, he removed it from the fire and cut it up with his hunting knife. But just as he was about to take the first bite, he woke up.

Tekayo looked around him, wondering what had happened to the meat! Could it be that he was dreaming? 'No, no, no,' he cried. 'It was too vivid to be a dream!' He sat upright and had another look around, as if by some miracle he might see a piece of liver roasting on the log fire beside him. But there was nothing. All he saw were the large roots of the old tree protruding from the earth's surface like sweet potatoes in sandy soil.

The cattle had wandered a long way off. Tekayo got up and followed them. They reached the river bank, and the thirsty cows ran to the river. While the cows drank, Tekayo sat on a white stone cooling his feet and gazing lazily at the mightily swollen river as it flowed towards the plain.

Beyond the river stood the great 'Ghost Jungle'. A strong desire for the rich meat came back to Tekayo, and he whispered, 'The animal with that delicious liver must surely be in that jungle.' He sat there for a while, thinking. The temptation to start hunting for the animal nagged him. But he managed to suppress it. The afternoon was far spent and they were a long way from home.

The next morning Tekayo left home earlier than usual. When

his wife begged him to wait for his lunch, he refused. He hurried from home, taking his hunting spears with him.

Tekayo made it impossible for the cows to graze. He rushed them along, lashing at any cow that lingered in one spot for long. They reached the edge of the Ghost Jungle and there he left the cows grazing unattended.

Tekayo could not see any path or track leading into the Ghost Jungle. The whole place was a mass of thick bush and long grass covered with the morning dew. And, except for the sounds of mating birds, there was a weird silence in the jungle that frightened him. But the vehement desire within him blindly drove him on, through the thick wet grass.

After walking for some time, he stood and listened. Something was racing towards him. He turned round to look, and sure enough a big impala was running frantically in his direction. Warm blood rushed through Tekayo's body and he raised his spear to kill the animal. But the spear never landed. He came face to face with a big leopardess that was chasing the impala. The leopardess roared at Tekayo several times challenging him, as it were, to a duel. But Tekayo looked away, clutching the spear in his trembling hand. There was no one to fight and the beast went away after her prey.

'What a bad start,' Tekayo said slowly and quietly when his heart beat normally again. 'That wild cat will not leave me alone now.'

He started to walk back towards the plain, following the track he had made. The roaring leopardess had taken the life out of him.

He saw another track that cut across the forest. He hesitated a little, and then decided to follow it, leaving his own. The track got bigger and bigger, and without any warning Tekayo suddenly came upon a baby wildebeest which was following a large herd grazing at the foot of a hill. He killed it without any difficulty. He skinned the animal and extracted its liver, leaving the rest of the carcass there.

Tekayo returned to his herd, and he sat down to roast the meat on a log fire. When the meat was cooked he took a bite and chewed it hurriedly. But he did not swallow it; he spat it all out! The liver was as bitter as the strong green herbs given to constipated children. The back of his tongue was stinging as if it had been burned. Tekayo threw the rest of the meat away and took his cows home.

He arrived home tired and disappointed; and when his young wife set food before him he refused to eat. He pretended that he had stomach ache and did not feel like eating. That night Tekayo was depressed and in low spirits. He did not even desire his young wife who slept by his side. At dawn the young wife returned to her hut disappointed, wondering why the old man had not desired her.

The doors of all the huts were still closed when Tekayo looked out through his door. A cold east wind hit his face, and he quickly shut himself in again.

It was getting rather late and the calves were calling. But it was pouring with rain so much that he could not start milking. He sat on the hard bed looking at the dead ashes in the fireplace. He longed to get out to start hunting.

When the rain stopped, Tekayo milked the cows in a great hurry. Then he picked up the lunch that had been left for him near his hut, and left the village. His wife, disappointed by the previous night, watched him till he disappeared at the gate.

When he reached the Ghost Jungle, it was drizzling again. The forest looked so lonely and wet. He left the cows grazing as usual and entered the bush, stealing his way through the dripping leaves. He turned to the left to avoid the thick part of the jungle. Luck was with him. He spotted a family of antelope grazing not far from him. He crawled on his knees till he was quite close to them, and then threw his spear killing one animal instantly. After skinning it, he extracted its liver, and also took some delicate parts for the family.

When he sat down under the tree to roast the meat, Tekayo was quite sure that he had been successful. But when he tasted the meat he shook his head. The meat was tender, but it was not what he was looking for.

They reached the river bank. The cows, after drinking, continued to graze and Tekayo, without realizing it, wandered a long way from his herd, still determined to discover the owner of that wonderful liver.

When he suddenly looked round, the herd was nowhere to be seen. The sun was sinking behind Mount Pajulu, and Tekayo started to run, looking for his cows.

The cows, heavy with milk, had gone home without Tekayo. For one day when Tekayo's children got lost in the forest, the cows had gone home without them, following the old track they knew well. On that day the whole village came out in search of the children in fear that the wild animals might harm them.

It was getting dark when Tekayo arrived home. They started to milk and Odipo remarked. 'Why, Father, you are late coming home today.'

'It is true,' replied Tekayo thoughtfully. 'See that black bull there? He went to another herd across the river. I didn't miss him until it was time to come home. One of these days, we shall have to castrate him – he is such a nuisance.'

They milked in silence until one of the little girls came to fetch some milk for preparing vegetables.

At supper time the male members of the family sat around the log fire waiting and talking. One by one, baskets of millet meal and earthen dishes of meat and vegetables arrived from different huts. There was fish, dried meat, fried white ants, and herbs. A little food was thrown to the ground, to the ancestors, and then they started eating. They compared and contrasted the deliciousness of the various dishes they were having. But Tekayo kept quiet. All the food he tasted that evening was bitter as bile.

When the meal was over, the adults told stories of war and the clans to the children who listened attentively. But Tekayo was not with them: he was not listening. He watched the smoky clouds as they raced across the sky.

'Behind those clouds, behind those clouds, rests my great-grandfather. Please! Please!' Tekayo beseeched him. 'Please, Father, take this longing away from me. Give me back my manhood that I may desire my wives. For what is a man without this desire!'

A large cloud covered the moon giving the earth temporary darkness. Tears stung Tekayo's eyes, and he dismissed the family to sleep. As he entered his own hut a woman was throwing small logs on the fire.

He offered many secret prayers to the departed spirits, but the craving for the mysterious liver never left him. Day after day he left home in the morning, taking his cows with him. And on reaching the jungle, he left them unattended while he hunted. The rough and disappointed life that he led soon became apparent to the family. He suddenly became old and uninterested in life. He had nothing to tell his sons around the evening fire, and he did not desire his wives. The sons of Tekayo went to Lakech and told her, 'Mother, speak to Father, he is sick. He does not talk to us, and he does not eat. We don't know how to approach him.'

Though Lakech had passed the age of child-bearing and no longer went to Tekayo's hut at night, she was his first wife and he loved her. She therefore went and asked him, 'Man, what ails you?'

Tekayo looked at Lakech, but he could not look into her eyes. He looked at her long neck, and instead of answering her question he asked her, 'Would you like to get free from those heavy brass rings around your neck?'

'Why?' Lakech replied, surprised.

'Because they look so tight.'

'But they are not tight,' Lakech said softly. 'I would feel naked without them.'

And Tekayo looked away from his wife. He was longing to tell Lakech everything, and to share with her this maddening craving that was tearing his body to pieces. But he checked himself. Lakech must not know; she would not understand. Then he lied to her.

'It is my old indigestion. I have had it for weeks now. It will soon pass.'

A mocking smile played on Lakech's lips, and Tekayo knew that she was not convinced. Some visitors arrived and Lakech left her husband.

Tekayo hunted for many months, but he did not succeed in finding the animal with the delicious liver.

One night, as he lay awake, he asked himself where else he could hunt. And what animal would he be looking for? He had killed all the different animals in the Ghost Jungle. He had risked his life when he had killed and eaten the liver of a lion, a leopard and a hyena, all of which were tabooed by his clan.

A little sleep came to Tekayo's heavy eyes and he was grateful. But then Apii stood beside his bed calling: 'Grandpa, Grandpa, it is me.' Tekayo sat up, but the little girl was not there. He went back to sleep again. Apii was there calling him: 'Can't you hear me, Grandpa?'

Tekayo woke up a second time, but nobody was there. He lay down without closing his eyes. Again the child's fingers touched his drooping hand, and the playful voice of a child tickled the skin of the old man. Tekayo sat up a third time and looked round the room. But he was alone. The cock crew a third time, and it was morning.

And Lakech died without knowing her husband's secret, and was buried in the middle of the village, being the first wife. Tekayo sat at his wife's grave morning and evening for a long time, and his grief for her appeased his hunger for the unknown animal's liver. He wept, but peacefully, as if his craving for the liver was buried with his wife.

It was during this time of grief that Tekayo decided never to go hunting again. He sat at home and looked after his many grandchildren, while the younger members of the family went out to work daily in the fields.

And then one day as Tekayo sat warming himself in the early morning sun near the granary, he felt slightly sick from the smell of grain sprouting inside the dark store. The shouting and singing of his grandchildren attracted his attention. As he watched them playing, the craving for the liver of the unknown animal returned powerfully to him.

Now among the children playing was a pretty little girl called Apii, the daughter of Tekayo's eldest son. Tekayo sent the other children away to play and, as they were going, he called Apii and told her, 'Come my little one, run to your mother's hut and bring me a calabash of water.'

Apii ran to her mother's hut to get water for her grandfather. And while she was fumbling in a dark corner of the house looking for a clean calabash, strong hands gripped her neck and strangled her. She gave a weak cry as she struggled for the breath of life. But it was too much for her. Her eyes closed in everlasting sleep, never to see the beauty of the shining moon again.

The limp body of the child slipped from Tekayo's hands and fell on the floor with a thud. He looked at the body at his feet and felt sick and faint. His ears were buzzing. He picked up the body and, as he staggered out with it, the air seemed black, and the birds of the air screamed ominously at him. But Tekayo had to eat his meal. He buried the body of Apii in a nearby anthill in a shallow grave.

The other children were still playing in the field when Tekayo returned with the liver in his bag. He roasted it in his hut hastily and ate it greedily. And alas! it was what he had been looking for for many years. He sat lazily resting his back on the granary, belching and picking his teeth. The hungry children, back from their play in the fields sat in the shade eating sweet potatoes and drinking sour milk.

The older people came back in the evening, and the children ran to meet their parents. But Apii was not amongst them. In great desperation they asked the grandfather about the child. But Tekayo replied, 'Ask the children, they should know where Apii is. They were playing together in the fields.'

It was already pitch dark. Apii's younger brothers and sisters sat in front of the fire weeping with their mother. It was then that they remembered their grandfather sending Apii to fetch water for him. The desperate parents repeated this information to the old man, asking him if Apii had brought water for him that morning.

'She did,' Tekayo replied, 'and then ran away after the others. I watched her go with my own eyes. When they came back, I was asleep.'

The grief-stricken family sat near the fireplace, their heads in their hands. They neither ate nor drank. Outside the little crickets sang in chorus as if they had a secret to tell.

For many days Apii's parents looked for their child, searching every corner and every nook. But there was no trace of her. Apii was gone. Months went by, and people talked no more about the disappearance of Apii. Only her mother thought of her. She did not lose hope of finding her child alive one day.

Tekayo forgot his deed. And when he killed a second child in the same way to satisfy his savage appetite, he was not even conscious of what he was doing. And when the worried parents asked the old man about the child, Tekayo wept, saying, 'How could I know? The children play out in the fields; I stay here at home.'

It was after this that Tekayo's sons said among themselves, 'Who steals our children? Which animal can it be? Could it be a hyena? Or a leopard? But these animals only hunt at night. Could it be an eagle, because it hunts during the day? But no!

Father would have seen the eagle; he would have heard the child screaming.'

After some thought, Aganda told his brother, 'Perhaps it is a malicious animal brought upon us by the evil spirits.'

'Then my father is too old to watch the children,' put in Osogo.

'Yes, Father is too old, he is in danger," the rest agreed.

And from that time onwards the sons kept watch secretly on the father and the children. They watched for many months, but nothing threatened the man and the children.

The sons were almost giving up the watch. But one day when it was the turn of Apii's father to keep watch, he saw Tekayo sending away the children to play in the field – all except one. He sent this child to fetch him a pipe from his hut. As the child ran to the hut, Tekayo followed him. He clasped the frightened child and dragged him towards the fireplace. As Tekayo was struggling with the child, a heavy blow landed on his old back. He turned round sharply, his hands still holding the child's neck. He was facing Aganda, his eldest son. The child broke loose from the limp hands of Tekayo and grabbed Aganda's knees as if he had just escaped from the teeth of a crocodile.

'Father!' Aganda shouted.

Seeing that the child was not hurt, Aganda pushed him aside, saying, 'Go to your mother's hut and lie down.'

He then got hold of the old man and dragged him towards the little windowless hut built for goats and sheep. As he was being dragged away, the old man kept on crying, '*Atimo, ang' o? Atimo ang' o?*' (What have I done? What have I done?)

Aganda pushed the old man into the little hut and barred the door behind him, as you would to the animals. He went to the child, who was still sobbing.

The rest of the family returned from the fields, and when Apii's father broke the news to them, they were appalled. The family wore mourning garments and went without food.

'Tho! Tho!' they spat towards the sun which, although setting on them, was rising on the ancestors.

'Great-grandfathers, cleanse us,' they all cried.

And they lit the biggest fire that had ever been lit in that village. Tekayo's eldest son took the old greasy drum hanging above the fireplace in his father's hut and beat it. The drum throbbed out sorrowful tunes to warn the clan that there was sad news in Tekayo's home. The people who heard the drum left whatever they were doing and ran to Tekayo's village following the sound of the drum. Within a short time the village was teeming with anxious-looking relatives.

'What news? What news?' they asked in trembling voices.

'And where is Tekayo?' another old man asked.

'Is he in good health?' asked another.

There was confusion and panic.

'Death of death, who will give us medicine for death? Death knocks at your door and, before you can tell him to come in, he is in the house with you.'

'Listen!' Someone touched the old woman who was mourning about death. Aganda spoke to the people.

'Men of my clan. We have not called you here for nothing. Listen to me and let our sorrow be yours. Weep with us! For several months we have been losing our children when we go to work in the fields. Apii, my own child, was the first one to disappear.'

Sobbing broke out among the women at the mention of the children's names.

'My people,' Aganda continued, 'the children in this clan get sick and die. But ours disappear unburied. It was our idea to keep watch over our children that we might catch whoever steals them. For months we have been watching secretly. We were almost giving up because we thought it was probably the wrath of our ancestors that was upon us. But today I caught him.'

'What man? What man?' the people demanded angrily.

'And from what clan is he?' others asked.

'We must declare war on his clan, we must, we must!'

Aganda stopped for a while, and told them in a quavering voice, 'The man is in that little hut. The man is no one else but my father.'

'*Mayo!*'[2] the women shouted.

There was a scuffle and the women and children screamed as if Tekayo was around the fire and they were afraid of him. But the men kept quiet.

When the commotion died down, an old man asked, 'Do you speak the truth, man?'

The son nodded. Men and women now shouted, 'Where is

the man? Kill him! He is not one of us. He is not one of us. He is an animal!'

There was nothing said outside that Tekayo did not hear. And there in the hut the children he had killed haunted him. He laid his head on the rough wall of the hut and wept.

Outside the hut the angry villagers continued with their demand, shouting, 'Stone him now! Stone him now! Let his blood be upon his own head!'

But one of the old men got up and calmed the people.

'We cannot stone him now. It is the custom of the clan that a wicked man should be stoned in broad daylight, outside the village. We cannot depart from this custom.'

'Stone me now, stone me now,' Tekayo whispered. 'Take me away quickly from this torture and shame. Let me die and be finished with.'

Tekayo knew by the angry shouting of the men and the shrill cries of frightened women and children that he was banished from society, nay, from life itself. He fumbled in his leather bag suspended around his waist to find his hunting knife, but it was not there. It had been taken away from him.

The muttering and shouting continued outside. There was weeping too. But Tekayo was now hearing them from afar as if a powerful wave were carrying him further and further away from his people.

At dawn the villagers got up from the fireplace to gather stones from nearby fields. The sun was not up yet, but it was just light enough to see. Everyone in the clan must throw a stone at the murderer. It was bad not to throw a stone, for it was claimed that the murderer's wicked spirit would rest upon the man who did not help to drive him away.

When the first rays of the sun appeared, the villagers had gathered enough stones to cover several bodies. They returned to the village to fetch Tekayo from the hut and to lead him to his own garden outside the village. They surrounded the hut and stood in silence, waiting to jeer and spit at him when he came out.

Aganda and three old men tore the papyrus door open and called Tekayo to come out. But there was no reply. They rushed into the hut to drag him out to the people who were now demanding, 'Come out, come out!'

At first it was too dark to see. But soon their eyes got used to the darkness. Then they saw the body of Tekayo hanged on a short rope that he had unwound from the thatched roof.

The men came out shaking their heads. The crowd peered into the hut in turn until all of them had seen the dangling body of Tekayo – the man they were preparing to stone. No one spoke. Such a man, they knew, would have to be buried outside the village. They knew too that no new-born child would ever be named after him.

NOTES

Ober tree[1] – *A very common tree in south Nyanza. The Luo use its bark and leaves for medicinal purposes.*

Mayo[2] – *(Dholuo) Exclamation of horror, literally 'My mother!'*

EXERCISES

1. After Tekayo has tasted the liver dropped by the eagle, he is filled with a craving which gradually leads to his moral disintegration. This is seen in how Tekayo progressively cuts himself off from his own better nature, from his relations, community and work. In murdering the children entrusted to his care and in his eventual suicide, he effectively cuts himself off, in life, death and for all time, from his community.
Read the story carefully. Then outline the various steps in Tekayo's disintegration, in his severing himself from moral and human ties. Enter your points under three broad headings: Tekayo's disintegration in relation to his:
   a) own inner integrity;
   b) relations and community;
   c) work

2. In the course of the story Tekayo has two dreams (p. 86, pp. 90–91). Closely examine the sections which relate the content of these dreams. Then suggest the way(s) in

which they further the action of the story in relation to Tekayo's decline into evil.

3. An American cartoonist once had one of his cartoon characters declare, 'We have met the enemy and he is us.' Very often, while we are busy looking for external enemies and scapegoats to blame, the essential evil that must be faced and conquered is really *within* us.
   Study 'Tekayo' to determine the different ways in which the author shows that because Tekayo blinds himself to the evil within, he is eventually overcome and destroyed by it. Here are some points you will need to consider:
   a) Tekayo the hunter who himself becomes a predator. "He came face to face with a big leopardess . . . 'That wild cat will not leave me alone now.'" (p. 87) How can the leopardess be seen as a symbol of the evil within Tekayo?
   b) Tekayo's greed for the meat. Notice the language the author uses to describe this; we get the impression that Tekayo eagerly nourishes the evil craving within himself.
   c) He projects on to his innocent wife Lakech his own sense of being enslaved to the evil craving (p. 90).
   d) He breaks various taboos of the clan without giving any thought to what he is doing (p. 90). Later, as he becomes more inured to evil and unwilling to rescue himself or be rescued from his terrible craving, Tekayo loses all moral sense of right and wrong. He murders Apii. 'Tekayo forgot his deed. And when he killed a second child in the same way to satisfy his savage appetite, he was not even conscious of what he was doing.' (p. 92)

4. "Outside the hut the angry villagers continued with their demand . . . 'We cannot depart from this custom'." (p. 95)
   What is the significance in this story of the clan elders strictly observing the community's rules even at a time of great crisis in their communal life?

5. 'Tekayo' gains much of its impact and resonance from the way Grace Ogot uses irony.

a) Read the following sections of the story and explain why they can be considered ironic.
   (i) 'The cows, heavy with milk . . . might harm them.' (p. 89)
   (ii) 'Though Lakech had passed the age of child-bearing . . . Then he lied to her.' (p. 90)
   (iii) 'It was during this time of grief . . . daily in the fields.' (p. 91)
   (iv) 'It was after this . . . the rest agreed.' (pp. 92–93)
b) Select other instances of irony in 'Tekayo' and explain how they are ironic.

Departure at Dawn

SAMUEL KAHIGA

(KENYA)

MUGO CAME HOME drenched to the skin. He was panting hard as he kicked the little wooden gate back and hurried along the path to his hut, his suffering head bent low. He was cursing bitterly – cursing the rain, cursing himself and even the Memsahib.[1]

'Drown me,' he hissed under his breath, probably to the angry heavens. He added, 'Maybe I will be better off dead.'

A gust of wind howled across the yard and for a moment he thought it would sweep him away. With it the rain increased, roaring in his ears and blinding him.

He staggered across the bare muddy space of ground. His boots squelched in the mud, and in his hurry he almost fell. But now the old hut was only a few yards away; shelter and peace were only a few yards away.

Peace . . .?

He almost stopped in his tracks. Would there be peace for him anymore? Was he ready to go into the old hut and tell a wounded man – his own brother – that he must go, go sick as he was? And when he went would there be peace . . .?

He ran the few final yards to the old hut. He pressed his body to the damp crumbling wall thankful for the comparative safety under the eaves of the hut.

Inside the hut were his brother, Ndonga, and his seventeen-year-old son, Karanja. Until he heard their voices Mugo was not aware of his son's presence in the hut. In fact what with all the hurry and the worries of the day he had forgotten that Karanja was due to come home from school that day for the holidays.

Karanja had arrived home two hours before. From the onset his holiday had been overshadowed by a threatening cloud. As usual he had passed through the farm on his way home to have a word with his father. The Memsahib's house, large and majestic on the little hill on which it stood, had been a refreshing and indeed thrilling sight after three long months of absence.

A path skirted the homestead and ran down the hill to the labourers' camp which squatted in the valley below. Through the fence he could see Peter and Cynthia, two of the Memsahib's children riding their tricycles on the lawn. They certainly seemed to have grown! He stood watching them with a smile until he was aware of the weight of the box he carried. Then he had turned and walked down the path to the labourers' camp to look up the headman's family. He would leave his box with the wife and go out to the ranch looking for his father.

The headman's children were playing in the dust when he came up. They ran up to him excitedly and clutched at his clothes and arms, soiling him all over. But he was not displeased. It was wonderful coming home again, for the ranch was a second home to Karanja.

It was the headman's wife who told him about his father's dismissal.

Now in the dimness of the hut he sat by his uncle's bedside listening to him talk. It all seemed like a dream – the presence of this strange man whom they said was his father's brother. There might have been some likeness between him and his father but with his very long hair and rough beard it was difficult to believe the relationship existed. But when he spoke one was immediately convinced for the voice was the same: quiet, rather husky.

'Don't go to him!' his mother had warned earlier on. 'Don't meddle with the man.'

'All right,' he had replied. 'I'll just peep in and have a look at him.'

'But do not –'

'I'll just look, Mother. After all, is he not my uncle?'

It had been drizzling when he went out from the new large house towards the old hut. Then suddenly, without warning, the heavens had opened and the rain had roared in his ears. He had run on into the hut shutting the door behind him hurriedly. Then he was staring at the man on the bed. The man was staring back . . .

Here he was. A *real* terrorist. That hair . . . Those eyes . . . For a moment, there was a tight feeling in his breast and his hand felt for the door handle. Then the terrorist grinned.

'*Niu ucio*?, And who is that?'

Karanja swallowed twice.

'Mugo's eldest son, no doubt. My biggest nephew. You were named after my father, I suppose?'

Karanja nodded. 'Yes, I am Karanja.'

He had awkwardly gone across to the bed and shaken the hard strong hand the terrorist offered.

That had been almost two hours ago. It was still raining and so he had not gone back yet. He was in no hurry to go back. He watched his uncle roll up some tobacco with a light piece of brown paper. Tough man, this, if all those stories he'd been telling were true.

'How is your leg, now?'

'Terrible,' Ndonga replied with a wry smile.

Karanja wondered how his uncle had been shot. In a night raid no doubt. He looked at his uncle thoughtfully. How come a terrorist could be a pleasant fellow? Why, he was quite human. Terrorists burn, rape and cut off people's heads. Somehow Karanja could not imagine his uncle hacking off people's heads. Some burning, some raping maybe. But not the other thing.

'When I get back I shall be all right,' Ndonga went on. 'I shall be treated with herbs. It's just –'

'Who shot you?' Karanja asked, unable to contain his curiosity.

Ndonga turned and for a moment Karanja was frightened. The eyes had slightly narrowed, the nostrils were dilated.

'A white bitch,' said the terrorist. 'A white bitch. *Ngai*[2], she might have killed me!'

Karanja stared at him. He didn't know what to think. He could not understand the look on the man's face. Was it fury? It looked more like fear. He managed a feeble smile.

'You might have killed *her*' he pointed out. He was glad of the line the conversation was taking. Soon, he hoped, his uncle would start talking like a real terrorist. All those stories about hares and bees were all very funny but he had to have something *bloody* for his school mates when he got back to Kikuyu.

'She might have killed me,' Ndonga said and this time his face broke into a little amused smile. 'But fortunately she only got me in the leg.' He shook his head. 'That's not the way to die – by a woman's hand.'

'Death is always a fearful thing. To me it would make no difference whence it comes,' said Karanja, 'Whoever kills deserves death too. Don't you think so?'

His uncle smiled. 'You are a big fellow. You look sensible too. So I shall talk frankly to you, but no –' he said checking himself. 'Your father would not like it.'

'I know,' said the boy. 'But how will he ever know what you told me?'

'Ah, no,' said Ndonga seriously. 'Your father is risking his life to save me. That is not something a man easily forgets. I would very much like a youth like you to see the truth and the light – what I fight for and why I have lived like a beast in my own country for many years. But your father and your mother would not like it. Their way of thinking is so different from mine.'

Karanja did not insist. Instead he changed the subject. 'Mother tells me some shocking news. My father has lost his job. When I passed through the farm on my way here the headman's wife told me the same thing. But neither of them know why my father lost his job.'

Ndonga chuckled. Why, Karanja had no idea.

'The woman is scared. All the white people are now scared stiff. They trust no black man. I believe she mistrusted your father.'

'But that just isn't possible!' Karanja exclaimed. 'Father isn't Mau Mau. His family isn't Mau Mau. Nob –' he stopped. His eyes met his uncle's. That was it! Someone knew about his uncle. Whoever that someone was he did not know his uncle's present whereabouts or they would surely have come for him, but they knew that his father had a relative who was a terrorist. The Memsahib, like many other settlers, had informers among her 'wogs' and one of them must have told her that his father could not be trusted. In her state of mind (which could easily be imagined after so many settlers had been cut to pieces or shot) the Memsahib could not have argued. Strange that she had not had him arrested or shot . . .

Karanja felt fear creeping through him. Suddenly the idea of a terrorist in their home ceased to be exciting and became a serious, frightening business. The homeguards[3] were always searching houses for hidden guns and ammunition. If they chanced to swoop down upon their house their uncle would surely be found. He would be shot – and so would Karanja's father. The fate of the rest of the family would be something awful too.

'Uncle,' he said quietly – and somehow the word did not sound strange, 'how is your leg now?'

'Terrible,' Ndonga replied and Karanja remembered he had already asked the question before.

'How . . . soon can you walk?'

His uncle turned and looked at him sombrely.

'I don't know. I can't say,' he replied. 'A week more, maybe.'

'A week! But that is – they will come searching this place and will find you. And then –'

'They will shoot me.' His uncle's voice was cool.

Curse the man. He could only see himself being shot. Besides him he could not see Karanja's poor father. With one bullet they would finish off his innocent father whose only mistake had been having too soft a spot for his murdering brother.

He must go, Karanja decided. If Father can't see that I am very surprised . . . His uncle's voice broke into his line of thought.

'Needless to say,' he said, 'your lives are in danger because of me. If they find me here they will be very cruel to you. They might even finish off your father along with me.'

'How can we stop this? Uncle, why can't you just cut your hair and turn over a new leaf? Give yourself up – surrender and be a good man again?'

The man on the bed, looking a little surprised at the question, shook his head. Then he spoke bitterly.

'Today your father went to the farm where he was employed. He went to beg the Memsahib to take him back on the farm. I don't know if he has returned yet. But my guess is that the Memsahib struck him in the face and told him to clear off. The black man in his own country has been turned into a dog. If we do not fight, the situation will never be remedied.'

I see, Karanja thought grimly. It sounds heroic. But all you blighters really do in the way of fighting is to burn villages and kill other black men. The other day at Lari[4] you brutally murdered lots of innocent folk. Black folk. If you fellows had been educated you would certainly know better. You have blood on your hands. If they come to shoot you it's a fair game. My father is a peace-abiding citizen and is not in this. Why should he die along with you? I have a soft spot for you but you must go . . .

'Uncle,' Karanja said and stopped. His uncle's eyes were closed and he had fallen asleep. On his face was a look of pain, almost as if he had only closed his eyes and not sunk into peaceful slumber. For him sleep seemed not to unravel the worried sleeve of care.[5]

Mugo had decided against taking shelter in the old hut. For the two talking in the hut he had bad news. Ndonga had to leave in the night. It would be foolish and dangerous to let him stay any longer. God had kept the guards away. It was unlikely that He would help much longer. They had to come to their senses and help themselves.

Fresh trouble had broken out early that morning not very far from their home. The homeguards had been searching all day – and were still searching – for a gang of terrorists who had raided Bwana[6] Eric Thomsett's farm. They had managed to kill a dog and mess up a few cows with *simes*[7]. But Bwana Thomsett and his son had managed to hold them at bay until the security forces had come to the scene. The gang had melted away.

The Memsahib's headman had told him the story when he had gone to the farm. Mugo had watched him closely. He was the headman: could he have arranged to have him sacked?

'Thandi,' he had said gravely, 'do you know why I lost my job?'

'No,' Thandi had replied. 'It was a great surprise to me. Since her husband died the Memsahib has not been herself. She has been very queer, you know. Now she sees in Mau Mau Fate's way of finishing her family off. She does not know which black man to trust. So she trusts nobody. Why she fired you I really do not know, but she has been rough with all of us. I believe if it were possible to run the farm without us she would do just that.'

'It is a great curse, this Mau Mau,' Mugo said. 'But tell me, Thandi, is it wise to go to the Memsahib and try to convince her of my innocence?'

'You cannot. At the mere sight of you she will be furious and might even strike you. You know the way their faces turn red like the eastern sky at dawn. – Have you got any snuff on you?

'... Thank you – The Memsahib has reached a point where if you annoy her greatly enough she could pull the trigger on you.' Thandi slapped his own shotgun affectionately.

Still I will try, Mugo thought to himself. What can I do without my job? The garden might yield enough food for our stomachs if it rains well, but we need money for clothes and school fees. I wish this had come earlier – before I had built that new house with all my savings . . . But the Memsahib might take me back – if I convince her of my innocence . . .

Innocence? Mugo sat up. For two nights he had harboured a dangerous gangster under his roof. That was enough to get a man hanged. What a fool he was! What a senseless, blundering fool he was to think of going to the Memsahib! A search might be arranged in his house before the Memsahib could take him back.

And Mugo would go to the gallows.

'What is the matter? You look frightened,' Thandi said.

'No,' Mugo replied.

'You know, if you really want to see the Memsahib –'

'No!' Mugo replied.

Feeling sick he had taken leave of the headman. He had taken the path that led across the bridge to the rocks on the other side of the river. He had walked out of the Memsahib's property with the sad heart of an exile. Somewhere high up on the rocks he had turned and looked back. The cattle, small moving specks in the distance, were grazing down below. He had lain down on the rocks, his face in his hands. He had not wept. He had slept.

They sat talking round the fire: his mother, father and sister. Karanja was deep in thought in a corner and did not talk much. The whole family had debated upon the fate of his uncle and had finally agreed to give him one more day. Karanja wondered what good that would do. As his uncle was not receiving any medical attention, his leg was not improving at all; in fact it was getting worse. Although everybody wanted him to go, they all lacked the courage to tell him to leave seeing the condition he was in. His father was agitated, frightened – and helpless.

His mother and father discussed the family's future in hushed voices.

'We shall manage somehow,' said his mother optimistically.

'With the help of God we shall manage. Mugo, many years ago you were a craftsman. You used to make –'

'I cannot go back to that, if that is what you are suggesting,' Mugo said in alarm.

His wife served the food in silence. She was a tactful woman and never foolishly argued with her husband. She said, 'Well, the Lord helps those who help themselves. In difficult times He doesn't drop manna from heaven as He did for the children of Israel.'

'Certainly I shall look for work,' her husband said defensively. 'But I do not have very high hopes. All the Europeans are suspicious of any strangers and would hardly employ me just like that.'

'But your old trade? Carpentry . . .'

'I failed in that. I cannot go back to it. The nights of hunger and misery still haunt me to this day. I can only work on a farm, Muthoni. That is the work I was made for.'

Mugo sighed. Possibly he was thinking of the fine, sturdy cows he had left on the farm. The Memsahib had entrusted them to his care and he had loved them almost as if they were his own. He understood cows and cows understood him. Many years back he had been born in a small hut many hills and valleys away. His earliest memories were linked with cattle, for he had spent his boyhood looking after his father's herd. In those days, of course, you roamed all over the place looking for the best pasture for your cows. Provided your cows did not wander into someone's *shamba* nobody cared where they grazed. In those days grass was grass, and grass was for all. Life was never monotonous or precarious. There was companionship and lots of fun.

When his brother Ndonga was big enough he had helped him with the herd – and Mugo had taught him lots of boyish tricks. But they had had very few years together really and had never grown to understand each other. When their father died Mugo had drifted into the city to look for his fortune. Some years later his brother had followed but then Mugo, frustrated and disillusioned, had left the city to work on a farm. From there he went to another farm where he had decided to remain permanently. Then of course *this* . .

Perhaps if their father had lived . . . But Ndonga had always been rather wild. It might not have changed things . . .

Cows were cows, no matter who owned them – white or black. And Mugo had been as much at home with the Memsahib's cattle as with his father's herd. Now he was like a fish that someone had seized from its water to examine in his hand. He lay in the hand of Fate, wondering into what sea he would find himself tossed next.

'Let us pray for the food.' His wife's voice awakened him from his meditations. They all closed their eyes and she prayed. She thanked God for the food and then with increasing emotion asked Him to provide for them always in those dark times. Their lives had been thrown into a turmoil through which only His guiding hand had the power to lead them.

As she prayed Karanja in his corner opened his eyes and looked at them. No one was certain of the future any more.

He took two hot plates of food into the old hut. The hut was in darkness, but after groping round in the dark he found a matchbox on a stool and lit an oil lamp. Then he shook his uncle by the shoulder till he woke up with a violent start.

'What is it! What's happened?' said his uncle, sitting up.

'I've brought your supper.'

'It's you, Karanja,' he said in great relief.

Karanja looked at him carefully. He observed a change in him from the afternoon. He looked tired and sick. And that softness seemed to have disappeared. What Karanja had seen the moment he had woken up with a start was a desperate, wild man. A man with wild eyes, a wild face and wild stringy hair.

'Eat,' Karanja said. He sat on one of the stones of the cold hearth and started on one of the plates. There was silence between them. But probably their thoughts were similar. Perhaps each was wondering what Fate held in store for him.

'It's cold in here,' Karanja said. 'Don't you feel it? Too bad Mother finished up all the dry wood in the house. All the wood outside is wet. Curse this rain.'

His uncle continued staring at the ceiling. Then he spoke.

'It does not matter,' he said.

Karanja looked down. It does not matter . . . Karanja understood. In a short time his uncle would have to leave. Death no doubt awaited him, for with his leg he would not go far. What did a little warmth or food matter now?

'The wages of sin is death' his mother had said that evening.

'When Ndonga came here staggering and bleeding in the leg he had probably murdered. There is nothing we can do for him, Mugo. Nothing whatsoever. He has killed and God saw it. We shall only be punished if we shelter him any longer.'

All right, Karanja now thought, we might die for sheltering this man. He himself will die, I suppose. But for what? For fighting for his rights – or what he calls his rights. He is a fighter – an enemy of the Memsahib and other white people. The Memsahib has fired my father. Because of that all my dreams have come tumbling down because I know that there'll be no more school for me. My father can't afford the fees now. What a vicious little circle! I could complete it by killing the Memsahib. That's an idea.

'Uncle,' Karanja said, 'that woman who shot you in the leg. What did you do to her?'

His uncle seemed to emerge from great depths. He did not turn.

'Let us not talk about it,' he said rather curtly.

'Because, Uncle,' Karanja went on, 'there is one woman on my mind. She has spoilt my life. What hurts most is the thought that she does not even know what she has done to me. She merely pushed a little button as it were, and machines started to turn. A lot of things came tumbling down. She does not know every little thing that tumbled down. I'm one of the little things. She can't notice me because I am in the dust at her feet.'

Slowly his uncle turned. His eyes glistened a little in the yellow light of the smoky lamp.

'The white Memsahib?' he asked. His voice sounded dull and flat.

Karanja nodded. His uncle looked again at the ceiling.

'It is like that,' he said at last, 'when a little insect hums around you, intruding upon your calm and peaceful meditations, you absent-mindedly slap it against your leg, killing it. To the white race, we are insects. But Karanja, we have learnt to sting. So, my boy, sting . . .'

Karanja stared at him for a moment.

'Well,' he said, 'I am really very upset, Uncle. I don't know what to do with my life. My father was a carpenter when he was my age. He failed miserably. Mother says he should start again. Well I have been thinking. I could go into partnership with him.

'Mugo and Son' sort of thing. Eat your food. It's getting cold. What do you think of the idea?'

His uncle made no reply.

'And do you know what we shall make if –' He stopped. His uncle was breathing quietly. He had fallen asleep again. He had not touched his food and Karanja thought of waking him. Then he thought better of it. He himself had hardly touched his food and had no appetite. He could understand his uncle not wanting food.

With his uncle asleep the hut was deathly quiet. The little smoky flame that lit up the hut flickered unsteadily. A sad feeling seized Karanja and suddenly he pushed his food away.

'Sting . . .' he said softly to himself. 'If I knew it would serve any purpose I would sting . . .'

But Karanja felt that it would serve no purpose. Yes, it would complete the little vicious circle – but that would be all. Nobody's position would be improved. He would only become a hunted man like Uncle Ndonga. He did not think that his uncle was a man to envy, especially in his present situation.

Karanja ate as much as he could and then threw the rest of the food outside. With the plate he covered his uncle's food. Then be blew out the lamp and went out.

That night the rain poured gently on to the roof, and the sound lulled Karanja into slumber. But it was a troubled sleep. He dreamt that the homeguards had come to get his uncle. Everybody in the house was terrified as their footsteps came up to the house.

He woke up cold and frightened. He breathed a sigh of relief to find himself safe in his bed. He shook his head to disperse all memory of his dream, but to his surprise the footsteps persisted in his ears.

Karanja sat up in bed, his heart pounding madly against his ribs. Terror seized him and choked him in the throat. It was no dream. There *were* footsteps!

The footsteps, he soon realized, belonged to one person and were receding slowly. Occasionally they sloshed in the mud heavily. Quietly, without making any sound, Karanja opened the window and looked out. In the pale light of dawn he had a passing glimpse of a figure just before it staggered forward suddenly and disappeared through the wooden gate.

Karanja sighed again and closed the window. He smiled in the darkness. A drunkard who had missed his way, that was all, he decided. Still, he felt rather weak.

Afterwards, he often wondered what would have been the outcome had he stuck to his conclusion and gone back to sleep and not been struck, as he was a few minutes later, by the strangeness of it all – the idea of a drunkard at that hour. A sickening idea occurred to him and he got out of bed hurriedly. He put on a pair of shorts and his school pullover and went out of the house. The mud was thick and soft and his shoes sank disgustingly into it. He reached the hut and knocked upon the door. When there was no answer from within he pushed the door open.

He was not very surprised to find his uncle gone.

Thandi, the headman, stirred out of bed. It was early, for only one cock had crowed. He went outside and contemplated the world. It had really rained. He did not expect the terrorists had been able to carry out any plans they might have had for the night. If it always rained like that – but then every gangster would secure for himself a raincoat.

In the east the sky had cleared somewhat. It was the colour of blood. On the whole it promised to be a fine day.

Thandi yawned and stretched. Then he went back inside to start the fire and make some tea. The children were not going to school today for the holidays had begun and so his wife would sleep for another hour or so. He himself could not afford to wake up late. He had a job to do. The Memsahib would not tolerate laziness or slackness from her number one man.

To wake up in the morning these days gave him great relief. Sleep was no longer a pleasure. You slept in fear and dread of what might creep out of the night. You dreamt dreams that left you cold and shaken. To wake up and find that Mau Mau had not set the whole camp ablaze and that you still had your neck gave you a warm feeling inside.

As the water warmed up on the fire he went to the bed and carefully, so as not to disturb his wife, pulled out his shotgun.

He loved this gun. One day, he was sure, it would save his life. It was his practice to clean it every morning.

He had just sat down to start his work when he heard a sound outside the hut followed by footsteps. His grip tightened on the gun. All his senses were at once alert. Could it be . . .? Not so early in the morning really. Not in broad daylight . . .

But the headman was not taking any chances. He stood waiting, his gun ready.

There was a knock. A rather hesitant knock that somehow made his muscles relax a little.

'Who is it?' he asked

'It is me – Karanja,' said a breathless voice.

Thandi smiled to himself. This time at least there was no trouble. But there were times when he wished it would come and be done with. This waiting – for heaven knew what – was getting on his nerves.

Karanja stood waiting outside. He shot uneasy sideways glances at his uncle fearing he might fall. But he looked a little better. At least he could stand without support.

He had caught up with him halfway down the hill near the labourers' quarters. He could have caught up with him earlier but that had not been the idea. He had followed his uncle, on discovering that he had left the hut, out of curiosity. To his amazement his uncle had not bothered to keep to the bush. He had hobbled quickly along the road, staggering in a manner painful to watch. The crazy fool would not get far, Karanja thought.

Yet he could not run up to him and beg him to come back . . .

Quickly, like one with a purpose, his uncle had struggled along the muddy road. Then suddenly he had rushed into the bushes and hurled himself into the interior, and Karanja could see his head and shoulders as he desperately penetrated the rich growth of marigolds.

Karanja, feeling sick at the sight, had followed. Now he wanted to reach his uncle, though what there was to tell him he was not certain.

His uncle had left the bushes and stumbled upon a path. Perhaps he knew where he was going, Karanja thought. Perhaps he had a friend around here. Karanja felt happy at the thought. Then his uncle had fallen.

He had clung to a wayside bush and dragged himself into it, crawling in the dust. Karanja had watched with a bleeding heart and then run forward.

'I'm home! I am home . . .!'

The words, made with breathless gasps, seemed to cut the thick tense silence of dawn and hang heavily in the atmosphere.

'Uncle,' Karanja called as he walked up.

His uncle took no notice of him. He was busy trying to make himself comfortable inside the bush. All the time he talked incoherently to himself. He was not mad, Karanja knew. He was just sick and delirious.

He had crept deep inside the wet bush and snuggled in there, no doubt in the belief that he was home. The feel of the wet leaves on his face and the scratching of the twigs must have overwhelmed him. He had started to whimper. The sound was unpleasant and sickening.

Talking was futile, Karanja soon realized. With sudden determination he had seized him by the legs and dragged him from the bush. Then he had looked down at the labourers' camp down below.

Down there his uncle could rest – even if it was to await one of those quick trials that invariably seemed to lead, for people such as he, to the hangman's noose. The game was up for Ndonga, freedom fighter.

When the door opened a man stood in the shadows, framed in the doorway. For a moment he peered at those standing outside. Then he made a noise in his throat. The gun in his hand spurted flame, leaping and roaring in his hand.

Karanja sat up, surprised that he felt no pain and was alive. He listened to the throbbing of his heart. An acrid whiff of smoke came to his nostrils. All the time he stared at the man in the shadows – and the gun that was pointed down at him.

To his ears came the sound of excited voices and hurrying feet that squelched in the mud. He was in the mud himself and the water soaked through his pants. He tried to move. His hand rested on something soft . . . An arm behind him. Suddenly he did not care about the mud and the water any more.

'Karanja . . .' The man in the shadows said. Somehow he was a stranger now. He sounded astonished and incredulous.

Karanja looked round at the beginning of a crowd. His head seemed to swim. His mouth had already dried up. A sharp panic shot through him. He turned to the headman in desperation and opened his mouth to speak, to lie, to plead, to . . .

The headman's eyes had left his face and turned to the still, prostrate figure behind Karanja. A little smile of satisfaction came to his lips. He addressed a little boy in the gathering crowd.

'Go and call the Memsahib,' he said.

NOTES

Memsahib[1] – *A word of Indian origin used to address a married woman. In colonial Kenya a term of deference used to address white women, usually one's employer's wife. Rarely used today except ironically.*

Ngai[2] – *(Kikuyu) God.*

Homeguards[3] – *Also known as 'loyalists'. Africans who fought on the British side during the Kenyan freedom struggle in the 1950s.*

Lari[4] – *A Kikuyu settlement thirty miles from Nairobi where, on 26th March, 1953, nearly one hundred 'loyalists' were killed by Mau Mau forces.*

Sleep seemed not to unravel the worried sleeve of care[5] – *A reference to Shakespeare's* Macbeth II. ii. 35–40.

Bwana[6] – *(Kiswahili) A form of address roughly equivalent to 'Mister' in English but can also be used to mean 'Sir', 'Master'.*

Sime[7] – *(Kiswahili) Short, two-edged sword or long knife.*

EXERCISES

1. In this story we see events from the point of view of Karanja, a young man of seventeen. Go back to the Introduction and read the section on 'point of view' (p. 13). Then re-read the story and answer the following questions. In doing so you will begin to appreciate how writers can make us view a situation in a certain way by how they

filter the events of a story through the eyes, heart and mind of a selected character.
   a) What evidence is there to show that at the beginning Karanja is naive, selfish and sheltered from the grim realities of the situation in Kenya at that time?
   b) At what point in the story does Karanja's naivety begin to give way to a recognition of the gravity of Ndonga's presence on the farm? Initially, with whose security and welfare is Karanja more concerned? When and in what way does Karanja's concern for his uncle break through his selfishness?
   c) Notice that throughout the story the author reveals Karanja's innermost thoughts side by side (and most often conflicting) with his spoken words. Pick out instances of this in the story and explain how it helps us to understand Karanja better.
   d) In this story we have Karanja's point of view. Now try and imagine how different this story would be if the events in it were related by each of the following: the white woman owner of the farm; Thandi, the headman; Karanja's mother; Karanja's father. Write the story from the perspective of any *one* of these characters.

2. An important part of the function of literature is to help us understand individuals in all their human complexity, to go beneath and beyond commonly-held stereotypes. Let us see how Kahiga helps us to do this in relation to Ndonga:
   a) What is Karanja's initial reaction to the presence in his home of his uncle Ndonga? In what ways does Karanja's initial reaction to Ndonga change in the course of the story?
   b) What general image comes to your mind when you hear or read the phrases 'Mau Mau terrorist' and 'Mau Mau freedom fighter?' After you had finished reading 'Departure at Dawn', did you see Ndonga as a 'terrorist' or a 'hero' – or in a different light?

3. Read the section on time-span in the Introduction (p. 11). Now answer the following questions:
   a) What is the time-span of 'Departure at Dawn'?

b) How does the author signal the passage of time in the story?

c) How does the brief time-span of this story affect its impact on you as a reader?

4. We can describe 'Departure at Dawn' as being, as it were, 'sodden with rain'. How is the background of rain, slush, high winds and overcast skies appropriate for this story?

Moneyman

PETER NAZARETH
(UGANDA)

MR MANNA LEITAO had joined the civil service at a time when no Goans[1] owned cars. In those days, it was quite normal for him to be seen walking all over the place, holding his umbrella like a walking-stick. But now, decades later, when Goans had passed through the bicycle age and were affluent enough to own cars, it was strange to see him drifting doggedly along the footpaths and by-lanes. He seemed to creep along the edge of one's consciousness, until one suddenly wondered, 'Who is this odd-looking fellow?'

Odd-looking indeed he was. He had a large mouldy face. The hair on his head looked like one of those ferns you see at a swamp – pokers sticking out at the edges and disappearing into a disc at the centre. His ears italicized his head, hairs standing out of them like mini-television antennae. His lips looked sensual, lending credence to the story that he was secretly a satyr, although he had never married. The Goans thought that he had remained single because looking after a wife and children would cost too much.

He often boasted that he was the richest man in the little town of Apana. Incredible, for how could a lowly civil servant who never played the stock market get rich? Well, in two ways. The first was the straightforward one of usury. There were always other lowly civil servants in Apana, particularly Africans, who were dead broke around the third week of the month. The bankers never lent money to those who really needed it, so this was where The Man stepped in. He would lend money for a maximum period of two weeks at about forty per cent interest. Not per annum but per two weeks.

This is why Manna Leitao came to be known as Money Leitao and, finally, Moneyman.

Then there was the second way he made money. He did not spend any.

Late one evening, Mrs Carmen Dias heard a groaning outside her house. She told her husband and son to investigate. They found Moneyman lying in a gutter in their compound, holding his leg in agony. The story went round later that Moneyman was chasing a spry young African miss across the lawns when he fell into the gutter and broke his leg. Yes, he broke his leg, as the Diases discovered eventually. They would have discovered it sooner had they taken him to the Grade A hospital but, despite his pain, he insisted that they take him to Grade B, where the poor were treated free of charge. His leg was put in plaster, and he was put to bed.

The Diases wrote about Moneyman's plight to his only traceable relatives, who lived in a neighbouring country. They arrived post-haste. Moneyman refused to see them. 'They have come here hoping I will die,' he said. 'They only want to get my money. Well, I won't, and they won't. Off with them!' Despite all efforts, the relatives had to give up and return home in disgust.

So Moneyman had to be looked after by the Diases. They felt that he was their responsibility as they had found him on their doorstep, so to speak. Who would look after this stubborn old man if they refused? They even cooked his meals because he said he could not eat African food. Father and son had to take turns cooking the meals because Mrs Dias had already made plans to go to Goa to visit her parents, and Moneyman's leg took a long time to heal. Needless to say, Moneyman did not pay the Diases anything, taking advantage of traditional Goan hospitality. What is more, after he realized that he was assured of regular meals, he started telling father and son what sort of meals to cook!

Moneyman's brush with death must have made him realize what a lonely man a single man is. At any rate, not long after he left the hospital, he gave up his lonely house and moved in with a family, the Fernandeses. The Fernandeses consisted of mother, father and three sons. It was surprising that they should take him in at all. Mother was a hard-headed, tough-hearted woman. Her husband, who owned a printing shop, was an inveterate drunkard, and the eldest son was a playboy. The second son was taciturn and determined. Nobody knew what he was determined about, but it looked as though he had secret ambitions. The youngest son was kind-hearted, but he was painfully shy and it was difficult to imagine him breaking out of his shell and making contact with anybody.

Gradually, it was noticed in Apana that Mrs Fernandes was running the printing shop. Mr Fernandes could be seen hanging around, cast aside like an empty bottle of liquor. The creditors had been about to foreclose when Mrs Fernandes stepped in. She paid off some of the debts and promised to pay the others in due course. The creditors agreed to wait provided she undertook to run the business herself. She accepted, even though she did not know anything about printing.

One day, Moneyman turned up at the house of Mr Pobras D'Mello, one of the elders of the Apana Goan community. Mr D'Mello was puzzled to see him because Moneyman was not a social man, let alone a sociable one. After the formality of informal talk and drinks, Moneyman said, 'I would like your advice, Mr D'Mello.'

Surprised at this request, and secretly a little pleased, Mr D'Mello replied, 'Of course.'

'Please read this letter,' said Moneyman, handing over a sheet of paper.

'Mrs Fernandes,' read Mr D'Mello, 'you have abused my sympathy and my kindly nature . . .' and a few rude words followed. 'When you borrowed four thousand shillings from me in June, you promised to repay it, plus a small lending charge, within three months. But you have not paid anything, and I demand it all back immediately you . . .' and a few obscenities followed.

'Well?' said Moneyman.

'Well?' said Mr D'Mello.

'Don't you think it is a good letter?' said Moneyman.

Mr D'Mello was known for his tact, so instead of answering directly he said, 'Tell me a little more about this matter.'

'Mrs Fernandes was in trouble because of her husband's debts.

She begged me to do her a favour and lend her four thousand shillings to pay off the debts. Feeling sorry, I lent her the money. Besides, I had already stood guarantee for her son's purchase of petrol, and the other day I had to pay a bill of nine hundred shillings . . .'

'You mention a service charge in your letter,' said Mr D'Mello. 'What is this?'

'Well, you know,' said Moneyman, 'I lost interest by drawing my money from my savings account at the bank, so it is but fair that I should be compensated . . .'

'How much?' said Mr D'Mello.

'I . . . er . . . er,' said Moneyman.

'How much?' said Mr D'Mello, a little sharply. 'How much is the service charge?'

'Er . . . one . . . two thousand shillings . . .'

'Per annum?' asked Mr D'Mello, amazed.

'No, to be paid as soon as the money was due.'

'Well, do you want to know what I think?' said Mr D'Mello. 'I think you are a mean, miserable skinflint. However, you have asked for my advice in respect of this . . . this letter, and I shall give it. The letter is extremely rude and offensive and, if you send it, Mrs Fernandes can use it to take legal action against you. Besides, from what you say, I don't think you have it in writing that you gave her the loan –'

'I already gave her the letter this morning,' said Moneyman.

'Then I will ask you to kindly leave my house,' said Mr D'Mello.

Moneyman got back home in time for dinner. He sat at the dinner table, where the atmosphere was decidedly frosty. Finally, he said in Konkani[2], '*Udoi coddi*,' which should mean 'pass the curry' but, if translated literally, means 'throw the curry'. And the second son did just that. He picked up the dish of curry and threw it at Moneyman.

'You bastard,' he yelled at him. 'You have been staying with us, no? Do the few shillings you have lent us make up for the inconvenience? But you have the cheek to write an insulting letter to my mother! I'll teach you!' And he began beating up the old man.

The eldest and the youngest sons pulled the second son back, but not before Moneyman had had his other leg broken. The eldest son had to take him to the Grade B hospital. After all, the car contained Moneyman's petrol.

Moneyman was abandoned at Grade B. He sent word to the Diases, who found this time that they could leave a stubborn old man to his distress without any qualms of conscience. When Moneyman was finally discharged, he did not press charges. He had nothing in writing, while the Fernandeses had. Besides, the lawyer would cost too much.

But Manna Leitao has benefited from his experience; he has learnt his lesson. He does not trust people any more; people are not as dependable as money. He can still be seen walking around Apana, shabbily dressed and with his ubiquitous umbrella; and whenever he passes the thriving Fernandes Press, he mutters to himself and tightens his grip on his umbrella, as though it is a bankroll from which he does not wish to be parted.

NOTES

Goans[1] – *A small Indian-Christian community whose forebears immigrated to East Africa from Goa on India's west coast.*

Konkani[2] – *Goan mother tongue.*

EXERCISES

1. In the Introduction we said that what happens to the central character in a short story should change him in a significant way. If it does not, then it is not a short story but a sketch. Given this definition, would you categorize 'Moneyman' as a short story or a sketch? Explain your answer in detail. (In answering this question, read the first sentence of the story's final paragraph and decide whether you agree that the protagonist 'has benefited from his experience'.)

2. Consider the following stylistic points:
   a) How do the similes in the second paragraph signal to

us that the story is likely to be a comic rather than a tragic one?
b) 'His ears italicized his head' Explain the meaning of 'italicized' in this context.
c) One of the characters, Mr Fernandes, is described as being 'cast aside like an empty bottle of liquor' (p. 118). Why is this an appropriate simile to describe what happens to Mr Fernandes?
d) Explain why the term 'lending charge' in Mr Leitao's letter to Mrs Fernandes (p. 118) is a euphemism. What would be a more accurate word to describe Mr Leitao's 'lending charge'.

We Are Going Home

PAUL NGIGE NJOROGE
(KENYA)

THE SMALL CHURCH was old and desolate. The tin roof had long been browned by the years and by the weather and by the dust; the clay plaster that had been applied on top of the mud walls had flaked off here and there and the reddish caked mud underneath was exposed.

Mugaa church overlooked the village. It stood on the crest of a hillock; the village lay in the depression below. Mugaa village was old and lonely, its scattered mud-and-thatch huts almost falling to the ground. And all around the dust lay, with tufts of parched grass appearing here and there.

Samuel Kibunja drove up to the church through the village. He steered the small Volkswagen through the dust slowly, but could not avoid stirring the dust and making it blow. The heat of the sun fell heavy on the land. He could see people quietly entering the church. But he made no hurry to join them, for he longed to be the last and did not want to be noticed.

A few other cars covered with dust were parked fifty yards from the entrance of the church to the left. He stopped his car there and got out slowly. Then he saw the car that had brought the body. It stood about ten yards from the church door and it was turned so that the back faced the church. A small group clustered round the car. The clergyman, in a black robe and white collar, stood with them staring at his black-jacketed Bible.

Kibunja avoided looking at these people and walked wearily into the church, his eyes downcast, his hands linked at his back. The church was full. A soft murmur vibrated among the congregation and several eyes turned to look at him when he entered, but Kibunja did not meet them. He went and sat beside a girl he had seen before, although he could not remember where. He had not intended to sit there but it was the only free place, all the other wooden forms were fully occupied.

He bowed his head and supported his forehead with his right hand, imitating prayer. The rare times he went to church he would bow his head, pretend he was talking to God, but in fact make no attempt to do anything of the kind. Perhaps other people did pray. He realized that his gesture was empty but he elected to remain a slave to it. He was still in his feigned prayer when he heard her whisper, 'Why did you come so late?'

Surprised, he looked at the girl sitting on his right. He sensed anger in her. But he could not summon such a strong feeling, only a dull and persistent resentment.

He avoided looking at her and his eyes surveyed the church. The walls, originally white, were now brown and almost black where the plaster of clay had worn off. Dust had also settled on the walls and in the corners cobwebs thrived, as they also did where the roof joined the walls.

But in front it was different. The floor here was made of stone, in contrast to the rest which was of beaten earth. The church furniture was well arranged and polished. Behind the pulpit a table stood, covered with a beautiful cloth made of fine linen.

The continuous drone was suddenly hushed, the congregation stood up, their eyes turned towards the church door at the back. The usual procession – a minor procession. The coffin was coming in, followed by the clergyman.

Then the confident words burst forth and they sounded strange in the desolate atmosphere: 'I am the resurrection and the life . . . he who believes in me, though he die, yet shall he live . . .' Kibunja watched the man who was asserting this message of hope. He was fat; his lips moved mechanically and the voice betrayed false emotion – or was it the monotony of words repeated too often? Perhaps if you didn't see the fat black priest and his moving lips and his dignified walk, if you only heard the words throbbing with their own rhythm . . . perhaps you would be comforted?

They put the coffin upon two stools that stood in front of the covered table. The coffin-bearers seated themselves on two reserved forms just below the altar. Here, also, were the dead girl's brothers and sisters.

Then the funeral service was conducted. The clergyman told the congregation how their life was merely a journey towards a home. The door to the eternal home was death. Death might seem frightful to those who had not been fully emancipated by Christ from the ways of this world, a world of bodily pleasures, bodily suffering. But Christ showed that death is not to be feared; it opens the door to eternal rest. 'Our sister Esther' was now receiving her reward in Heaven.

Then the friends and parents were invited to say a word about Esther whom God had called from their midst. In this part of a funeral service people remind themselves of how good the dead person was when alive. They express their conviction that the dead person has gone to Heaven, for the person was deserving of it and, after all, God has infinite mercy.

Kibunja sat still as if fearing to stir. He was tense and hot and his clothes stuck to him with sweat. He listened and stared in front of him. When he saw her father walk up to speak to the congregation, he shifted a little on the form where he sat. His forehead felt hot and feverish. He fished out a red handkerchief and slowly wiped his brow. And, in front, her father talked.

He told how Esther had helped her parents. How from birth she had been a blessing. She had been a beautiful baby and she had grown to be beautiful. She possessed the loveliness of the heart. For she loved her parents and obeyed them. She was beloved of her brothers and sisters and her friends had been drawn to her very strongly.

He told of how Esther had helped her brothers and sisters with school fees when she started working – before she had finally decided to go for training in nursing. As he told this his narrow bony forehead lit up. And there was a smile on his face. Even in the nursing school those who instructed her and those she studied with came to love her. And the people around the small hospital where the student nurses worked had come to know her and to like her. This is why they came to give her back to God in this particular country church where the country friends she had made lived.

Kibunja listened intently. Rooted to his form, he felt the girl sitting to his right burning him with her eyes. His throat was dry, but he listened on.

'And now God has called her to Himself. Some people would say she is dead. But *we* know she is not dead and we shall join her when we enter Heaven. Rather than weep and mourn we rejoice that God has given her the blessing of eternal life. And we exult in our God-given conviction that she has attained the joy that we who are left can hardly picture in its magnitude.'

There was a pause. Kibunja released a long breath. He thought: 'The man is a preacher. He should now sit down for he has spoken. He has concluded.'

But the old man did not stop. He continued and now you felt the pain. He stumbled over the words with barely masked effort.

'Esther's death was . . . quick and unexpected. God decided on it . . . no man could have decided on it . . .'

The congregation flinched under the inappropriateness of the words. Esther's father seemed to be aware of the same error but continued grimly to the end.

'For, if a man could decide on the death of somebody we love . . . well, we would not find it easy to forgive him.'

Tiny beads of sweat stood on his nose and around his mouth as he walked heavily to sit down beside his wife and children. And now the congregation seemed to cower together as sheep might do when it starts raining and they are out in the open.

Kibunja kept thinking: 'So there is truth! So the damned rumour contains some truth.'

The service ended. They took out the coffin. The congregation spilled out but again Kibunja was slow in following. There in the open the girl who had sat beside him came over.

'She was your friend, wasn't she?' she said in a tight voice.

'Yes,' he mumbled.

'She was my friend too. I'll miss her. Many people will miss her.'

And then Kibunja remembered where he had met the girl. It had been at the nursing school during one of his visits. He did not want to talk to her. But she added with surprising vehemence: 'I hate to think of the way she died.' Kibunja walked away from her. He re-entered the church and got out through a side door. Leaning against the wall he heard the cars driving off. There were no people here now. Everybody was leaving for the burial. Shortly Kibunja was alone at the small Mugaa church. It was all quiet around him.

He was not going for the burial, he told himself. They were taking her fifteen miles from here to her father's garden to bury her. He was not going with them. He slowly shuffled to his lone car and got in. Taking it through the blinding dust, he avoided the road which the funeral procession had taken and told himself he was going home.

A week had crawled on to its close. It was late on Sunday afternoon and Kibunja sat in a narrow compartment drinking. It was dark in the small cardboard cubicle, one of a series that lined the two walls of Gikeno Bar and Restaurant. A bottle of lukewarm beer stood in a growing pool of stale beer, on a tiny table in the small room. And underneath the table were five empty beer bottles.

As he continued drinking, he could hear noises from the other cubicles, some harsh and sharp noises that cut through the thin makeshift walls, some drunken moans that tumbled into his cubicle. Wonderful privacy the Gikeno Bar and Restaurant offers, he thought bitterly, as he reached for his glass listlessly.

There had been no peace since the girl died. He repeatedly told himself that he was not responsible for her death, that somebody else must be. But it did not help.

Kibunja drained the bottle into his glass. Here was life reduced to two simple operations: pouring and swallowing. He felt warm and a little nauseous from the rancid air in the place and from the beer.

He emptied his last glass and raised his eyes, and inwardly wondered whether he should call for more. It was then that Kibunja saw *him*, and the cloying warmth of the drinks instantly deserted him. The cardboard walls, the small grimy table, the roof, all seemed to swirl before his staring eyes.

No it could not be him, he thought. No, the figure he had just seen pass could not be Esther's father! Esther's old man was a Christian and didn't, wouldn't drink . . . Yes, he once used to drink but then he had belonged to the old ways . . . But Esther's father would not come to a bar to drink!

He had to make sure. He had to see the man who had just

passed by. Or was the man leaving the bar, and would Kibunja be left in perpetual doubt? This questioning did not continue for long; Kibunja again saw him amble past the narrow entrance to his drinking cubicle. The old man slumped into a chair in the opposite cubicle. Kibunja stood up and crossed to the bent figure of the old man. When he saw his face he could not think what to say or do; the face which only a week ago expressed firmness and dignity was now sagging and broken.

He retraced his steps to his place. Suddenly he wasn't interested in beer. He rested his head on the table; there was a sour taste in his mouth, his head felt heavy and he was slowly sinking into sleep, only his mind could not stop. When the waiter touched him on the shoulder he straightened up with a jolt.

'Young man,' the waiter said, 'if you have finished you might as well go. The police may be calling on us any time now, it is getting late.'

'Have you seen the *mzee*[1] – the one in the opposite cubicle?' Kibunja asked in a low, dull voice.

The waiter smiled, jerking a finger towards the cubicle occupied by Esther's father. 'He has been coming here for a whole week and looks as if he is interested in continuing his visits.'

Gripping the top of the table, Kibunja said, 'If those mean law people come for a raid the old man might be taken.'

The barman raised his eyes in mock concern.

'Well, I don't want him taken, Chief!' Kibunja said irritably.

'I am going to warn him,' replied the barman, puzzled. He walked away. Presently he came back and sat on top of the small table.

'He doesn't want to go,' he explained. 'He is not in the mood, or in the condition – come to think of it – to go home.'

Kibunja took out a twenty-shilling note for his beer and threw it on the table. He again walked to the old man's compartment.

Now Esther's father was resting his bulky body against the wall. Kibunja touched him and the old man grunted. Kibunja looked at the face and saw tears in the eyes and on the cheeks. He said softly, 'Let me take you home.'

The old man's words came across harshly but not too clearly. 'Who are you?' he demanded.

Kibunja whispered urgently in his ear, 'The law people are coming.'

He supported the old man out of the bar. Again he had the same agonizing sensation he had felt in church a week ago: eyes burning him with horror at what he had done. He walked Esther's father to the Volkswagen and helped him into the passenger seat in front and drove the old man home.

Esther's father sat sprawled beside Kibunja, breathing heavily and mumbling things. Kibunja did not feel the urge to say anything. The headlamps picked out the footpath that led to the homestead and Kibunja slowed down for the bumpy short ride to the front of the house.

As he branched off from the main road his left arm was suddenly gripped. He started. The car swerved. He swore, steadied the car and braked.

He asked very calmly, 'Do you want to get off here?'

The old man looked very disagreeable as he demanded, 'Where do you think *we* are going?'

'Home. Your home. I am taking you home.'

'And who asked *you* to bring me home? Who, young man, told you I wanted to be brought home?'

Kibunja sat silent. He felt anger stirring in his heart. And the anger was mixed with vague and general resentment at the strange reaction everybody had adopted towards him lately.

'I am asking, who appointed you to bring me home!'

Kibunja said, very softly, 'Well, you didn't object. And the police were coming.'

The old man's voice suddenly softened but he couldn't contain his bitterness. 'My wife and children . . . I don't want them to see me the way I am. And I cannot stop drinking. Since my daughter died . . . it is the way she died.'

Kibunja nodded sympathetically but he did not speak. He was, however, getting impatient – yes, a girl he felt warmly towards had died, but why the constant reminder?

Esther's father repeated: 'It is the manner of her death! A man sleeps with my daughter and then abandons her when he knows she is with child, so my daughter kills herself when trying to destroy the seed of this deceiving devil! God, I would like to know the man.'

He moaned, then very suddenly stared at Kibunja, who flinched and felt frightened. Maybe there were people in the neighbourhood, hidden, listening.

Kibunja now knew what he wanted to do. He wanted to depart from here. He wanted to forget Esther, and her father and the whole affair. He wanted to go home and rest.

'*Mzee*,' Kibunja said, 'you had better go. I am going home and it is late.'

'I am not going,' the old man said loudly. 'You do not know me. You offered yourself to bring me here. I am telling you to take me back where you brought me from,' Esther's father was almost shouting now.

Then Kibunja instinctively sensed the presence of listening ears and his desire to get away became urgent. The old man lived here, he told himself. This was his home. With quiet resolution, Kibunja extended his arm across the old man's chest and turned the handle of the door; the door flew open. But the man sitting beside him did not move.

Kibunja shoved him to the ground. He almost fell, but Kibunja helped him to a sitting position away from the car.

Esther's father growled words at Kibunja. But the latter did not stop to listen; he made haste to get into the car. He didn't stop to look around him when he heard somebody shout from the cover of the darkness, 'What is going on? What is it?'

He started the car and reversed quickly. As he changed gears, outside the gate he saw people coming from the direction of Esther's home: the dead girl's family. Esther's father lay on the ground shouting and a crowd was forming round him.

Kibunja drove slowly as a passer-by would. The people who were crowding in to answer to the shouting had to squeeze to get out of the way of the slowly but resolutely advancing car. He drove past without even glancing at them.

And then he heard a cry behind him and the noise grew in volume. And he knew there were eyes out there, piercing eyes, accusing eyes.

The memory of Esther would not leave him. Or the memory of her father. And there was this persistent feeling that he had done some wrong, although *he* hadn't been responsible for Esther's death. Perhaps he should have explained, he thought. The hopelessness of the situation hit him with terrifying finality. Perhaps he should never have met Esther in the first place . . .

As the car picked up speed he made a deliberate effort to shake off these thoughts. There was some shady comfort in the idea of going home – so he reminded himself that he was going home.

NOTES

Mzee[1] – *(Kiswahili) Old man.*

EXERCISES

1. Samuel Kibunja, the protagonist of this story, is tortured by contradictory emotions of guilt and the need to deny his guilt.
   a) We can say that Kibunja is 'ambivalent' in his guilt. Explain the meaning of ambivalence in this context. How exactly is Kibunja ambivalent in his guilt?
   b) Offer evidence from the story which points to guilty and resentful behaviour on Kibunja's part.
   c) Is it clearly stated in the story of *what* Kibunja is guilty? To what do *you* attribute his guilt?

2. The action in the story takes place in two settings: Esther's funeral at the dilapidated village church and a sleazy bar where her drunken father is grieving. Explain how the background in both cases is appropriate to the theme of the story.

3. Consider the following instances of irony in the story. Explain where the irony lies and what purpose it serves in the particular example and for the story as a whole.
   a) 'Death might seem frightful . . . bodily suffering.' (p. 124)
   b) "'Rather than weep and mourn . . . in its magnitude.'" (p. 125)
   c) "'God decided on it . . . easy to forgive him.'" (p. 125)
   d) "'It is the manner of her death! . . . God, I would like to know the man.'" (p. 128)

4. Consider the significance of the title 'We Are Going Home'. The idea of 'going home' is suggested in different ways in the story: when Kibunja is assailed by guilt at Esther's funeral, he 'told himself he was going home' (p. 126); a week later in Gikeno Bar he tells Esther's father 'I am taking you home' (p. 128); Esther herself is brought to her rural home to be buried; euphemistically, she 'goes home' to her Creator. Why is there this repeated emphasis on 'going home' in the story?

The Town

ENERIKO SERUMA
(UGANDA)

'THE PARK IS too crowded today. I wish I could afford to stay in bed on Saturdays,' the taxi driver said as he stopped the car in the Nakivubo car-park, his eyes wandering over the crowd. 'But of course the more crowded it is, the more money there is to be earned,' he added, laughing to himself.

None of his passengers said anything; he had had a quiet load this run. His caller started calling out for new passengers in a quick, hoarse voice. 'Passengers for Wandegeya, Makerere, Bwaise, Kawempe; this way please. Makerere, Wandegeya . . .' His voice faded as he moved among the crowd.

The passengers got out of the cab, handing the fare to the driver. Each passenger, except the last one, disappeared into the crowd as soon as the change was handed back. The last passenger, a man who was a villager, stood some feet away from the car and watched the distant caller. 'And they *like* the town!' he thought. 'Instead of owning a small place in the village and farming for a better living, look at what they do. How can a man spend all day barking like a crazy dog?' He wondered how much the caller earned and walked over to the driver who was sitting in his car whistling to himself as he waited for passengers.

'How much does the caller earn?' he asked the driver.

'Fifty cents per car-load. That's some money, you know. About eight, nine, maybe even ten shillings a day. And that's earned without any manual labouring too.'

The man thanked the driver and moved away. 'Yes,' he thought, 'that's the trouble with town people: they are always afraid of manual labour. They don't realize that because I dig from sunrise to midday I can sell five to six bags of coffee for a lot of money, and I save because I don't have to buy food like they do. They spend all their money buying villagers' farm produce.' He took his eyes from the caller and walked away, squeezing among people of all sorts. 'What a gathering of characters!' he marvelled. 'They are all like vultures over a carcass.'

The man wished he could shut off the noise of the crowd; it was maddening. Not even at weddings and feasts – or even drinking parties – had he heard so much noise. Everybody seemed to be shouting; the noise seemed as if a cloud was hanging over the park and was striking him with bolts of noise.

'Here, miss, over here! I have the latest style . . .'

'Over here, good lady! I have the latest fashion . . .'

'Natete! Natete! Passengers for Natete over here!'

'Here's a real nice cab. Over here, passengers, quick! It's comfortable; it has a radio; listen to your favourite songs as you go to Nakulabye.'

'This one is *faster*. You'll be there in a few minutes.'

'That's how they kill themselves,' the villager thought, 'driving fast as if bees were chasing them! Like that driver who brought me, how fast he had been driving – with one hand! One is safer in buses these days.' The man concluded his thoughts about the fast cars as other shouts hit his exhausted ears.

'Handkerchiefs! Handkerchiefs! Only forty cents, two for eighty cents. From your shilling you will be left with twenty cents for peanuts and popcorn. Two handkerchiefs for . . .'

'Here, my lords, here! Pure woollen trousers for only thirty-five shillings. Only thirty-five shillings – cheaper than in the Asian shops. Here my . . .'

'Katwe, Kibuye, Najja. Passengers for Katwe, Kibuye. The bus has just left, so don't miss this chance of a faster arrival. Katwe . . .'

The villager stood and stared in wonderment. 'This is too much to believe! Do these men wake up in the morning to tell their wives they are going to work? Look at them, all shouting their heads off. What a way to earn a living!' He shook his head at the men who rushed at him with yards of cloth on their arms. There were so many of them. 'How can they make money with such competition?'

He looked out in the distance. All he could see were heads that bobbed and mouths that shouted. Here and there were some unfortunate travellers caught in a competition between callers, who were each shouting the experience of the driver they were working for. The poor travellers stood between them with worried looks on their faces, like prisoners standing in court while the defender and the prosecutor battle over their fate. Some travellers, caught between cloth-sellers, were entangled in rolls of cloth as the sellers showed off the quality of the materials.

The man turned his head and looked at the road and the entrance to the park. There was a traffic jam of cabs as they turned off the main street to enter the park. Horns hooted from cars that were full of impatient bewildered people, who stared out of the windows just like the monkeys that stared at the man every morning he went digging. Some of the passengers got out of the cars and walked the rest of the way. Dwarfing the cabs, that were mostly the small cars the villager called tortoises but which the town people called Volkswagens, were the double-decker buses that had both decks full of people going to all corners of Kampala city. The bus depot was opposite the taxi park; the man could see people lining the platforms and others scrambling to get into buses.

'How man does produce!' the man wondered. 'What thousands and thousands of people! One would think that there are no people left in homes.' His heart missed a beat as he saw a young man run beside a bus and jump on to it. 'The fool' he thought, remembering the man he once saw who missed when he tried to jump and got run over by the bus. 'Why are town people always in haste?' he wondered. 'Is it because they are living and working with the white people who always hurry as if they are afraid they won't make it to the outhouse?'

'Here you, all people, hear!' a voice interrupted the man's thoughts. 'This is your chance to buy this incredible medicine. If your wife is unfaithful, if you are troubled by spirits, if your children are always sick, if you are impotent, if girls don't fall for you, if you have a constant headache, stomach ache, mumps, dizziness, if you want to pass your exams successfully – everything, ladies and gentlemen, anything you want to get rid of, this is the medicine. Buy this medicine, this rare *mumbwa*[1], and everything will be better.'

The villager looked toward the clear, booming voice. 'That is some strong medicine,' he thought to himself, 'curing all those ailments. I wonder if it's just another way for the town people to earn money, or whether it is true.' He walked over to where the medicine-seller was sitting on a leopard skin, with all kinds of assortments laid out in front of him. Everything that looked odd seemed to be there, from live things like an eagle, a hawk, a snake, a rabbit, and other little animals, to dead things like a hyena, an antelope and a jackal.

'Yes?' the medicine-seller was looking at him. He had bloodshot eyes that never seemed to blink.

'You were just talking about a *mumbwa* . . .'

'Yes, yes. Are you impotent?' the medicine-seller asked. 'Is your wife running away? Are you troubled by your in-laws? Or are you after your neighbour's wife? She'll be yours tonight if you buy this *mumbwa*. And what's more, he won't do a thing about it. But perhaps you've spirits of your grandparents disagreeing with the way you are spending the family fortune, uh? Oh, I know! You would like to win over one of these white things clicking around the city, wouldn't you, huh?'

'No, sir. White girls are for students at Makerere, not for people like me. They don't know how to bend their backs to cultivate. How can I, a farmer, have a wife who doesn't dig? No, all I wanted . . . you see, sir, I've had a lot of trouble with burglars, I thought . . .'

'Oh, yes, of course, yes, yes, my friend,' the medicine-seller said, without a smile. 'This is the medicine for your troubles. Buy this and you are rid of them. If they ever . . .' the medicine-seller stopped suddenly and cocked his head to one side. Then he sprang up with surprising speed and started running. Everybody was running and shouting, except the villager, who stood there staring stupidly at the place where the medicine-seller had been sitting. 'What is happening?' he asked himself.

'Run, everyone, run! Tax!'

'Tax raid! Run everybody! It's the entire blasted police force!'

The villager started running. There were so many people, he kept bumping into fear-crazed people who seemed blind, unable to distinguish women from men. The noise cloud seemed to have burst into ear-splitting fragments that whistled shrilly and shouted and cried hysterically. Among the crowd the villager could see the khaki uniforms of the policemen as they spread their huge arms wide apart to stop the fleeing tax-defaulters.

The villager ran because he had not paid his annual tax yet. 'What lousy luck!' he thought as he jumped over abandoned spreads of merchandise. Of all days, the police had chosen to raid on this one, when he was in town! Back in the village he could always avoid the less experienced village chief and his helpers. But here, with white officers commanding the policemen, they came so swiftly and silently like a dark cloud engulfing the sun. One never knew what was happening until the whole park was surrounded by policemen. They surrounded the park first, and then brought in more truckloads of policemen armed with short, effective clubs.

NOTES

Mumbwa[1] – *(Luganda) Clay and fine sand mixed with crushed medicinal leaves, shaped into small cylinders and dried. The 'mumbwa' is grated into a little water and the mixture drunk to cure various kinds of ailments.*

EXERCISES

1. In this story, life in town is observed through the critical eyes of a villager. What different methods does the writer use to make vivid the man's experience of town life? (Examine Seruma's use of description, dialogue, similes.)

2. In his detailed criticism of urban life the man directly and indirectly claims the superiority of rural life. What, according to him, are the virtues of country life when compared to life in the town?

3. Write a piece (or you could organize a class debate) rebutting the villager's view of the town by arguing for its positive aspects.

Transition

PETER JOHN BOSCO
(TANZANIA)

IF YOU STOOD down there in the plain, facing up the river, you could have a good view of both sides of the wide valley. On your left side, starting at the edge of the plain, hills would rise steeply like strong, solid walls, culminating in a series of jagged summits: the hills of Giza. And on one of those hills you would not fail to see the hut, standing alone, surrounded by solitude. But on your right the land would rise gradually, rounding off into an undulating plateau with green valleys and low, conical hills. And at one point along the gentle slope you would see Umoja[1]. The village spread up and down one of the green valleys and, if you happened to look at it in the evening, you would see white columns of smoke spiralling up from the score of thatched roofs into the placidity of the softening light and, higher up, dissolving into the calm, endless sea of deep blue.

In the lengthening shadow of the hut sat a man. He was strongly built, despite his age – he might be in his late forties. He had a strong, protruding jawbone and deep-set eyes. His nose was wide and flat and his lips were thick and as black as coal. His forehead was wrinkled and this, together with the thick beard he never shaved, gave him a fierce look. All around him fell the craggy shadows of the jagged hills and huge boulders.

Sitting on his stool, Amri[2] watched his wife, Taabu[3]. She was struggling up the steep hill, with a *debe* of water gingerly balanced on her head. She was tall and thin, and wore a haggard look. The cheap cloth covering her body was drenched by the dripping *debe*. Her feet were small and lined with cracks. Hands long and thin. Palms chapped. Her look weary and distant. Twenty years ago, then newly married to Amri, she was plump, beautiful and proud. But six births had emaciated her and the hazards of life reduced her carriage to its present listlessness.

Taabu went with the water past her husband, into the hut. Soon she came out and squatted on the bare ground. She sighed. She was exhausted by the countless hardships of life, by the countless duties of the day, by the thousands of depressing memories.

She suddenly became angry.

'Amri,' she started, her voice a bit sharper than usual, 'we can't go on like this forever. You may find it easy, but I don't find it so. We are going to join them this season!'

'What!' And his voice was thin and edged.

But she would not be deterred. Her endless suffering would have expression and the rancour of many sleepless nights would find vent.

'I said we are going to leave this place this season,' she repeated adamantly.

Then she was surprised by her own courage. She and Amri spoke little to each other, and, when they did, it was either he giving an order or she reporting that something ordered was done. Amri was, as his name indicated, a man of orders: easily offended and hard to please.

'And where do you want us to go?' he growled.

'I have already said we are going to join the others in Umoja.'

She saw his eyes contract and the lines on his face get harder, as they had always done when a storm was gathering. Yes, it was not the first time she had talked to him about that issue. But each time it had ended in rough words and high-pitched tones.

'You never draw the water. So you don't know what it is like to slip and fall down that steep slope with a *debe* on your head. You can't see the suffering of the children who have to get up at dawn each morning to go to school and come back late in the evening. You don't see how dangerous it is for them crossing that river, or what they lose when the river is in flood and they can't go to school for a whole week.'

She saw the disbelief in his eyes. But she would not stop yet.

'What sort of man do you think you are? How much money do you get from scratching the bare slopes of the hill for your tobacco crop? Look at what we are wearing: mere rags. The children don't even have uniforms. Look at your friends in Umoja. Look at their healthy children. Look at what their wives wear. You yourself are still wearing *magwanda*[4] when everybody else is wearing trousers. Don't you feel ashamed going among your fellow men?'

'Shut up, woman!' Amri hissed. But Taabu wouldn't shut up just like that.

'For how long do you want to keep us down? What makes you stick to this barren desert? You are poor. Your hut is rotting away and falling. All of us are suffering, but you would stick to the place like a tick . . .'

'I said you shut that gaping mouth, woman! I brought you here with my money. I am keeping you here, and I could send you away any time I wished to. Are you now telling me where to build a new hut, or what to do with my house?'

'I didn't tell you that,' she retorted. 'I said that we are suffering here for nothing and that I am not going to suffer anymore.'

'Listen, woman. I have told you several times already: we are not going to join those fellow fools of yours in Umoja. I am the man here, and a woman is not going to change my word!'

Taabu had now tasted the bitter-sweet liquor of daring and courage; she would not budge.

'Say what you wish, but I have also told you that I am not going to die for somebody else's lack of sense!'

'What!'

Amri's eyes were blazing. He was on his feet and his long whiskers heaved up and down at her. He remembered Nguvumali[5], the Chairman of Umoja Ujamaa[6] village, and the incident of twenty years ago. The memory stabbed at him like a sharp knife and he once again re-lived the very feelings he had experienced that day. Again the shock of discovery pricked into his flesh like a thousand pin-pointed thorns. Again he felt the opium of rage and humiliation go to his head and intoxicate his brains to madness. He trembled with emotion and struck his wife hard on the mouth. He hit her on one cheek and again on the other. He rained blows on her and forgot that he was beating her. Taabu didn't emit a single sound. She just collapsed under her husband's blows. He drummed on her sides and lashed at her backside.

Then abruptly he stopped and turned away from the disorderly heap sprawled on the ground. He felt limp. He went back to his stool and sat with drooping shoulders, his fury spent. He stared into a black abyss: into a dark past of nothingness and into a future that had become featureless. Even the hope pinned on Tumaini[7] faded into the obscure distance for a moment. The noises of the children returning from school brought him back to the present. He saw that it was already dark; he saw that the disorderly figure was still sprawling where he had left it.

'Woman! Go and cook!'

Taabu heard the voice of her husband. She also heard the noises of the children. Then she remembered the children. If she was tired of life then the children at least had to live. And if they had to live, her first duty was to live too, not to die. She got up with difficulty, wiped the blood from her mouth and limped into the hut. Soon complete darkness was embracing every object in fear and uncertainty: the jagged summits, the solitary hut and the agitated figure hunched on the three-legged stool.

Three years back Umoja village hadn't existed. Most of the people lived on the other side of the river, on the Giza hills, and Amri shared with them everything: the barren hillsides, the fickleness of the river and the poverty of the place. Then there had come people carrying the message of the new prophet, Nyerere[8]. Nguvumali had taken up the cry.

'*Umoja ni Nguvu*. Unity is Power'.

From hill to hill he had walked, spreading this new word.

'Let us shake off this poverty that is on our backs like wet bark cloth! Let us abandon barren hills and, together, go to a new land of fertility!'

Some people had listened to him. With a handful of others Nguvumali had crossed the river. Umoja Ujamaa village had been born. Then, one after the other, the remaining people had crossed the river too and followed him.

Fools, stupid fools, Amri had decided. They knew nothing. The thing was not new to Amri. When Nguvumali had called his first meeting to urge the people to join him in the new venture he, Amri, had told the people the story of the two villages of the Wakoti and Wamasoka people.

Some people among the Wakoti, a tribe living further down the river, had come to build an *ujamaa* village. They had built their huts and opened one large *shamba*. But a heavy storm had soon poured down and washed away all the new crops, with some of the huts. They failed to start anew and, disillusioned, they dispersed. Among the Wamasoka, too, a village had sprung up. But soon children had started dying in the village. Some great *wachawi*[9] had been included among the villagers. The people had started quarrelling among themselves and the village had broken up.

The people had listened to Amri, but they had failed to grasp the meaning of his words. They had flocked behind Nguvumali like a herd of cattle. Fools. They did not even know who Nguvumali was, or what his motives were.

When Amri's father was on his death-bed he had warned him of Nguvumali's father, then a very old man. 'Beware of him,' he had said, 'and watch your family.' Owls hooted over his roof at night and mysterious beasts shrieked in the bush surrounding his hut. Amri's first two children had died at the age of a few months. The three witch-doctors Amri had consulted had all pointed their finger at the old man. When the third pregnancy had ensued, however, Taabu and Amri had gone to some witch-doctors and medicine-men for insurance against any further calamity. The child that had been born had lived, and his parents had named him Tumaini, Hope. When the wizened old man died, people had sighed with relief.

And now the son of the same old man was calling on the people to come together, like a cattle-owner gathering his herd of cows and calves on the eve of a great feast-day . . . Let them follow him, Amri had told himself, and pay for their folly with their wives and children.

Amri and Nguvumali were old enemies. This enmity had been born twenty years back, and the incident that had sparked it would ever burn in Amri's mind and endlessly gnaw at his peace. Then, Taabu had only recently been married to him. One evening returning from a drinking spree, Amri had found his domain broken into and his most precious vessel being defiled. He had found Nguvumali lying on top of his new bride.

People had arrived at the scene just as Amri was about to drive the spear into the trespasser's heart and they had prevented him from administering his crude form of justice. Nguvumali had apoligized and paid Amri a fine of a cow. But how could a cow restore to a man his wife's impaired loyalty, or cure the insult inflicted on a husband's manhood?

In addition, there had been the death of his two children at the time of Nguvumali's father. Their latest quarrel, however, had been over their sons.

Amri's son, Tumaini, studied in a big school in the city. Nguvumali also had a son who went to the same secondary school as Tumaini. At the time the two men were the only people in Giza with children in a secondary school. But when the examination had come and Tumaini had passed and qualified to go to the big school, Nguvumali's son had failed. He had been unable to secure even a messenger's job. So Amri had beaten Nguvumali! Intense jealousy had developed between the two of them and the old enmity had been fanned anew.

There was a man, Toma, whom everybody knew. He was a wealthy man. He lived in a big brick and iron-roofed house, and owned a big shop. He had a large herd of cattle and goats. He never worked on the poor land like all the others. But only three or four years back he had been as poor as anybody else in Giza. Where had he obtained all this wealth? His son. He had been educated and now he worked in the big city and had become a big man.

Nguvumali knew Toma, and so he knew what Tumaini's going to the big school meant to Amri. His campaign to start Umoja Ujamaa village was therefore primarily directed against him. He would draw all the others across the river after himself and isolate his adversary. It was a personal struggle between Nguvumali and Amri. But the others had no idea about these secret motives. They just followed Nguvumali. Like sheep.

He, Amri, was determined to remain where he was and bide his time. When the moment was ripe he would cross the river too. He would choose a site near Umoja village, Nguvumali's creation, and erect his new brick and iron-roofed house. He did not want any shop. He would have, instead, a diesel flour-mill installed beside his new house. People would then flock to him with their grain and for every *debe* of maize he milled he would charge a shilling – Amri knew a man who had quickly become rich in this way. He would then leave it to Nguvumali to decide who was the winner between them.

Amri had tried to explain matters to Taabu, but a woman would never understand these things. She kept nagging at him and pestering him to follow the others. How could Amri go there to be told to do this or that by Nguvumali? How could he let his wife be ordered about by other men and still call himself master of his family? Perhaps her son would make her understand. The rains had already broken out and Tumaini would soon be home for his holidays.

At the foot of the hill Tumaini put down his heavy suitcase and sat down on a rock to regain his strength for the final effort. His had not been a good journey. The rains had broken out and for some two or three days had poured down in unabated fury. All the roads had turned into a quagmire, and the journey that normally took him three days by bus had taken him six days. His white, long-sleeved shirt and blue, striped trousers had become muddy brown, and his new black shoes were two lumps of caked mud. The three-mile walk from the motor track had completely exhausted him, and he had nearly fallen off that rickety bridge when crossing the stream.

Now sitting on the rock, he watched the sickly animals grazing on the stony slopes of the hill. Three cows and six goats. One of the cows had calved but its udders hung flabbily between its hind legs, like empty sacks. He knew his father milked it every morning; and the calf had long feet and swollen joints, and its rack-like ribs were clearly visible. Once again Tumaini wondered why his father continued in this poverty and hard life. Why couldn't he cross the river too and follow the others to prosperity? He must talk to him tonight. He rose and with great resolution lifted the leaden suitcase to his head.

The bright red embers glowed like the angry eyes of some fierce beast. And the glow they radiated faintly revealed the shins of two dark figures hunched on low, three-legged stools. Father and son sat alone by the evening fire, surrounded by darkness.

Amri was lost in thought. Tumaini tried to think too, attempting to get to the core of the whole issue. But one thought collided against another and his mind became jumbled. He would never get to the root of his father's obstinacy. The people of Umoja village were much better off than he. Their land was more fertile than the bare hill slopes of Giza. Their children were much nearer to the school. The Government had already given them a dispensary, although a small one, and a nurse. It had promised them tap water, and the pipes had already been brought. The people there farmed and sold their crops on a co-operative basis. A truck came to take the crops to the market, and they got good prices. The houses they built were stronger and more durable and a few of them were already iron-roofed. Wasn't this what the Government was awakening the masses of the people to see?

His father saw all this, lived near it; but he would still stick to the barren hills. His hut was rotting away, but he would never change his mind. All Tumaini's arguments had fallen on deaf ears. Was it always as difficult as this to change old minds? If it was, then the task facing the new blood of this nation was great indeed.

The fire now made a little crackling noise and his father cleared his throat to speak.

'It is true that it has not always been easy to stay here.' His father spoke slowly, deliberately, with a heavy and deep voice that seemed tinged with the solemnity of the night and the mysteriousness of the darkness surrounding them. 'It is also true that the soil here doesn't produce much. But that is no reason to blind us or make us cast caution from our step. Don't forget that a man has got to be alive first before he can live a better life. Nguvumali is not our friend.'

Here Amri paused and to Tumaini it seemed the name Nguvumali had rather agitated him. He waited for him to continue.

'Your grandfather, lying on his death-bed, had warned me to beware of Nguvumali's family. Your two brothers who had come before you passed away. And it had been on account of Nguvumali's father. It was only with great difficulty that we prevented him from taking your life too. But now luck has been on our side. Nguvumali and his family have crossed the river and we have been left alone in peace. Are we now again to run after him?'

Nonsense, utter nonsense, Tumaini thought. But he said

nothing. Nyerere's words rang in his mind: 'We have now to fight our three great enemies: Disease, Poverty and Ignorance . . .'

'Look, Tumaini,' his father went on after a pause, 'you know Toma, don't you?'

'Oh, yes! Toma Makombo. His son is working with the Ministry of Education. He is a great friend of mine.'

'Yes. Toma sent his son to school and now that son has become a big man. He has built him a big brick and iron-roofed house. He has given him a big shop and a large herd of cattle. Now Toma is rich. Today you won't find him toiling and sweating in the *shamba* like the rest of us.'

All this time Amri had spoken with his head bowed low. Now he sat upright and looked directly into his son's eyes. For a moment Tumaini resisted his father's piercing look but then he winced and looked down. He would never grow out of his fear of his father.

Amri said, 'You have now been in school as long as him, haven't you?'

And now at last it dawned on him. Tumaini's jaw fell and for a moment he did not know what to say.

He had known Toma's son, the Education Officer, but he had never once related his father's wealth to his position. It had never once crossed his mind that his own father had all this time looked on him as an asset! And now as he thought of it it seemed most absurd, contrary to all the principles he had so far cherished. Was he to shut his eyes to the glaring poverty of the masses and rob them even of the little they had? Was he now to use his education to make his father a small capitalist, growing fat on the sorrows and miseries of the very people who had paid for that education?

Betrayal was in the air between him and his father; he smelt betrayal. But then what of his father who had, for all the years of his education, built high hopes on him? Here was ideology *vis-à-vis* the reality.

'Perhaps,' Tumaini began, 'I should tell you the truth right away. When I finished my secondary education I applied to an agricultural school, and for the last three years I have studied at this new school. When I go back now I am going to complete my course. Now the thing is that I have applied to come to stay in Umoja Ujamaa village and work with the people there.'

Amri jerked up his broad shoulders and sat upright on his stool, as if struck by a thunder-bolt.

'What!' he hissed. 'Are you joking?'

'No, Father. In fact I had hoped that you would join . . .'

'You are not going to let me down just like that, are you?'

'I don't mean to let you down, father. This is now the call to the people all over the country. The people have to come together in *ujamaa* villages. Together they have to open bigger farms, build better houses and take the new road to development. Villages are springing up all over the country. It is our pride that we, the people of Giza, too, have answered this call.'

'You said the villages are starting all over the country?'

'Yes, father.'

'And many people are joining them?'

'Not very many as yet. Some, for one reason or another, are hesitating. Some are rich and they don't want to share riches with others, so they refuse to join. Others, because they don't know what an *ujamaa* village is like, think if they join one they are going to be ruled over and ordered around like school children. But more and more people are starting to understand, and one day, we hope, most of the people in this country will be living in such villages.'

'And who is telling the people to go into villages? Is it this Nyerere they talk about so much?'

'Not only Nyerere. It is the policy of the Government –'

'Government! Government! Alas, my son! They are cheating you. Tell me: who among the people you call Government is living in an *ujamaa* village himself? Don't we see them wearing expensive clothes, riding in beautiful cars? Don't they live in the towns, where they own large, beautiful houses? Do their wives ever know what it is like to pound maize in the mortar or fetch water from the river? They are cheating you, my son! They don't want you to share the wealth with them.'

'Things are changing, Father. Some of the big men now leave their offices to go to villages to work with the people on better farming methods . . .'

'To push me into Umoja, to be shouted at and ordered about by Nguvumali, to be taunted and despised by everyone, to be pointed and giggled at by school children.'

Now Amri was shouting at Tumaini, at the darkness behind

him, and at all those forces that had conspired against him. 'You are shattering all my dreams for a better future. I have spent all I had on your education. I have gone hungry and naked to make you what you are today. Now at last, like an ungrateful calf with stomach full, you are kicking me in the face, butting the hand that has fed and reared you. Can my own son treat me like that?'

The father's speech had ended in a cry of anguish. The son said nothing. He couldn't find the words to say. Had his father deserved that disillusion at all? But then on the other hand, was there any alternative to it?

The wave of emotion spent, Amri slumped back on his stool and stared blindly at the embers that had now gained a layer of grey ash on them. They were slowly dying, growing cold.

Later that night Tumaini lay awake in his creaking bed, thinking of what had passed between him and his father that evening. He did not know whether to accept the guilt he was now feeling or not.

Since his outburst of emotion his father hadn't spoken another word. Tumaini had found it safer to keep quiet too. They had stayed like this for a long time, until a wind had started blowing dust particles into their eyes. His father had slowly risen and gone into the hut. He had followed his example, but now sleep would not come. He listened to the leaves of the trees outside sighing in the wind that had become much stronger now. Thunder rolled in the distance and the hut trembled under its impact. A heavy storm was gathering.

His three younger brothers slept on the floor beside his bed. He could hear their snores above the hissing wind. Soon, however, the storm burst out. The raindrops came clattering down on the grass roof and drowned the snores. The wind fiercely hurled the leaden drops against the roof and mud walls, and he could hear the rivulets of water gurgling as they collected into bigger and stronger streams and found their way down the hill. Flashes of lightning came through the cracks in the walls and the thunder roared. Through a leak in the roof water dripped down and struck Tumaini's foot. He shifted his feet, but another leakage found his bare shoulder. He shifted his body and listened. Hundreds of drops thudded everywhere on the floor.

Now the whistling wind, the roaring thunder and the pouring

rain formed one continuous, dull, rumbling sound that shook the hut and inspired fear in Tumaini's heart.

The fierce storm raged on for hours. Tumaini had shifted his position on the bed a hundred times or more. At last he gave up the attempt and let the rain drench him as it wished. He wondered how his younger brothers could sleep undisturbed in the dripping rain. He wondered whether his father was awake too and, if he was, what he could be thinking. The difficulty of the period of transition! The suffering of the generation in transition! It had never once occurred to him that the policy directed at changing a life of poverty and misery to one promising affluence and betterment could also mean disillusionment and disappointment – even to the ones it was supposed to benefit! If this was being experienced in all the other parts of the country, then the dream that had been so vivid and real in his imagination and the imagination of his friends back at school would be much more difficult to realize than they had known. The leap from today into tomorrow was going to be much more difficult than they had known. The leap from today into tomorrow was going to be a difficult feat to perform.

Suddenly there was a sharp crack. Tumaini jumped up and cried above the fury of the storm: 'Father! Father! Kalombi! Doto! Get up! Quick!'

In a few moments the house was in commotion. Everyone was carrying out of the hut what he could lay hands on: mats, baskets, pots, bits of clothing, implements. The roof of the hut gaped open in the middle and sagged dangerously over their heads. Rain flooded into the hut. Taabu was shouting at the children to keep out of the way. Just as Amri was dragging out the large earthen pot, the last item remaining in the hut, the roof collapsed, bringing down two of the walls with it. At once a swirling torrent hit at the remaining walls which, like melting wax, yielded to its erosive power and collapsed in a heap. The relentless drops of rain pelted at the prostrate walls and little by little carried them away as chunks of mud.

Amri and the family clustered together in the streaming rain. Lightning flashed and thunder rocked the earth they stood on. A few paces from where they stood something heavy fell with a dull thud. When lightning flashed again they saw their granary being slowly washed down the hill in a strong current. The goats bleated and the cows lowed in their byre. And now the deep, rumbling mourning of the thunder caught hold of them too, and the fear of the dark night and the storm assailed their hearts.

Tumaini found himself standing beside his father. He peered at his face and in the flash of lightning saw the defeat in his eyes. Tumaini was suddenly filled with compassion. He braced his shoulders and resolved to stand by him through the hazards of the night and together with him await the break of a new day.

> To cross the river, as wide and deep
> That 'tween opposing worlds doth sweep,
> To jump across with one clear leap
> It never once shall be as cheap.
> But must always a storm them force,
> The strong-willed ones that are loath to cross?

NOTES

Umoja[1] – (Kiswahili) Unity.

Amri[2] – (Kiswahili) Command.

Taabu[3] – (Kiswahili) Troubles, difficulties.

Magwanda[4] – (Kiswahili) A calico garment sometimes worn by men in Tanzania. It is like a smock or shirt-kanzu reaching to the knees.

Nguvumali[5] – (Kiswahili) A rich, powerful man.

Ujamaa[6] – (Kiswahili) A form of African socialism based on traditional concepts of the extended family, the social community and self-help projects. A co-operative village or farm established on the ujamaa principle.

Tumaini[7] – (Kiswahili) Hope.

Nyerere[8] – Dr Julius Nyerere, President of Tanzania 1962–85. The architect of Tanzania's ujamaa policy.

Wachawi[9] – (Kiswahili) Witches.

EXERCISES

1. The conservative Amri regards his son as an 'asset', someone who will bring him wealth. Tumaini gives his father a preachy little political lecture to persuade him to change his attitude and move to the *ujamaa* village.
   a) Do you sympathize with either of these two characters and the position each holds?
   b) Are children in East Africa widely considered as assets by their parents? How particularly? Is this an attitude to be deplored in *all* circumstances?

2. Amri, in justifying his determination not to move to the new village, tells the story of the Wakoti people. Why is this story ironical considering the fate that eventually befalls Amri himself?

3. Read the story again and try to determine how images of nature and the natural scene 'work' in the story. Consider the following in answering the question:
   a) the description of where Amri lives;
   b) the description of the *ujamaa* village's situation;
   c) the storm that occurs at the end.

4. The author uses several methods to tilt our sympathy a certain way. Examine the following points and explain how precisely they affect our emotions as readers:
   a) the choice of significant Kiswahili names for the characters and where they live;
   b) the description of the natural environment;
   c) the physical descriptions of Taabu and Amri.

5. The last paragraph mentions 'the break of a new day'. What is Tumaini thinking about?

A Mercedes Funeral

NGUGI WA THIONG'O

(KENYA)

IF YOU EVER find yourself in Ilmorog, don't fail to visit Ilmorog Bar and Restaurant. There you're likely to meet somebody you were once at school with and you can reminisce over old days and learn news of missing friends and acquaintances. The big shots of Chiri District frequent the place, especially on Saturday and Sunday evenings after a game of golf and tennis on the lawn grounds of the once FOR EUROPEANS ONLY Sonia Club a few miles away. But for a litre or two of Tusker or Pilsner[1] they all drive to the more relaxed low-class parts of Ilmorog. Mark you, it is not much of a restaurant; don't go there for chicken-in-the-basket and steak cooked in wine; it is famous only for charcoal-roasted goat meat and nicely dressed barmaids. And, of course, gossip. You sit in a U-shaped formation of the red-cushioned sofa seats you find in public bars all over Kenya. You talk or you listen. No neutrality of poise and bearing, unless of course you pretend; there's no privacy, unless of course you hire a separate room.

It was there one Saturday evening that I sat through an amusing story. Ever heard of a Mercedes-Benz Funeral? The narrator, one of those of our dark-suited brothers with a public opinion just protruding, was talking to a group, presumably his visitors, but loudly for all to hear. A little tipsy he probably was; but his voice at times sounded serious and slightly wrought with emotion. I sipped my frothy beer, – I am a city man if you want to know – I cocked my ears and soon I was able to gather the few scattered threads. He was talking of someone who had once or recently worked in a bar:

. . . not much . . . not much I confess, he was saying. The truth of the matter, gentlemen, is that I too had forgotten him. I would not even have offered to tell you about him except . . . well . . . except that his name surfaced into sudden importance in that ridiculous affair. But, gentlemen, you must have read about it . . . no? Is that so? Anyway the affair was there all right and it really shook us in Ilmorog. It even got a few column inches in the national dailies. And that's something, you know, especially with so many bigger scandals competing for attention. Big men fighting it out with fists and wrestling one another to the ground . . . candidates beaten up by hired thugs . . . others arrested on nomination day for mysterious reasons and released the day after, again for mysterious reasons. A record year, gentlemen, a record year, that one. With such events competing for attention, why should anyone have taken an interest in a rather silly story of an unknown corpse deciding the outcome of an election in a remote rural town? And yet fact number one . . . not, gentlemen, that I want to theorize . . . yet the truth is that his death, or rather his funeral, would never have aroused so much heat had it not come during an election year.

Now, let me see, count rather: there was that seat in parliament: the most Honourable John Joe James . . . would you believe it, used to be known as John Karanja but dropped his African name on first being elected – standards, efficiency and international dignity demanded it of him you know – anyway he wanted to be returned unopposed. There was also the leadership of the party's branch: the Chairman . . . wait, his name was Ruoro but he had been the leader of the branch for so long – no meetings, no elections, ran the whole thing himself – that people simply called him the Chairman . . . he too wanted a fresh, unopposed mandate. There were vacancies in the County Council and in other small bodies, too numerous to mention. But all the previous occupants wanted to be returned with increased majorities, unopposed. Why, when you come to think of it, why do a few people out of jobs they had done for six years and more? Specialists . . . experience . . . all that and more. And why add to unemployment? Unfortunately there were numerous upstarts who had different ideas and wanted a foot and a hand in running the very same jobs. Dynamism . . . fresh blood . . . all that and more. Naturally gentlemen, and I am sure this was also true in your area, the job which most thought they could execute with unique skill and efficiency was that of the Honourable MP for Ilmorog. See what I mean? More Tusker beer gentlemen? Hey Sister . . . Sister . . . these barmaids! . . . *baada ya kazi jiburudishe na Tusker*.[2]

Well, after the first round of trial runs and feelers through a whispering campaign, the field was left to the incumbent and three challengers. There was the university student . . . you know the sort you find these days: a Lumumba goatee,[3] weather-beaten American shirts and jeans. . . . they dress only in foreign clothes, foreign fashions, foreign ideas . . . You remember our time in Makerere under De Bunsen?[4] Worsted woollen suits, starched white shirts and ties to match . . . now that's what I call proper dressing. Anyway, our student challenger claimed to be an intellectual worker and as such could fully understand the aspirations of all workers. There was also an aspiring businessman. An interesting case this one. Had just acquired a loan to build a huge self-service supermarket here in Ilmorog shopping centre. It was whispered that he had diverted a bit of that loan into his campaign. He would tell his audience that man was born to make money: if he went to parliament, he would ensure that everybody had a democratic chance to make a little pile. He himself would set an example; a leader must lead. Also in the arena was a Government Chief, or rather ex-Chief, who had resigned his job to enter the race. He claimed that he would make a very good chief in parliament. Sweat and sacrifice, he used to say, were ever his watchwords. As an example of S and S, he had not only given up a very promising career in the civil service to offer himself as a complete servant of the people, but had also sold three of his five grade cows to finance his campaign. His wife protested of course, but . . . Sister, I asked you for some beer . . . we all have our weaknesses, eh?

Each challenger denounced the other two, accusing them of splitting the vote. If they, the other two that is, were sincere, would they not do the honourable thing: stand down in favour of one opponent? The three were however united in denouncing the sitting member. What had he done for the area? He had only enriched himself and his relatives. They pointed to his business interests, his numerous buildings in the area and his many shares in even the smallest petrol station in the constituency. From what forgotten corner had he suddenly acquired all that wealth, including a thousand-acre farm, asked the aspiring businessman? Why had he not given others a democratic chance to dip a hand in the common pool? The student demanded: what has he done for us *wafanyi kazi*[5]? The ex-Chief accused him of never once visiting his constituency. His election had been a one-way ticket to the city. They all chorused: let the record speak, let the record speak for itself. Funnily enough, gentlemen, the incumbent replied with the same words – yes, let the record speak – but managed to give them a tone of great achievement. First he pointed out what the Government had done: the roads, hospitals, factories, tourist hotels and resorts, Hilton, the Intercontinental and all that. Anybody who said the Government had done nothing for *wananchi*[6] was demagogic and indulging in cheap politics. To the charge that he was not a minister and hence was not in Government, he would laugh and fly-whisk away such ignorance. From where did the Government derive its strength and power? From among whom was the Cabinet chosen? To the charge that he had made it, he answered by accusing the others of raging with envy and congenital idleness. A national cake on the table . . . some people too lazy or too fat to lift a finger and take a piece . . . waited to have it put into their mouths and chewed for them, even. To the ex-Chief he said: didn't this would-be MP . . . a man without any experience . . . didn't he know that the job of an MP was to attend parliament and make good laws that hanged thieves and repatriated vagabonds and prostitutes back to the rural areas? You don't make laws by sitting in your home drinking Chang'aa[7] and playing draughts. For the student he had only scornful laughter: intellectual workers . . . he means intellectuals whose one speciality is stoning other people's cars and property! Gentlemen . . . there was nothing in the campaign, no issues, no ideas . . . just promises. People were bored. They did not know whom to choose although the non-arguments of the aspiring businessman held most sway. You, your bottle is still empty . . . you want to change to something stronger? Vat 69? No? . . . oh . . . oh . . . Chang'aa, did you say? Ha! ha! ha! . . . Chang'aa for power . . .

Kill-Me-Quick[8] . . . no, that is never in stock here . . . Sister, hey, Sister . . . another round . . . the same.

You mention Chang'aa. Actually it was Chang'aa, you might say, that saved the campaign. Put it this way. If Wahinya, the other watchman in Ilmorog Bar and Restaurant, had not suddenly died of alcoholic poisoning, our village, our town, would never have been mentioned in any daily. Wahinya dead became the most deadly factor in the election. It was during a rather diminished public meeting addressed by the candidates that the student shouted something about 'We workers'. The others took up the challenge. They too were workers. Everybody, said the incumbent, everybody was a worker except the idle, the crippled, prostitutes and students. A man from the audience stood up. By now people had lost their original awe and curiosity and respect for the candidates. Anyway this man stands up. He was a habitual drunk – and that day he must have broken a can or two. Who cares about the poor worker, he asked, imitating in turn the oratorical gestures of each speaker. These days the poor die and don't even have a hole in which to be put, let alone a burial in a decent coffin. People laughed, applauding. They could well understand this man's concern for he himself, skin and bones only, looked on the verge of the grave. But he stood his ground and mentioned the case of Wahinya. His words had an electric effect. That night all the candidates singly and secretly went to the wife of the deceased and offered to arrange for Wahinya's funeral.

Now I don't know if this is true in your area, but in our village funerals had become a society affair, our version of cocktail parties. I mean since Independence. Before 1952, you know, before the Emergency, the body would be put away in puzzled silence and tears. People, you see, were awed by death. But they confronted it because they loved life. They asked: what's death? because they wanted to know what was life! They came to offer sympathy and solidarity to the living and helped in the burial. A pit. People took turns to dig it in mutual silence. Then the naked body was lowered into the earth. A little soil was first sprinkled over it. The body, the earth, the soil: what was the difference? Then came the Emergency. Guns on every side. Fathers, mothers, children, cattle, donkeys – all killed and bodies left in the open for vultures and hyenas. Or mass burial. People became cynical about death; they were really indifferent to life. You today; me tomorrow. Why cry my Lord? Why mourn the dead? There was only one cry: for the victory of the struggle. The rest was silence. What do you think, gentlemen? Shall we ever capture that genuine respect for death in an age where money is more important than life? Today what is left? A showbiz. Status. Even poor people will run into debt to have the death of a relative announced on the radio and funeral arrangements advertised in the newspapers. And gossip, gentlemen, the gossip. How many attended the funeral? How much money was collected? What of the coffin? Was the pit cemented? Plastic flowers; plastic tears. And after a year, every year there is an ad. addressed to the dead.

> *In loving memory. A year has passed but to us it is just like today when you suddenly departed from your loved ones without letting them know of your last wish. Dear, you have always been a guiding star, a star that will always shine, etc., etc.*

You see, our man was right. It was a disgrace to die poor; even the Church will not receive the poor in state, though the priest will rush to the death-bed to despatch the wretch quickly on a heaven-bound journey, and claim another victim for Christ. So you see where Wahinya's death, a poor worker's death, comes in!

I don't know how far this is true, but it is said that each candidate would offer the wife money if she would leave all the funeral arrangements and oration in their sole hands . . . You say, she should have auctioned the rights? Probably . . . probably. But those were only rumours. What I do know for a fact, well, a public fact, was that the wife and her husband's body suddenly vanished. Stolen, you say? In a way, yes. It was rumoured that J.J.J. had had a hand in it. The others called a public meeting to denounce the act. How could anybody steal a dead body? How dare a leader show so little respect for the dead and the feelings of the public? The crowd must also have felt cheated of a funeral drama. They shouted: produce the body; produce the body! The meeting became so hot and near-riotous that the police had to be called. But even then the tempers could not be cooled. The body, the body, they shouted. J.J.J., normally the very picture of calmness, wiped his face once or twice. It was the student who saved the day: he suggested setting up a committee not only to investigate the actual disappearance but to go into the whole question of poor men's funerals. All the contestants were elected members of the committee. Well, and a few neutrals. There was a dispute as to who would chair the committee's meetings. The burden fell on the Chairman of the branch. Thereafter all the candidates tried to please him. Rumours became even more rife. Gangs of supporters followed the committee and roamed through the villages. And now the miracle of miracles. As suddenly as she had disappeared, Wahinya's wife now surfaced and would not disclose where she had been. More, the body had found its way to the city mortuary. This started even more rumours. No beer-party was complete without a story relating to the affair. Verbal bulletins on the deliberations of the committee were daily released and became the talking points in all the bars. People, through the Chairman, were kept informed of every detail about the funeral arrangements. Overnight, so to speak, Wahinya had, so to speak, risen from the dead to be the most powerful factor in the elections. People whispered: who is this Wahinya? Details of his life were unearthed; numerous people claimed special acquaintance and told alluring stories about him. Dead, he was larger than life. Dead, he was everybody's closest friend.

Me? Yes, gentlemen, me too. I had actually met him on three different occasions: when he was a porter, then as a turnboy[9] and more recently as a watchman. And I can say this: Wahinya's progress from hope to a drinking despair is the story of our time. But what is the matter, gentlemen? You are not drinking? Sister, hey, Sister . . . see to these gentlemen . . . well, never mind . . . as soon as they finish this round . . . Yes, gentlemen . . . to drink, to be merry . . . Life is – but no theories I promised you . . . no sermons, although I will say this again: Wahinya's rather rapid progress towards the grave is really the story of our troubled times!

There was a long pause in the small hall. I tried to sip my beer, but half-way I put the glass back on the table. I was not alone. Half-full glasses of stale beer stood untouched all round. Everybody must have been listening to the story. The narrator, a glass of beer in his hand, stared pensively at the ground, and somehow in that subdued atmosphere his public opinion seemed less offensive. He put the glass down and his voice when it came seemed to have been affected by the attentive silence:

I first came to know him fairly well in the 1960s, he started. Those, if you remember, were the years when dreams like garden perfume in the wind wafted through the air of our villages. The years, gentlemen, when rumours of *uhuru*[10] made people's hearts palpitate with fearful joy of what would happen tomorrow: if something should – ? But no, nothing untoward would possibly bar the coming of that day, the opening of the gate. Imagine: to elect our sons spokesmen of black power, after so much blood . . . so much blood . . .!

He too, you can guess, used to dream. Beautiful dreams about the future. I imagine that even while sagging under the weight of sacks of sugar, sacks of maize flour, sacks of *magadi* salt and soda,[11] he would be in a world all his own. Flower fields of green peas and beans. Gay children chasing nectar-seeking bees and butterflies. A world to visit, a world to conquer. Wait till tomorrow, my Lord, till tomorrow. He was tall and frail-looking but strong with clear dark eyes that lit up with hope. And you can imagine that at such times the sack of sugar would feel light on his back, his limbs would acquire renewed strength, he was the giant in the story who could pull mountains by the roots or blow trees into the sky with his rancid breath. Trees, roots, branches and all flew into the sky, high, high, no longer trees but feathers carried by the wind. Fly away bird, little one of the courtyard, and come again to gather millet grains in the sand. He would lay down the sack to watch the bird fly into the unknown and no doubt his dreams would also soar even beyond the present sky, his soul's eye would scan hazier and hazier horizons hiding away knowledge of tomorrow. But from somewhere in the shop a shout from his Indian employer would haul him back to this earth. Hurry up with that load, you lazy boy. Money you want, work no! You think money coming from dust or fall from sky. *Kumanyoko*.[12] No doubt Wahinya would sigh. He was after all only a porter in Shukla and Shukla Stores, an object like that very load against which he had been leaning.

Shukla and Shukla: that's where I used to meet him. I was

then a student in Siriana boarding school. A missionary affair it was in those days, I mean the school and its numerous rules and restrictions. For instance, we were never allowed out of the school compound except on Saturday afternoons and even then not beyond a three-mile radius. Chura township, a collection of a dozen Indian-owned shops and a post office, was the only centre within our limits, both physical and financial. With ten cents, fifty cents or a shilling in our pockets, we used to walk there with determination as if on a very important mission. An unhurried stroll around the shops . . . then a Fanta soda, or a few madhvani gummy sweets[13] from Shukla and Shukla . . . and our day was over. Well, I used never to have more than two shillings pocket money for a whole term. So I would often go to Chura without a hope of crowning my Saturday afternoon outing with Fantas, *mandazis*[14] or madhvanis. A sweet, a soft drink then was a world. You laugh. But do you know how I envied those who strode that world with showy impunity and suggestions of even greater well-being at their homes? As soon as I reached the stores, friends and foes had to be avoided. I lied and I knew they knew I lied when I pretended having important business further on. Still, can you imagine the terror in case I was found out and exposed?

Wahinya must have seen through me. I can't remember how we first met or who first spoke to whom. I remember, though, my initial embarrassment at his ragged clothes and his grimy face. It seemed he might pull me down to his level. What would the other boys think of me? How quickly school could separate people! At home in order to preserve my school uniform I wore similarly ragged clothes and often went to bed hungry. From our conversations I soon found that we shared a common background. We came from Ilmorg. We were both without fathers: mine had died of Chang'aa poisoning; his had died whilst fighting in the forest. So we were brought up by mothers who had to scratch the dry earth for a daily can of *unga*[15] and for fees. We attended similar types of primary schools: Karing'a Independent. But while mine came under the Colonial District Education Board, his was closed and the building burnt down by the British. All African-run schools were suspected of aiding in the freedom struggle.

Thus, blind chance had put Wahinya and me on different

paths. And yet with all our shared past, I felt slightly above him, superior. Deep in my stomach was the terror that he might besmirch my standing in school. But occasionally he would slip twenty cents or fifty cents into my hands. For this I was grateful and it of course softened my initial repugnance. So I, the recipient of his hard-earned cents that helped me hide my humiliation of lies and pretence and put me on an equal footing with the other boarders, became the recipient of his dreams, ambitions and plans for the future.

'You are very lucky,' Wahinya would always start, his eyes alight. He would then tell me how he loved school and what positions he had held in the various classes. 'From Kiai to Standard Four, I was never below number three. Especially English . . . aah, nobody could beat me in that . . . and in history . . . you remember that African king we learnt about? What was his name . . . Chaka[16], and Moshoeshoe[17] . . . and how they fought the British with stones, spears and bare hands . . . and Waiyaki[18], the Laibon[19], Mwanga[20], the Nandi struggle against the British army[21] . . .' He would become excited. He would reel off name after name of the early African heroes. But for me now educated at Siriana this was not history. I pitied him really. I wanted to tell him about the true and correct history: the Celts, the Anglo-Saxons, the Danes and Vikings, William the Conqueror[22], Drake[23], Hawkins[24], Wilberforce[25], Nelson[26], Napoleon[27] and all these real heroes of history. But then I thought he would not understand secondary school history and Siriana was reputed to have the best and toughest education. He would not, in any case, let me slip in a word. For he was now back with his heroes gazing at today and tomorrow: 'Do they teach you that kind of history in Siriana? Only it must be harder to understand . . . I used to draw sketches of all the battles . . . the teacher liked them . . . he made me take charge of the blackboard . . . you know, duster, chalk and the big ruler in the shape of a T. You know it?' He would question me about Siriana: what subject, what kind of teachers. 'Europeans, eh? Do they beat you? Is it difficult learning under white men who speak English through the nose?' Often as he spoke he would be eyeing my jacket and green tie; he would touch the badge with the school motto in Latin and I often had the feeling that he enjoyed Siriana through me. I was the symbol of what he would soon become, especially with the rumoured departure of white men.

And that, gentlemen, was how I would always like to remember Wahinya: a boy who had never lost his dreams for higher education. His eyes would often acquire a distant look, misty even, and he seemed impatient with his present Shukla surroundings and the slow finger of time. 'This work . . . only for a time now . . . a few more days . . . a little bit more money . . . aah, school again . . . you think I will be able to do it? . . . Our teacher . . . he was a good one . . . used to make us sing songs . . . I had a good voice . . . you should hear it one day . . . he used to tell us: boys, don't gaze in wonder at the things the white man has made: pins, guns, bombs, aeroplanes . . . what one man can do, another one can . . . what one race can do, another one can, and more . . . One day . . . but never mind!' He always cut short the reference to his teacher, his eyes would become even more misty and for a few seconds he would not speak to me. Then, as if defying fate itself, he would re-affirm his teacher's maxim: what one man can do, another one can. Newspapers, well, printed words, fascinated him. He always carried in his pockets an old edition of *The Standard* and in between one job and the next he would struggle to spell out words and meanings. 'You think one day I'll be able to read this? I want to be able to read it blindfolded even. Read it through the nose, eh? Now you see me stumbling over all these words. But one day I will read it . . . easy . . . like swallowing water . . . Here tell me the meaning of this words . . . de . . . de . . . deadlo . . . ck . . . deadlock . . . how can a lock die?' I must say I could not help being affected by his enthusiasm and his unbounded faith especially in those days of lean pockets and occasional gunsmoke in the sky.

Gentlemen, you are no longer touching your drinks. What's left to us but to drink? Drinking dulls ones fear and terror and memories . . . and yet I cannot forget the last time I saw him in Chura. Same kind of Saturday afternoon. He was waiting for me by the railway crossing. I was embarrassed by this and I affected a casual approach and cool words. He was excited. He walked beside me, tried the customary pleasantries, then whipped out something from his pocket. An old edition of *The Standard*.

'See this . . . see this,' he said, opening a page. 'Read it, read it,' he said, thrusting the whole thing into my hands. But still he tried to read over my shoulder as we walked towards Shukla and Shukla stores.

> *Did you miss the student airlift abroad?*[28]
> *Study abroad while at home.*
> *Opportunities for higher education.*
> *Opportunities for an attractive career.*
> *All through correspondence.*
> *Apply:*
> *Quick Results College,*
> *Bristol,*
> *England.*
> *P.S. We cater for anything from primary to university.*

It was the days of those airlifts to America and Europe, you remember. Wahinya was capering around me. He fired many questions at me. But I knew nothing about correspondence schools. I dared not show him my ignorance though. I tried to make disparaging comments about learning through the post. But he was not really interested in my defeatist answers. His dream of higher education would soon be realized. 'I can manage it . . . I will manage it . . . *uhuru* is coming, you see . . . *uhuru* . . . more and better jobs . . . more money . . . might even own part of Shukla and Shukla . . . for these Indians are going to go, you know . . . money . . . but what I want is this thing: I must one day read *The Standard* through the nose . . .' I left him standing by Shukla and Shukla, peering at *The Standard*, his eyes probably blazing a trail that led to a future with dignity. Nothing, it seemed, would ever break his faith, his hopes, his dreams, and that in a land that had yet to recover from guns, concentration camps and broken homes.

I went back to my studies and prepared for the coming exams. Most of us got through and were accepted in Makerere, then the only University College in East Africa . . . no, not quite true . . . there was Dar es Salaam . . . but then it had only started. No more fees. No more rules and restrictions. We wore worsted gaberdines and smoked and danced. We even had pocket money.

Uhuru also came to our countries. We sang and danced and wept. Tomorrow. *Cha. Cha. Cha. Uhuru. Cha. Cha. Cha.* We streamed into the streets of Kampala. We linked hands and chanted: *Uhuru. Cha. Cha. Cha.* It was a kind of collective madness, I remember, and those women with whom we linked our loins knew it and gave themselves true. The story was the same for each of us. But none of us I am quite sure that night fully realized the full import of what had happened. This we knew in the coming years and perhaps Wahinya had been right. And what years, my Lord! Strange things we heard and saw: most of those who had finished Makerere were now being trained as District Officers, Labour Officers, Diplomats, Foreign Service – all European jobs. *Uhuru. Cha. Cha. Cha.* Others were now on the boards of Shell, Caltex, Esso and other oil companies. We could hardly wait for our turn. *Uhuru. Cha. Cha. Cha.* Some came for the delayed graduation ceremonies. They came in their dark suits and their cars, with red-lipped ladies in heels. They talked of their jobs, of their cars, of their employees, of their mahogany-furnished offices and of course their European and Asian secretaries. So this was true. No longer the rumours, no longer the unbelievable stories. And we were next in the queue.

We now dreamt not of sweets, Fanta and ginger-ale. The car was now our world. We compared names: VW, DKW, Ford Prefects, Peugeots, Flying 'A's. Mercedes-Benzes were then beyond the reach of our imagination. Nevertheless, it all seemed a wonder that we would soon be living in European mansions, eat in European hotels, holiday in European resorts at the coast and play golf. And with such prospects before my eyes, how could I remember Wahinya?

Travelling in a bus to the city one Saturday during my last holidays before graduation, I was dreaming of a world that would soon be mine. With a degree in Economics and Commerce, any job in most firms was within my grasp. Houses, cars, shares, land in the settled area . . . these whirled through my mind when suddenly I noticed my bus was no longer alone. It was racing with another called *Believe In God No. 1* at a reckless pace. I held my stomach in both hands, as we would say. The two buses were now running parallel making on-coming vehicles rush to a sudden stop by the roadside. It seemed my future was being interfered with by this reckless race to death. And the turnboys: they banged the body of the bus, urging their driver to accelerate – has the bus caught tuberculosis? – at the same time jeering and hurling curses at the turnboys of the enemy bus. They would climb to the luggage rack at the top and then swing down, monkey-fashion, to the side. They were playing, toying with death, like the death-riders I once saw in a visiting circus from India. You could touch the high-voltage tension in the bus. At one stage a woman screamed in an orgasm of fear and this seemed to act like a spur on the turnboys and the driver. Suddenly *Believe in God. No. 1* managed to pull past and you could now see the dejected look of the turnboys in our bus, while relief was registered on the faces of the passengers. It was then, when I dared to look, that I saw that one of the turnboys was none other than Wahinya.

He came into the bus, shaking his head from side to side as if in utter disbelief. He was now even more frail-looking but his face had matured with hard lines all over. I slunk even further into my seat instinctively avoiding contact. But he must have seen me because suddenly his eyes lit up, he turned towards me shouting my name for all in the bus to hear. 'My friend, my friend,' he called, clasping my hands in his, sitting beside me, slapped me hard on the shoulders. He was much less reserved than before and despite an attempt to keep our conversation low his voice rose above the others. 'Still at Makerere. You are lucky, eh! But remember our days in Chura? Those Indians . . . they never left . . . dismissed me just like that . . . it's good our people are rising . . . like the owner of these buses . . . the other day he was a *Matatu*[29] driver . . . now see him, the owner of ten buses. In one day he can count over 100,000 passengers. Not bad, eh? You better finish school soon, man . . . educated people like you can get loans. You start a business like the owner of these buses . . . do you know him? The MP for the area . . . John Joe James, or J. J. J. . . . To tell you the truth, this is what I want to do . . . a little money . . . I will buy a Peugeot . . . start a *matatu* . . . I tell you no other business can beat transport business for quick money . . . except buying and renting houses . . . Driver, more oil.' And suddenly, to my relief I must say, he stood up and rushed along the unpeopled aisle. He had spied another bus. The race for passengers would soon be over.

I went away slightly sad. What had happened to the boy with hopes for an education abroad? While at home I soon dismissed this sudden jolt to my own dreams and tried to re-experience that sweetness in the soul at the prospect of a tasty meal. But the death-race had dampened my spirits.

Eh? A glass to recover my breath? Welcome sweet wine . . . sweet eloquence . . . but what's the matter gentlemen? Drink also . . . I say a good drink, in a way, is the staff of life.

You should have seen us a week after graduation. We drank ourselves silly. Gates of heaven were now open because we had the key . . . the key . . . Open Sesame into the great world. Mark you it was not as rosy as it had seemed once we started working. I worked with a commercial firm and all the important ranks were filled with whites . . . experts, you know . . . and we stayed for so long in training, it tried one's patience . . . especially four years after Independence . . . Is it still the same? In a way, yes. Experts who are technically under you and still are paid more . . . and make real decisions . . . still I can't say I have been disappointed . . . If you work hard you can get somewhere . . . and with Government and bank loans . . . the other day I got myself a little *shamba* . . . a thousand acres, a few hundred cows . . . and with a European manager . . . the 'garden' is doing all right. And that's how I get a few cents to drink now and then . . . My favourite bar has always been this one . . . gives me a sense of homecoming . . . and I can observe things you know . . . homeboy . . . after all man has ambitions . . . And occasionally they employ beautiful juicy barmaids . . . man must live . . . mustn't he? There was one here . . . huge behind . . . Mercedes they used to call her . . . I prefer them big . . . Anyway one day I wanted her so bad, I winked at the watchman. I bent down to scribble a note on the back of the bill: would she be free tonight? Then I raised my head. The watchman stood in front of me. He had on a huge *kabuti*[30], with a *kofia*[31] and a *bokora* club[32] clutched firmly in his hands. This was a new one, I thought. Then our eyes met. Lo! It was Wahinya.

He hesitated that one second. A momentary indecision. 'Wahinya?' It was I who called out, automatically stretching out my hand. He took my hand and replied rather formally, 'Yes,

Sir,' but I did detect the suggestion of an ironic smile at the edges of his mouth. 'Don't you remember me?' 'I do.' But there was no recognition in his voice or in his manner. 'What did you want?' he asked politely. My heart fell. I was now embarrassed. 'Have a drink on me?' 'I will have the bill sent to you. But if you don't mind, we are not allowed to drink while customers are in, so I will take it later.' And he went back to his post. I had not the courage to give him the note. I went home, driving my Mercedes 220S furiously through the dark. What could I do for the man? What had happened to his dreams? . . . broken . . . and there was not the slightest sparkle in his eyes. And yet the next weekend I was back there. That barmaid. Her whole body looked like the juicy thing itself, crying: do it to me, do it to me. But whom could I send? I again called out for the watchman. I argued; he was after all employed for little services like that. And he was taking messages for others, wasn't he? I gave him the note and nodded in the direction of the fat barmaid. He smiled, no light in his eyes, with that mechanical, studied understanding of his job and what was required of him. He came back with a note: 'YES. Room 14. CASH.' I gave him twenty shillings and well, how could I help it, a tip . . . a tip of two shillings . . . which he accepted with the same mechanical precision. Wahinya! Reduced to a carrier of secrets between men and women!

Occasionally he would come to work drunk and you could tell this by the feverish look in his eyes. He would talk and even boast of all the women he had had, of the amount of drink he could hold. Then he would crawl with his voice and ask for a few coins to buy a cigarette. I soon came to learn how he lost his job as a turnboy. His bus and another collided while racing for a cargo of passengers. A number of people died, including the driver. He himself was severely injured. When he came back from the hospital, there was no job for him. J. J. J. would not even give him a little compensation . . . he would talk on like that as in a delirium. And yet when he had not taken a drop, he was very quiet and very withdrawn into his *kofia* and *kabuti*. But as weeks and months passed, the sober moments became rarer and rarer. He became a familiar figure in the bar. At times he would drink all his salary in credit so that at the end of the month he was forced to beg for a glass or fifty cents. He had already started on Kiruru[33] and Chang'aa. At such moments, he would be full of drunken dreams and impossible schemes. 'Don't worry . . . I will die in a Mercedes-Benz . . . don't laugh . . . I will save, go into business and then buy one . . . easy . . . the moment I buy one, I will stop working. I will live and die like Lord Delamere'.[34] People baptized him Wahinya Benji. Often, I wondered if he ever remembered the old days in Chura.

One Saturday night he came and sat beside me. This boldness surprised me because he was very sober. I offered him a drink. He refused. His voice was level, subdued, but a bit of the old sparkle was in his eyes.

'You now see me a wreck. But I often ask myself: could it have been different? With a chance – an education, like yours. You remember our days in Chura? Aah, a long time ago . . . another world . . . that correspondence school, do you remember it? Well, I never got the money. And it was harder later saddled with a wife and a child. Mark you, it was a comfort. Aah, but a little money . . . a little more education . . . school . . . our teacher . . . you remember him? I used to talk to you about him. What for instance he used to tell us? What one man can do, another one can; what one race can do, another one can . . . Do you think this true? You have an education, you got to Makerere, you might even go to England to get a degree like the son of Koinange[35]. Tell me this: is that really true? Is it true for us ordinary folk who can't speak a word of English? Put it this way: I am not afraid of hard work; I am not scared of sweating. He used to tell us: after *uhuru*, we must work hard. Europeans are where they are because they work hard; and what one man can do, another one can. He was a good man, all the same, used to tell us about great Africans. Then one day . . . one day . . . you see, we were all in school . . . and then some white men came, Johnnies[36], and took him out of our classroom. We climbed the mud walls in fear. A few yards away they roughly pushed him forward and shot him dead.

Wahinya's drinking became so bad that he was dismissed from his job. And I never really saw him in that ruined state because my duties with the Progress Bank International took me outside the country. But even now as I talk, I feel his presence around me, his boasts, his dreams, his drinking and, well, that last encounter.

The narrator swallowed one or two glasses in quick succession;

I followed his example. It was as if we had all witnessed a moving scene and we wanted to drown the memory of it. The narrator after a time tried to break the sombre atmosphere with exaggerated unconcern and cynicism: 'You see the twists of fate, gentlemen. Wahinya dead had become prominent, even J. J. J. his former employer, was fighting for him.' But he could not deceive anybody. He could not quite recapture the original tone of light entertainment. There was, after all, the Chura episode behind us. Wahinya, whom I had never met but whom I felt I knew, had come back to haunt our drinking peace. Somebody said: 'It's a pity he never got his Mercedes-Benz – at least a ride.'

You are wrong, said the narrator. In a way, he got that ride. You shake your heads, gentlemen? Give us a drink, Sister, give us another one.

It was thanks to the rivalry among the candidates. Although they were all members of the committee charged with burial arrangements, they would not agree to a joint effort. Each, you see, wanted only his own plan adopted. Each wanted his name mentioned as the sole donor of something. After one or two riotous sessions, the committee finally decided on a broad policy.

Item No. 1: Money. It was decided that the amount each would give would be disclosed and announced on the actual day of the funeral.

Item No. 2: Transport. J. J. J. had offered what he described as his wife's shopping basket, a brand-new, light-green Cortina GT, to carry the body from the city mortuary, but the others objected. So it was decided that the four would contribute equal amounts towards the hire of a neutral car – a Peugeot family saloon.

Item No. 3: The pit. Again the four would share the expenses of digging and cementing it.

Item No. 4: The coffin and the cross. On this they would not agree to a joint contribution. Each wanted to be the sole donor of the coffin and the cross. Mark you, none of them was a known believer. A compromise: they were to contribute to a neutral coffin to transport the body from the mortuary to the church and to the cemetery. But each would bring his own coffin and cross and the crowd would choose the best. Participatory democracy, you see.

Item No. 5: Funeral oration. Five minutes for each candidate before presenting his coffin and cross.

Item No. 6: Day. Even on this, there was quite a haggling. But a Sunday was thought the most appropriate day.

That was a week that was, gentlemen. Every night, every bar was full to capacity with people who had come to gather gossip and rumours. Market-days burst with people. In buses there was no other talk; the turnboys had a field-day regaling passengers with tales of Wahinya. No longer the merits and demerits of the various candidates; issues in any case there had been none. Now only Wahinya and the funeral.

On the Sunday in question, believers and non-believers, Protestants, Catholics, Muslims and one or two recent converts to Radha Krishnan[37] flocked to Ilmorog Presbyterian Church. For the first time in Ilmorog, all the bars, even those that specialized in illegal Chang'aa, were empty. A ghost town Ilmorog was that one Sunday morning. Additional groups came from villages near and far. Some from very distant places had hired buses and lorries. Even the priest, Rev. Bwana Solomon, who normally would not receive bodies of non-active members into the holy building unless of course they were rich and prominent, this time arrived early in resplendent dark robes laced with silver and gold. A truly memorable service, especially the beautifully trembling voice of Rev. Solomon as he intoned: 'Blessed are the meek and poor for they shall inherit the earth; blessed are those who mourn for they shall be comforted.' After the service, we trooped on foot, in cars, on lorries, in buses to the graveyard where we found even more people seated. Fortunately loudspeakers had been fixed, through the thoughtful kindness of the District Officer, so that even those at the far outer edges could clearly hear the speeches and funeral orations. After the prayers (again Rev. Solomon with his beautifully trembling voice captured many hearts) the amount of money each candidate had donated was announced.

The businessman had given seven hundred and fifty shillings. The farmer had given two hundred and fifty. J. J. J. had given one thousand. On hearing this the businessman rushed back to the microphone to announce an additional three hundred. A murmur of general approval greeted the businessman's additional gift. Lastly the student. He had given only twenty shillings.

What we all waited for with bated breath was the gift of coffins and crosses. There was a little dispute as to who would open the act. Each wanted to have the last word. Lots were cast. The student, the farmer, the businessman and J. J. J. followed in that order.

The student tugged at his Lumumba goatee. He lashed at wealth and ostentatious living. He talked about workers. Simplicity and hard work. That should be our national motto. And in keeping with that motto, he had arranged for a simple wooden coffin and wooden cross. After all Jesus had been a carpenter. A few people jeered as the student stepped down.

Then came the farmer. He too believed in simplicity and hard work. He believed in the soil. As a Government Chief he had always encouraged *wananchi* in their patriotic efforts at farming. His was also a simple wooden affair but with a slight variation. He had already hired the services of one of the popular artists, who painted murals or mermaids in our bars, to paint a picture of a green cow with udders and teats ripe with milk. There was amused laughter from the crowd.

What would the businessman bring us? He, in his dark suit with a protruding belly, rose to the occasion and the heightened expectations. People were not to be bothered that a few had never had it so good. What was needed was a democratic chance for all the Wahinyas of this world. A chance to make a little pile so that on dying they might leave their widows and orphans decent shelters. He called out his followers. They unfolded the coffin. It was truly an elaborate affair. It was built in the shape of a Hilton hotel complete with storeys and glass windows. Whistles of admiration and satisfaction at the new turn in the drama came from the crowd. His followers unfolded the cloth: an immaculate white sheet that elicited more whistling of amused approval. The businessmen then stepped down with the air of a sportsman who has broken a long-standing record and set a new one that could not possibly ever be equalled.

Now everyone waited for J. J. J. His six years in Parliament had made him an accomplished actor. He took his time. His leather briefcase with bulging papers was there; he collected his ivory walking stick and fly-whisk. His belly though big was right for his height. He talked about his long service and experience. People did not in the old days send an uncircumcised boy to lead a national army, he said, slightly glancing at the opponents . . . He had always fought for the poor . . . But he would not bore people with a long talk on such a sad occasion. He did not want to bring politics into what was a human loss. All he wanted was not only to pay his respects to the dead but also to respect the wishes of the dead. Now before Wahinya died, he was often heard to say . . . but wait! This was the right cue for his followers. The coffin was wrapped in a brilliantly red cloth. Slowly they unfolded it. People in the crowd were now climbing the backs of others in order to see, to catch a glimpse of this thing. Suddenly they saw the coffin raised high. It was not a coffin at all, but really an immaculate model of a black Mercedes-Benz 660S complete with doors and glass and maroon curtains and blinds.

He let the impact made by this revelation run its full course. Only the respect for the dead, he continued as if nothing had happened. Before Brother Wahinya had died, he had spoken of a wish of dying in a Benz. His last wish . . . I say let's respect the wishes of the dead. He raised his fly-whisk to greet the expected applause while holding a white handkerchief to his eyes.

But somehow, no applause came; not even a murmur of approval. Something had gone wrong, and we all felt it. It was like an elaborate joke that had suddenly misfired. Or as if we had all been witnesses to an indecent act in a public place. The people stood and started moving away as if they did not want to be identified with the indecency. J. J. J., his challengers and a few of their hired followers were left standing by the pit, no doubt wondering what had gone wrong. Suddenly J. J. J. returned to his own car and drove off. The others quickly left.

Wahinya was buried by relatives and friends in a simple coffin which, of course, had been blessed by Rev. Solomon.

About the elections, the outcome I mean, there is little to tell. You know that J. J. J. is still in Parliament. There were the usual rumours of rigging, etc., etc. The student got a hundred votes and returned to school. I believe he graduated, a degree in Commerce, and like me joined a bank. He got a loan, bought houses from non-citizen Indians and he is now a very important landlord in the city. A European-owned estate agency takes care of the houses.

The businessman was ruined. He had dug too deep a pit into

the loan money. His shop and a three-acre plot were sold in an auction. J. J. J. bought it and sold it immediately afterwards for a profit. The farmer-chief was also ruined. He had sold his grade cows – all Friesians – in expectation of plenty as an MP. J. J. J. saw to it that he never got back his old job as a Location Chief.

You go to Makueni Chang'aa Bar where Wahinya used to drink in his last days and you'll find the ruined two, now best friends, waiting for anybody who might buy them a can or two of KMK – Kill-Me-Quick. It costs fifty only, they'll tell you.

J. J. J. still rides in a Mercedes-Benz – this time 660S, just like mine – and looks at me with, well, suspicion! Four years from now . . . you never know.

Gentlemen . . . how about one for the road?

NOTES

Tusker or Pilsner[1] – *Two popular Kenyan beers.*

Baada ya kazi jiburudishe na Tusker[2] – *(Kiswahili) After work, relax with Tusker. An advertisement for Tusker beer.*

Lumumba goatee[3] – *A reference to the goat-like beard worn by Patrice Lumumba (1925–61), a leading nationalist in the Belgian Congo (now Zaire). He was the independent Congo's first prime minister (1960) but was murdered in mysterious circumstances in February 1961 by his political enemies. Even today Lumumba is a hero of radical nationalist Africans.*

Makerere under De Bunsen[4] – *Sir Bernard De Bunsen was the Principal of Makerere University College, Uganda, 1949–63.*

Wafanyi kazi[5] – *(Kiswahili) Workers.*

Wananchi[6] – *(Kiswahili) The common people, countrymen.*

Chang'aa[7] – *An intoxicating local liquor.*

Kill-Me-Quick[8] – *A potent and illegal local brew.*

Turnboy[9] – *Tout.*

Uhuru[10] – *(Kiswahili) Independence from colonial rule, freedom.*

Magadi salt and soda[12] – Salt and soda ash mined at Lake Magadi in southern Kenya. It contains the world's largest natural deposit of sesqui-carbonate of soda. Soda in Kiswahili is 'magadi'.

Kumanyoko[12] – Kikuyu word of abuse.

Madhvani gummy sweets[13] – Candy manufactured locally by the Madhvani Group.

Mandazi[14] – (Kiswahili) A kind of doughnut.

Unga[15] (Kiswahili) Flour.

Chaka[16] – (Also spelled Shaka.) (c. 1787–1828) Founder of the Zulu Kingdom, one of the most powerful kingdoms in 19th century Africa.

Moshoeshoe[12] – (c. 1785–1870) Founder-king of Lesotho. He exploited the political upheavals of the 1820s in southern Africa to build the Sotho state.

Waiyaki[18] – Waiyaki wa Hinga, a hero of the Kikuyu. He opposed the Imperial British East Africa Company officials and their plundering soldiers in the early 1890s. He was exiled to the coast but died on the way at Kibwezi. The IBEAC officials claimed he committed suicide but the Kikuyu, whose first political martyr he became, insisted he had been buried alive.

Laibon[19] – Title of the religious and military leader of the Masai people of Kenya and Tanzania. It is uncertain here to which Laibon Ngugi is referring.

Mwanga[20] – Mwanga II (c. 1866–1903), last independent ruler (1884–99) of the Baganda. He opposed the British before they finally took over control of his kingdom.

The Nandi struggle against the British army[21] – The Nandi, under their great leader Koitalel, fiercely resisted various punitive British army expeditions between 1895 and 1905 when they were at last defeated.

William the Conqueror[22] – Son of the Duke of Normandy (1027–87). He successfully invaded England in 1066 and had himself crowned king.

Drake[23] – Sir Francis Drake (1540–96). The greatest of Elizabethan seamen. Circumnavigated the globe, 1577–80. Defeated the Spanish Armada in numerous sea battles.

Hawkins[24] – *Sir John Hawkins (1532–95). The first Englishman to traffic in slaves. He was knighted for his services to the state, especially for repelling the Spanish Armada and disrupting the Spanish West India trade.*

Wilberforce[25] – *William Wilberforce (1759–1833). English philanthropist, MP and anti-slavery crusader.*

Nelson[26] – *Viscount Horatio Nelson (1758–1805). British naval hero of the sea battles of the Napoleonic era. He was killed at the Battle of Trafalgar in which the British triumphed over the French.*

Napoleon[27] – *Napoleon Bonaparte (1769–1821). Brilliant military leader who, in the years following the French Revolution, brought most of Europe under his heel. He crowned himself Emperor of France in 1805 but was defeated by the British at Waterloo.*

Student airlift abroad[28] – *Tom Mboya, the Kenya politician, initiated this scheme in which hundreds of Kenyan students were 'airlifted' to the USA in the early 1960s to pursue university education.*

Matatu[29] – *(Kiswahili) Any vehicle used as auxilary transport in place of a bus or taxi in East Africa.*

Kabuti[30] – *(Kiswahili) Long coat.*

Kofia[31] – *(Kiswahili) Hat.*

Bokora club[32] – *(Kiswahili) A walking stick or club.*

Kiruru[33] – *A potent Kikuyu brew.*

Lord Delamere[34] – *(1870–1931). Wealthy leader of the English settlers in Kenya. He exerted great influence on successive colonial administrations in which he served as an elected member of the legislative council. He was a strong advocate of the paramountcy of white interests in Kenya.*

Son of Koinange[35] – *Mbiyu Koinange, son of Senior Chief Koinange of the Kikuyu. He left for America (not England) in 1927, returning to Kenya in 1938 with an MA from Columbia University.*

Johnnies[36] – *A derogatory term for white soldiers in colonial Kenya.*

Radha Krishnan[37] – *Hindu religious sect.*

EXERCISES

1. The careers of the bar-narrator and Wahinya run on parallel but vastly different tracks. Briefly outline their respective careers, one of which moves in a swift ascent while the other spirals ever downwards.

2. 'Wahinya's rather rapid progress towards the grave is really the story of our troubled times!' (p. 157)
   How and why can Wahinya's story be regarded as *representative* or *typical* of the general trends in our society? (In answering this question you will need to consider the kind of society the author describes and how, at the story's end, the Chief and the businessman are going the route Wahinya travelled.)

3. The bar-narrator draws into his orbit the writer of the story (the writer-narrator) and his two audiences: his immediate circle of listeners in the bar and his other audience, the readers of the story.
   a) Read through the story and note down the occasions when the bar audience is addressed directly (offered 'refills' by their storyteller-host, asked questions) and how it responds in varied ways (by giving answers, asking questions, offering suggestions). You will find that this story, like a traditional oral tale, is partly constructed by its audience's responses. Look out for instances when the narrator responds to his audience's puzzlement, indignation or questions by turning around and incorporating them into furthering the plot of his own story. One example is on pp. 154–155.

   You, your bottle is still empty . . . you want to change to something stronger? Vat 69? No? . . . oh . . . Chang'aa, did you say? Ha! ha! ha! You mention *Chang'aa*. Actually it was *Chang'aa*, you might say, that saved the campaign.
   b) Note down the occasions when the reader is addressed directly by the writer-narrator.
   c) Also note when the writer-narrator himself directly enters the story.

d) Now broadly try to sum up the impact made on the reader by the author's narrative method: he uses two narrators and the responses of different 'listeners' (the writer-narrator, the bar audience, the reading audience).

4. The *tone* used in this story is of central importance in our response to it as readers.
   a) Generally, what tone does the bar-narrator employ in telling his story? How is his tone affected by the atmosphere in which he tells his story? (Give examples from the text to illustrate your answers.)
   b) How does the story's tone affect your response to it?
   c) Notice how, as the story progresses, there is a change of mood. Explain when and why this happens.

5. 'A Mercedes Funeral' is given an edge by its satirically sharp, rather grim humour. The objects of Ngugi's satire are numerous. From the story select several examples of the satirical treatment of:
   a) the bar-narrator himself;
   b) various other characters;
   c) social customs and institutions.
   For each example chosen, briefly explain the purpose and effect of the satire.

Incident in the Park

MEJA MWANGI
(KENYA)

THE SKY WAS a hot clear blue. Not a promise of a drop of rain that August.

The drought had taken a heavy toll in the park. The ground was a deep dusty brown, bare and parched. Dried bits of grass stuck forlornly out of the numerous cracks like pleading tongues out of hell screaming for a drop of water. Dry leaves shed by the thirsty trees ran rustling in front of the light breeze. This city, in a desperate effort to keep itself beautiful, had watered the more delicate flowers planted like oasis islands at various points over the dirty brown park.

The vast park quietly shimmered in the oppressive sun. The boat-house sat sadly hunched over the shoulder of the lake, the dirty muddy water lapping softly at its withdrawn feet. Up the hill to the west the red-tiled roof of the cathedral was visible half-hidden among the tall dark blue gums, the gaunt walls giving it an appearance as ominous as the castle of Count Dracula[1]. Among the trees higher up the hill, there were more modern fortresses, the ministerial offices, towering over the aged blue gums with youthful impunity, hundreds of glass windows winking at the park below. Across the park from the ministerial offices was the city itself, lying low, a dormant dragon growling with clogged-up traffic. The huge highway stretched taut between them restrained the city from intruding on the park.

From the park grounds, if one lay facing east, one looked up straight into the frowning faces of the parliament and city hall clocks. Every hour on the dot the two struck suddenly together, regulating the tired city's pulse and reminding the park loungers just how many hours they had wasted lying idle, pleading with them to get up and be useful. Mostly the pleas went unheeded. But every now and then a misplaced person rose with a start, squinted up at the clocks' accusing fingers and, brushing grass and dust from his bottom, slunk defeatedly across the highway into the city maze. Others shook their heads defiantly at the insistent clocks, cursed them loudly and, facing the other way, went back to sleep. These were the insolent few. If they had anywhere to go at all, they did not want to go there.

Cars brayed on the highway. Brakes shrieked. Ambulances wailed away, racing against death. Half a kilometre away trains whistled urgently. Time to go. Go where? The park people were there to stay. They had arrived. The sounds were sounds from another world.

On the stroke of one the dam burst. A flood of hungry office workers gushed out of the ministerial offices, and in a furiously ravenous torrent swept down the hill. They came in armies.

Time had once again thrown the floodgates open. They swarmed down the hill into the park, past the first icecream man, round the lakes to the eastern exit. The second icecream man blocked the only way on to the highway, determined to make a sale today. The swarm swirled round him and over him and away. Today, like yesterday and the day before, not one bar of icecream was bought by the hungry ones. Once across the highway, the waves disintegrated into individuals and dispersed. Some rushed for the meat-roasting places down River Road, others joined the queues at the numerous fish-and-chip joints where they dutifully swallowed soggy fried chips with watered-down ketchup. In a few seconds the thousand or so strong swarm had been swallowed up by the yawning concrete jungle. With its usual idle curiosity the sleepy park witnessed this spectacle. The park waited. In an hour the tide would return.

The parched park was almost dead, alive only with a few idlers and the dust-raising wind, the dry fallen leaves scampering to hide from the hot breeze which, like the hungry humans, blew down the narrow path, across the highway and into the humming city. The icecream man's bell still rang lonely and unwelcome like a lost leper's warning bell.

Under the gnarled bare trees, in fact anywhere there was the slightest shade, a few men lay half awake hiding from the tormenting sun. A shaggy, thin man sat under a shrub, scratching numbers and letters on his black dry skin with a used match. By his side were the two oversize fruit baskets he had been selling from all morning and which he would resume hawking after the lunch break. Now he scratched his head with the matchstick and tried to balance the morning's sales. He mumbled to himself, cursed and, rolling up his trouser legs, continued writing on his thigh. Finally he flung the stick away and, wetting his palm with saliva, violently erased what he had scribbled. Then he fell unceremoniously on his back and covered his rough bearded face with two bony hands.

On the lake a couple of men paddled vigorously in two small hired boats. A few others sat on the cement bank, unshod feet swinging only a few inches above the dirty grey water and, ignoring the icecream man's cries, watched the boaters. With undivided interest they witnessed every move, every paddle stroke. Some sat alone muttering to themselves. Those who sat in twos or threes communicated only in monosyllables. Every day the same watchers watched the same rowers move their boats over the lake and under the bridges; every day unconsciously reacting to the maxim that spectating is the next best thing to participating.

A few metres above the lake was the fish pond, now dangerously overgrown with weeds. The yellow, blue and purple water lilies struggled with the colourless weeds. Where once there had been a blue and green surface there was now an ugly mishmash of pond weeds. Where the pond flowers had once stuck their buds out in thick colourful fingers and proclaimed order, there now was a riot of unclassifiable intruders, with bastard flowers. The park soil of the northern bank of the fish pond had collapsed and reclaimed it, thereby forcing the murky brown water and the bewildered fish to the deeper, further end.

A hairy loafer wearing worn slippers sat on a board inscribed with the words DO NOT FEED FISH – BY ORDER. He carelessly tossed debris, tiny bits of grass and soil at the hungry fish. The shoals of red, black and white fish – some only a few inches long, others almost a foot – fought for the fragments before they realized they were useless and let go. But every time a particle hit the water they all went for it. The idler sitting on the bank sniggered and threw more rubbish into the water. Every now and then he stopped, hand raised in the process of dropping something, and with sharp dark eyes followed the darting movement of the fish. He shook his head, dropped the twig and found another.

The reflection of another man materialized by that of his in the water at his feet. He glanced at it and dropped a piece of soil to the fish.

'Greetings', he said at the reflection.

'Greetings.'

'What do you suppose they eat?'

'Insects.'

'Insects? How do they catch them?'

'Insects drown.'

'Insects . . .' He looked around but could not find any. 'Too bad.'

He rolled up his torn trouser-legs exposing thin hairy legs. He scratched his long uncombed hair and returned to his business. But there were no insects anywhere near him. After a time he turned and, shielding his eyes against the hot sun, squinted up at the newcomer.

'Did you know fish are like people?'

'No.'

'They are.'

'How?'

'How?'

He turned and pointed at the frothing mass of fish.

'Look at them,' he said.

He picked up another loose piece of earth and dropped it into the water. The fish exploded after it.

'See that.' He turned to squint at the other man. 'They have been doing that all morning. Watch this . . .'

He picked up a huge piece of rock with his horny toes, realized it was too large for even the largest fish and left it. Again he scratched his long hair. He fed the fish population a flattened cigarette end, the only loose particle within reach. The largest fish, pitch black with vast pink blotches on its head and back, caught the cigarette-end and swam powerfully away from the others towards the centre of the pond. After two flicks of its big tail it dropped the useless butt and swam back to the feeding ground scaring the smaller ones away.

'How do you suppose they make children? I mean, do they have places they go to sleep after dark?'

The icecream bell cut sharply into their hearing. The sitting man looked past the one who was standing and pointed.

'Would you believe that man is crazy?'

'No.'

'He is. Always hammering the bell and no one wants to buy his icecream. He should go where the children are.'

He turned to feed the fish, and spoke, addressing them.

'There is this great big fish in the ocean, a great monster that is king of all the water. When it comes out to bask we see its image. The rainbow. When it drinks up the whole ocean there will be a great drought and the world will come to an end.'

'How do you know?'

'I heard some men talking once.'

He turned and, shielding his eyes from the sun as before, squinted at the man beside him.

'Do you suppose this is true?'

'No.'

'Have you seen the ocean?'

'Once.'

'How big is it?'

'Big.'

'Is it . . .' he waved a limp hand at the lake, 'a hundred times as large?'

'More.'

He licked his dry lips.

'A thousand times maybe?'

'Much more.'

'Oh,' he grimaced. 'The story of the king fish could be true then?'

'Could be.'

'But . . .' he scratched his head, 'what would such a huge monster eat?'

'Other fish.'

He turned to scrutinize the gliding fish curiously. Wondering. And for a long while he was silent. His stomach rumbled. Suddenly he turned, his red eyes hungrily set on the other man's cigarette. He rubbed his nose restlessly.

'Do you suppose you could allow me a puff on your cigarette, Mister?'

The stranger reached into his pocket and offered him an unsmoked one. Overwhelmed, the man gasped and rose to his creaking knees.

'Thank you,' he said declining the match. 'You are my brother!'

Then he suddenly bent and grabbing the large rock at his feet now hurled it violently at the confounded fish.

'Dumb bastards,' he said, before buzzing away across the park pocketing his cigarette.

The stranger dropped the fish his burning cigarette end.

The park was astir. The tide was returning. By the eastern exit two city constables demanded to see the icecream man's licence. As before, the returning crowd swirled around them unnoticing. The office workers trickled out of the rumbling city's streets and alleyways and collected at the edge of the highway waiting for a break in the heavy traffic. Slowly, they flowed back across the park and up the hill. Bodies rose like zombies from under the shrunken trees and shrubs, flung away the newspapers in which they had wrapped the potato chips and headed back to their stations. Those who had been able to afford to drink milk inflated the packets and exploded them under their right feet.

In this manner the fruit-seller expressed his opinion of the world. Stooping, he heaved the large fruit baskets to his shoulders, one on the left, one on the right. Slowly he slouched back to the path that crossed the park east to west, still muttering to himself. He had just regained the pathway when the two city constables accosted him. He stopped with a start, confused. He looked from one to the other and lowered his burden on to the path.

'Your licence?' the constable repeated.

'Licence.' The old man nodded uncomprehendingly and reached into his pocket. 'Licence.'

He searched himself for a few seconds. He shook his head, shrugged and helplessly spread his hands.

'Home,' he said faintly.

'Home,' the constable repeated. 'May we see your identity card?'

The old man made a shorter search this time. He looked up shaking his head sadly.

'Home,' he said extending his hand. 'I have five shillings.'

The constables now looked at the money in the old man's hand then looked at one another. One shrugged.

'That is all I have made today,' the fruit-seller said.

The constable grabbed him by the worn coat and shoved him along.

'You will explain to the judge,' he said harshly. 'No licence, no identification . . .'

The other picked up the fruit baskets. The three trudged along in the direction of the city.

'I swear by my mother that is all I have,' the old man pleaded with the one holding him. 'You can't take me back to that judge, the man will have me hung this time. You see, brothers, I've got this other case coming up next week and I was only selling this time to afford the fine. You know the way that judge is a tyrant . . .'

The two looked up sharply.

'Sorry . . .' the hawker said quickly. I mean the man is . . . crazy. I mean he will surely have me castrated this time. I have a wife and children and . . .'

They remained unimpressed.

'I have ten shillings,' he said desperately. That's the truth. I swear by my mother's . . . you got to let me go.'

The one with the heavy fruit baskets hesitated, but the other marched the old man right ahead.

'Take one,' the seller cried. 'One basket and ten shillings . . . you got to let me go. I promise I won't ever repeat the offence. Believe me, I will go straight home until I can afford a licence. Take both baskets, take everything. I have to go home.'

They said nothing.

The fruit-seller cursed them and their wives and children. Then swearing loudly he leaped and broke away leaving the surprised constable hanging on to a large piece of his torn coat. His surprise lasted a few short seconds. The constable shot after the fleeing man across the park shouting for help from passers-by. The one with the baskets took two quick steps, found it impossible to run with the baskets and followed slowly. He stopped to pick up his flying mate's fallen hat.

The fleeing hawker put a couple of hundred yards between himself and his pursuers. He was certain he could find sanctuary in the crowded city. As he slowed to cross the highway a man nabbed him, alerted by the constables' shouts. He hit out, breaking free once more. Another man lunged for him. Again he lashed out, savagely desperate, and tried to run. He stumbled, falling into the ditch by the side of the highway. People came by. More stones. He cried out, pleaded for mercy. In their thirst for blood no one listened. By the time the constable ran up, the fruit-peddler lay like a broken and twisted rag doll at the bottom of the ditch. A chunk of rock, as large as the one the disgusted loafer had hurled at the fish, had drawn thick red blood over the sparsely bearded face.

The constables looked furtively around for someone to blame. No one looked guilty enough. The word 'thief' hovered over the assembled crowd, and, just as it started to permeate through them, the constables conveniently withdrew across the highway into the city. The party hung aimlessly around until a passing police car drew up and demanded to know what was the matter. The inspector cut a path through the spectators, hopped into the ditch and went down on his haunches. He felt the victim's wrist, shook his head. He felt round the neck. Again he shook his head.

'Dead,' he said, rising to face the spectators. That was his verdict.

Those nearest him lowered their eyes, an automatic defence mechanism against being called upon to give witness. Some drew back and hurried back to their offices. Under the pressure from the police officer's forceful presence, the word 'thief' oozed out again from the back and spread like silent poisonous gas to the front, so quiet it was impossible to tell from which mouth the condemnation issued forth. Here lay a desperate thief, attired in the unmistakable uniform of his trade – dirty torn clothes and a mean hungry face.

Now it was the police officer's turn to feel uneasy and uncertain. A thief was a thief. Somewhere in the crowded streets and the twisted garbage-strewn back alleys there was an unwritten law that clearly set down the fate of apprehended thieves. Now there remained only one thing: to establish the man's identity.

The watching clocks struck two.

Justice, fairly, quickly and completely administered, the crowd broke, dispersing their various ways. The flood ebbed faster back up the hill and behind the guarded doors. But some stayed to watch the turn of events to their logical conclusion. Among them was the one interested in fish – the idler I had earlier given a full cigarette in the park. Subdued, we hung around, nervously shuffling our feet until the body of the unknown thief was carted off to the mortuary to await identification by the next of kin – his wife and children. Then we, the regular park loungers, a dark silence hovering over our conscience, drifted back under our bare trees to hide from the shame.

The vast park was once more calm and peaceful but for the sun and the dust-stirring wind. The weather men said it would rain in September.

We, we didn't particularly care.

NOTES

The castle of Count Dracula[1] – *Dracula, chief character in the novel* Dracula *(1897) by Bram Stoker, was a vampire. He was a corpse during the day but would come to life at night to suck the blood of living people. Count Dracula lived in a gloomy castle in Romania.*

EXERCISES

1. The writer includes what seems like an extraneous episode in the story, the one dealing with the two men chatting by the fish pond in the park.
   a) Do you feel that this episode is a digression and irrelevant to the story?
   b) If not, what is Meja Mwangi's purpose in including it? In answering these questions you will need to determine how this episode is linked with the story's main theme; how the world of the park is a microcosm of a larger uncaring society. Also notice this observation on p. 184: 'A chunk of rock, *as large as the one* the disgusted loafer had hurled at the fish, had drawn thick red blood over the sparsely bearded face.' (emphasis added)

2. Study closely the first seven paragraphs of the story. Try and decide why the author provides such a lengthy, detailed description of the environment (nature, the physical surroundings, the weather) in which the story is set.
   a) What *aspects* of these surroundings does he stress?
   b) How are these details significant when we consider the story as a whole?

3. Only at the very end of 'Incident in the Park' (in the second-to-last paragraph) do we discover that one of the two men by the pond (up to now anonymous and variously referred to as 'another man', 'the newcomer', etc.) is the narrator himself.
   a) How does this new knowledge (the narrator as one of the characters) affect our response to the fate of the hawker, all the other park loungers and to the society in which they live?
   b) Do you feel that the writer has 'cheated' you by springing this surprise regarding the narrator's identity on you?
   You might find it interesting to read a novel where, as in this story, the identity of the narrator is revealed only at the very end. Such a novel is the detective thriller *The Murder of Roger Ackroyd* by Agatha Christie. If you read this novel, you will find your feelings on completing the book very similar to those you have at the end of 'Incident in the Park' and for a similar reason.

4. Would you say that the word 'incident' in the story's title is appropriate in the context of the story? If not, why do you suppose Meja Mwangi uses it?

Her Only Child

T.S. LUZUKA
(UGANDA)

SHE WAS HAPPY, the mother was. She hummed as she peeled bananas, dropping them on to banana leaves placed in a small basket. The hum was deep and lively and her skin was smooth and rich. Her child sat on a mat playing with the mid-rib of a green banana leaf, twisting it and forming a hoop and then straightening it. The mother's hands were skilled hands. She could peel bananas without looking at what she was doing. She would sometimes gossip with the neighbouring women and laugh; but her hands would never gossip, would never laugh, would never listen or look; they would work. They would peel bananas methodically, yet tenderly and with much affection, until the basket was filled with well-peeled bananas. Her hands now peeled bananas – using a sharpened home-made knife – while she hummed. And the hum was very rich in the evening silence. Occasionally she glanced at her child. She fed him with anything good she could think of, and any scratch on him that might draw a line of blood would worry her and she would spend a sleepless, anxious night.

The mother stopped humming and sighed with satisfaction. Her avid eyes glowed as she looked at the pile of peeled bananas and then at her child. She would cook the bananas and would feed her child, and her child would grow fat and would not cry from hunger. Her eyes slid to the corner of the kitchen. There was a huge *sufuria*[1] resting on three stones. Firewood burned in gaiety between the stones, sending flames upwards and the flames licked the base of the *sufuria*. The water in it was getting warmer and warmer and then hot. The mother looked at it, ignoring the thin threads of smoke from a poorly dried piece of wood. She would bathe her child with warm water and Lifebuoy soap. She would do this when the sun sank behind the hills. This she always did. And then she would dry the water on her child with her cloth. Her child would be oiled. And she would kiss him and tell him stories of long ago and sing the songs that he loved. Yes. She would do this until the cooking-pot sent a strong, rich smell which meant that the food was ready and well-cooked.

The mother got up and fished out a sweet potato from under the banana leaves. She looked at it and brushed off with her fingers the dry soil that had stuck to it.

'Look,' she said in her warm voice, stretching out her arm, 'let me roast this for you. I am going to cut more banana leaves. Do not move near the fire, I will come back soon and give you the potato when it is ready.'

She bent down and buried the potato in the hot ash. Then she picked up a tin mug and a rusty tablespoon and these she gave to her child.

'Play with these,' she said, 'until I come back. Do not go away or else I shall not sing for you.'

She kissed him and held his cheeks reassuringly. She picked up a knife and laughed with joy. And she went out of the kitchen towards the banana plantation still singing. The mother was very happy.

Nalwoga, the mother, was still very young. It was three years since she had married a healthy young man who industriously worked in his coffee plantation. Now he had ridden to the city to sell his sweat to the Indian traders. He would return in the night. She would wait for him after her child had gone to sleep. Her man would bring home a few pounds of meat. Perhaps he would buy a new dress for his wife and a shirt for their child. Oh, yes, he would buy sugar and salt and oil and curry powder. Nalwoga would cook a good meal for him and this would make him happy. He would be glad that she appreciated his work.

Nalwoga remembered the potato in the hot ash and she hastily cut down good green banana leaves. She would roast a hunk of meat for her child tomorrow. The child would be pleased and would grow healthy and strong and fat. But not too fat. No. The child would grow in the way a child ought to when he is well fed. And as she worked. Nalwoga smiled and sighed happily and thought of all the good things that she wished for her child and her husband and herself. She hummed softly and her hands worked as if they had eyes.

But then Nalwoga tensed. She thought she had heard a cry, but she was not sure. Perhaps she had merely imagined it. No. She had not heard any cry. She had merely imagined it. She hummed again and gathered the bundle of banana leaves and walked back towards the kitchen.

The rays of the sun were quickly dying and the sun itself was sinking below the horizon. Nalwoga walked faster. She had better hurry up and bathe her child before the mosquitoes came. She did not want them to hurt her child. She came near the kitchen. It was very quiet. Perhaps her child had fallen asleep out of loneliness. She ought to have come back sooner. Next time she would return soon. It would be very difficult now to wake him up and bathe him. And she hated to disturb him in his sleep. How she hated to disturb him, even if it was all meant for his own good.

Inside the kitchen it was very dark. Nalwoga paused at the doorway to shift the bundle of banana leaves to her left arm. She glanced once at the setting sun as it disappeared below the horizon, and entered the kitchen.

Nalwoga looked at the mat on the floor and the light coming from the fire showed her that her child was not there. Neither were the tin mug and the spoon. She was worried. Had her child gone out to play in the dark? Oh, the darkness was dangerous. It hid so many evil things, so many spirits and devils. And Nalwoga, as she thought of these things, felt an ache in her heart. She gasped and dropped the bundle of banana leaves and the knife. She strode to the doorway and wanted to enter the dark night, but she decided against this. She was panting. Her sharp breasts heaved up and down. She turned around. She faced the fire directly and the three stones on which rested the *sufuria*. The water in the sufuria was boiling. She cried out. She gave a high-pitched shriek. Her mouth was wide open and her eyes strained against their sockets. The veins in her neck bulged and trembled. She shrieked in the air; and the night was hushed and listened to her shriek. The head, the shoulders, the arms and half the chest of her child were immersed in the boiling water, the legs protruding out into the air. A flame leaped up and showed the body of the child turning white. Nalwoga grabbed the hot limp body of her child and sat down and squeezed it between her thighs and against her bosom, shrieking with frenzy, her mouth thick with foam. The flames ceased licking the *sufuria* and seemed to shrink back into the ashes. The fire quickly died out. The night became pitch black.

NOTES

Sufuria[1] – (*Kiswahili*) Cooking pan.

EXERCISES

1. Read the story's first two paragraphs again carefully. They describe for us Nalwoga's feelings, her activities as a mother and housewife, her plans for her child and her sense of serene contentment.
   a) Select the words and phrases in these two paragraphs which help to construct the picture of a young mother at the centre of a warm domestic scene.
   b) In this story, how does food act as a symbol of Nalwoga's maternal and wifely feelings?

2. In the Introduction we said that the story-story writer often seeks to make an impression on the reader by the use of 'shock tactics'. The ending of 'Her Only Child' is a shocking one. How does the picture of tenderness, loving care and contentment in the first few paragraphs contribute to making the tragic ending even more shocking?

3. Towards the end of the story the author uses images of sunset, darkness and quiet.
   a) How did these images affect you as you read the story?
   b) Do they help prepare the reader for something? Explain how they do this.

4. As the anxious Nalwoga hurries back from the garden to her child, she promises herself 'Next time she would return soon'. (p. 189) This is an example of irony.
   a) Can you point to *two* other instances of irony in the story?
   b) In all three cases try and explain *why* these examples are ironic.

A Kind of Fighting

JOTHAM MCHOMBU
(TANZANIA)

THE WIND WAS blowing south, screeching protestingly. The pull of a void in the great land-mass of Southern Africa was irresistible. In the heavens above, the clouds twisted somersaults, grudgingly following the wind. Lower than the clouds, a horde of vultures cruised on the south-bound wind, peering speculatively at some objects moving on the ground.

The vultures' keen eyesight had spied a strange spectacle below. A group of men, numbering between thirty and forty, weighed down by packs on their shoulders and each one with a gun in his hand, was no everyday sight. They marched forward as the wind overtook them in its hurry.

They were being propelled by another void. A painful emptiness in their hearts craving for fulfilment. They wore no uniform attire except the uniform of shared suffering. There was an atmosphere of cement-like unity about them, stemming from the common experience of being hunted down, ferreted out of their homes like rats and, as if this was not enough, uprooted from the land of their birth and condemned to wander about like ghosts for the rest of their lives. Desperation and determination was stamped on every worn face.

The leader gave the signal to rest and the group wormed its way into the undergrowth to become completely invisible from the air. They crouched down, easing their guns to more comfortable positions.

'We are now in enemy-held territory.' The word was passed

from mouth to mouth. Everyone knew what this meant: extra precautions and a state of complete alertness.

The leader moved from man to man offering words of encouragement.

'It feels good to be in the land of our birth again, eh?' he said to Masanja, the oldest man in the group.

'Aim carefully when they show themselves,' he said to Maringo, the youngest member of the group, who was going into action for the first time.

'Take out lunch!' The order was given and repeated around the group. The haversacks were unbuttoned. Within a few minutes everyone had eaten.

The leader beckoned *mzee* Masanja and after a brief conversation the latter received his orders. He was to go ahead on scout duty. The rest would follow at a safe distance.

The old man detached himself from the others and was soon swallowed by the thicket. This was always the trickiest part of guerilla warfare. He was now entirely on his own. He moved cautiously, his eyes combing the rugged terrain for any moving object which might mean enemy soldiers. He strained his ears to catch the slightest sound. He hovered behind bushes, crouched there a moment before zig-zagging to the next one. This occupied him fully; every atom of his aged body was on the alert. A slight miscalculation and he would be a dead man. He shivered.

He was just about to dart across another open space when he was arrested by the suspicion of a movement in front of him. The movement was sensed rather than seen. He dropped to his belly behind the bush. He trained his binoculars on the spot where he had sensed the movement. For a few seconds he could make out nothing. Then he saw him.

The Portuguese soldier stood behind a bush trying to convince himself that the coast was clear. Apparently satisfied, he left his cover and came forward. His hand was placed on the butt of his gun. He stroked the smooth wood, imagination carrying him to the softness of a woman's thigh.

The old man watched the approaching soldier undecided. According to the rules he was to go back and report to the leader. As the soldier paced up the distance separating them, the anger and resentment he had nursed for so long boiled up in him. 'Hang the rules,' he whispered fiercely. 'I'll kill this one with my own hands.' His eyes clouded with emotion, his heart thumped with renewed vigour. It was as if salt had been put in an old wound; the pain was unbearable. A vision of his old home rose before his eyes, a home in a large prosperous village, into which disaster had struck like a thunderbolt: bombing, shooting, slayings, one great hell of bewildering pandemonium. The people had been cut down by the bullets like a herd of penned swine. Half the population had been buried in the smouldering cinders . . . The screams of frying children and mothers, the groans of strong men, the hopeless cries for help.

'Where was God on that day?' he thought as he swallowed to remove the lump that had formed in his throat.

The old man unstrapped his gun and laid it on the ground. It would only attract the enemy with its noise. He unsheathed his dagger, testing its sharpness with satisfaction. He was ready.

The soldier lumbered forward oblivious of the danger lurking behind the bush he was heading for. Masanja waited until the man was only a few paces away, then loomed up to block his path.

'Oh – what is – err . . .' the soldier stammered as he tried to master his confusion. Masanja looked at the soldier contemptuously, his teeth bared in a snarl which the other at first mistook for a smile: the smile of the vanquished, a philosophical acceptance of servitude. Suddenly the Portuguese's eyes alighted on the gun. An alarm bell started ringing somewhere in his head.

'You are going to die,' the old man whispered very softly. So softly that his lips did not move. The soldier saw the shabby clothes the man was wearing and the grenades attached to his belt. In the labour-cracked hand the dagger gleamed brightly. His own gun was strapped to his shoulder and he knew he couldn't hope to free it in time.

'Oh God, save me from this murderer!' he whined inwardly as the shabby man closed in on him. Then he turned and ran. The old man dived for his legs and they rolled together on the ground. It was an embrace which only death could break. The old man managed to get his knife into his mouth and he held it there with his teeth so as to leave both hands free. They crashed into the surrounding bushes like wild animals bent on destroying each other. Both were slippery with sweat and the breath hissed out of their labouring chests like water hissing out of a burst tap.

Masanja's age was showing its effect. His chest heaved painfully with the effort of muscular exertion. He realized that time was running out for him. He made desperate grabs for the soldier's throat but every time the streaming hot sweat made his hands slip off. He tried again, sending both hands forward, and with some difficulty his fingers held on to the soft fleshy throat. He pinned the soldier's head to the ground with one hand. His other hand moved for the knife. The arm rose and fell, rose and fell as the blade perforated the soldier's chest. Violent emotion overwhelmed any sense of brutality. Soon the body was reduced to a mess of gore. Quickly he dragged the mutilated corpse into a bush. He picked up his things and touched the Portuguese's brand-new gun reverently. As he turned to go the spectacle that met his eyes made his blood run cold.

A company of Portuguese soldiers, numbering more than two hundred, was so near that it was a miracle they hadn't seen him yet. He had no time to lose. The others had to be warned immediately. He dropped behind the bush, aware that any incautious movement would betray his whereabouts.

There was only one thing to be done. He lifted his gun and aimed carefully. The bullets crashed into the unsuspecting group. Two fell on the spot and the rest did what he had been counting on: dived crazily for cover. This was the breathing space he had been praying for.

He grabbed the corpse and lifted it on to his back. He held the cold elbows so that he was effectively covered from the rear. And then he ran, stumbling in his effort not to make himself an easy target. The slugs buried themselves harmlessly in the corpse.

He was almost beyond the line of fire when two bullets struck his right leg, breaking the bone. He fell forward, letting go his cumbersome burden. Having lost the use of one limb he was forced to crawl forward on hands and knee. The others had to be told that they could not risk a face-to-face clash with such superior numbers. The jittery Portuguese continued to pump the surrounding bush with fire, to soften it up before deciding whether to advance.

The wound was hurting him a lot. He crawled on like a half-squashed grub. Bitter sweat bit at his eyes. Tell-tale drops of blood on the ground charted the path of his desperate progress. He reached the others in time although to his weak body it felt as if he had spent a whole day on his feet. They tied his thigh to stop the bleeding. Briefly he told them what had taken place.

One thing could still save them: slip away before the enemy got wind of their whereabouts and caught them in a trap. They would have to move like lightning before the helicopters were called in to assist the hunt.

The old man reasoned that he would only be a burden if he allowed his friends to carry him along. It would slow them down and give the enemy time to find them and kill them all. He beckoned the leader to his side.

'The pain is too much. I can't see myself surviving this march.' A chorus of disapproval greeted the old man's words. He pointed to a small knoll nearby which had big boulders in a cluster at the top. 'Take me up there and go away,' he said sternly to override the mounting reluctance.

Precious minutes were slipping through their fingers. The leader looked at the old man's face – a contorted mask of pain. The eyes were pleading, repentant. He had erred. The old man knew this and knew that his leader knew it too. All he wanted now was a chance to rehabilitate himself, to lay down his life for the others.

The commander was thinking: 'The old fool nearly did for us all, but if we leave him here he's done for himself.' His mind raced ahead. He could see the old man fighting alone, utterly isolated, covering their retreat. He could picture those pus-licking jackals closing in all round, hemming him in, bayoneting him, tearing him apart limb from limb. Could they make a dash for it with him and get clear in time?

It was high time to come to a decision.

His eyes travelled over the faces around him – probing, sounding out. He was not going to impose decisions on anyone. It was as much their necks he was risking as his. He said: '*Mzee* Masanja has broken revolutionary discipline. By giving way to his emotions he has endangered the whole unit . . .'

The young man Maringo sensed the motive behind his commander's questioning gaze. The answer, he decided on an impulse, was action and not words. He freed himself from his pack and gave it to a companion. He walked deliberately over to where the old man was lying and knelt down.

'Strap him on my back quickly.'

Willing hands soon secured Masanja on to Maringo's strong young back. Maringo was surprised how light the old man felt. The others fell in behind as he went ahead. The leader stared at the wounded body of the frail old man. With his eyes closed he was like a slumbering child on the back of its mother. Now for the first time the heroic feat that the old man had accomplished pierced his disciplined heart like a needle. The more his thoughts dwelt on it the greater his conviction grew . . . 'Pah,' he said to himself, 'you're getting sentimental.' But it was his responsibility, wasn't it, to get Comrade Masanja out alive, so they had something to pin the damned medal on?

EXERCISES

1. There is a moral question posed in this story. In the guerilla group tight discipline is a matter of life and death. Does a single member of the group have the right to breach discipline for personal reasons? And if he does breach the rules, should he not suffer the consequences of his action?
   a) How did you react to *Mzee* Masanja breaking the rules?
   b) Considering that young Maringo's action could prove disastrous for the safety of the group as a whole, do you think he makes the right decision in saving Masanja's life?
   c) In the story's concluding paragraph there is an obvious tussle going on in the heart and mind of the group's commander: between the dictates of 'revolutionary duty' and the humane promptings of his heart. If the decision about what to do with the wounded Masanja had remained with the commander, what line of action do you think he would have taken?

2. 'The arm rose and fell, rose and fell *as the blade perforated the soldier's chest. Violent emotion overwhelmed any sense of brutality*. Soon the body was reduced to a mess of gore. Quickly he dragged the mutilated corpse into a bush. He picked up his things *and touched the Portuguese's brand-new gun reverently.*' (p. 195; emphasis added)

a) What is ironic about the sections emphasized in the passage above? Do you think the author intended this irony or was he unaware of it?
b) Do you agree with the view implied in the italicized sentence that strong feelings justify brutality?

3. Read the first two paragraphs of the story. Here we have, quite literally, a bird's eye view of the story's setting and its characters. Why is this a particularly effective opening for a story of this kind dealing with guerilla warfare? (In answering this question you will want to note, among other things, the following sentence on p. 196: 'They would have to move like lightning before the helicopters were called in to assist the hunt.')

4. The story is narrated mainly in short, terse sentences.
a) How is this narrative style suitable to the situation being described?
b) How does it affect our response when we are reading the story?

5. Make a close study of the *imagery* used in this story. Animal images predominate as do those drawn from the field of hunting, tracking and scouting. Given the story's theme, why are these images so appropriate?

The Spider's Web

LEONARD KIBERA
(KENYA)

INSIDE THE COFFIN his body had become rigid. He tried to turn and only felt the prick of the nail. It had been hammered carelessly through the lid, just falling short of his shoulder. There was no pain but he felt irretrievable and alone, hemmed within the mean, stuffy box, knowing that outside was air. *As dust to dust . . .* the pious preacher intoned out there, not without an edge of triumph. *This suicide, brethren . . .* They had no right, these people, had no right at all. They sang so mournfully over him, almost as if it would disappoint them to see him come back. But he would jump out yet, he would send the rusty nails flying back at them and teach that cheap-jack of an undertaker how to convert old trunks. He was not a third-class citizen. *Let me out*! But he could not find the energy to cry out or even turn a little from the nail on his shoulder, as the people out there hastened to cash in another tune, for the padre might at any moment cry *Amen*! and commit the flesh deep into the belly of the earth whence it came. Somebody was weeping righteously between the pauses. He thought it was Mrs Njogu. Then in the dead silence that followed he was being posted into the hole and he felt himself burning up already as his mean little trunk creaked at the joints and nudged its darkness in on him like a load of sins. *Careful, careful, he is not a heap of rubbish . . .* That was Mr Njogu. Down, slowly down, the careless rope issued in snappy mean measures like a spider's web and knocked his little trunk against the sides to warn the White Gates that he was coming to whoever would receive him. It caved in slowly, the earth, he could feel, and for the first time he felt important. He seemed to matter now, as all eyes no doubt narrowed into the dark hole at this moment, with everybody hissing *poor soul; gently, gently*. Then snap! The rope gave way – one portion of the dangling thing preferring to recoil into the tight-fisted hands out there – and he felt shot towards the bottom head downwards, exploding into the gates of hell with a loud, unceremonious *Bang!*

Ngotho woke up with a jump. He mopped the sweat on the tail of his sheet. This kind of thing would bring him no good. Before, he had been dreaming of beer parties or women or fights with bees as he tried to smoke them out for honey. Now, lately, it seemed that when he wasn't being smoked out of this city, where he so very much belonged and yet never belonged, he was either pleading his case at the White Gates or being condemned to hell in cheap coffins. *This kind of thing just isn't healthy* . . .

But he was in top form. He flung the blanket away. He bent his arms at the elbow for exercise. He shot them up and held them there like a surrender. *No that will not do*. He bent them again and pressed his fingers on his shoulders. They gathered strength, knitting into a ball so that his knuckles sharpened. Then he shot a dangerous fist to the left and held it there, tightly, not yielding a step, until he felt all stiff and blood pumped at his forehead. Dizziness overpowered him and his hand fell dead on the bed. Then a spasm uncoiled his right which came heavily on the wall and, pained, cowered. Was he still a stranger to the small dimensions of his only room even after eight years?

But it wasn't the first time anyhow. So, undaunted, he sprang twice on the bed for more exercise. Avoiding the spring that had fetched his thigh a blow yesterday morning between the bulges in the old mattress, he hummed *Afrika nchi yetu*[1] and shot his leg down on the bed. Swa – ah! That would be three shillings for another sheet through the back doors of the Khoja Mosque. Ngotho dragged himself out of bed.

It was a beautiful Sunday morning. He felt he had nothing to worry about so long as he did not make the mistake of going to church. Churches depressed him. But that dream still bothered him. At least they could have used a less precipitate rope. And those nails. Didn't he have enough things pricking him since

Mrs Knight gave him a five-pound handshake saying Meet you in England and Mrs Njogu came buzzing in as his new Memsahib borrowing two shillings from him?

Ngotho folded his arms at his chest and yawned. He took his moustache thoughtfully between his fingers and curled it sharp like a bull's horns. At least she could have returned it. It was not as if the cost of living had risen the way people borrowed from you these days. He stood at the door of the two-room house which he shared with the other servant who, unlike him, didn't cook for Memsahib. Instead Kago went on errands, trimmed the grass and swept the compound, taking care to trace well the dog's mess for the night. Already Ngotho could see the early riser as good as sniffing and scanning the compound after the erratic manner of Wambui last night. (Wambui was the brown Alsatian dragged from the village and surprised into civilization, a dog-collar and tinned bones by Mrs Njogu. Her friend Elsie Bloom, a widow, also kept one and they took their bitches for walks together.) Ngotho cleared his throat.

'Hei, Kago!'

Kago, who was getting frost-bite, rubbed his thumb between his toes and turned round.

'How is the dog's breakfast?'

'*Nyukwa!*'[2]

Ngotho laughed.

'You don't have to insult my mother,' he said. 'Tinned bones for Wambui and cornflakes for Memsahib are the same thing. We both hang if we don't get them!'

Kago leant on his broom, scratched the top of his head dull-wittedly and at last saw that Ngotho had a point there.

He was a good soul, Kago was, and subservient as a child. There was no doubt about his ready aggressiveness where men of his class were concerned it was true, but when it came to Mrs Njogu he wound his tail between his legs and stammered. This morning he was feeling at peace with the world.

'Perhaps you are right,' he said to Ngotho. Then diving his thumb between his toes he asked if there was a small thing going on that afternoon – like a beer party.

'The queen!'

At the mention of the name, Kago forgot everything about drinking, swerved round and felt a thousand confused things beat into his head simultaneously. Should he go on sweeping and sniffing or should he get the Bob's Tinned? Should he un-tin the Bob's Tinned or should he run for the Sunday paper? Mrs Njogu, alias Queen, wasn't she more likely to want Wambui brushed behind the ear? Or was she now coming to ask him why the rope lay at the door while Wambui ran about untied?

With his bottom towards Memsahib's door, Kago assumed a busy pose and peeped between his legs. But Memsahib wasn't bothered about him, at least not yet. She stood at the door, legs askew and admonished Ngotho about the cornflakes.

Kago breathed a sigh of relief and took a wild sweep at the broom. He saw Ngotho back against the wall of their servants' quarters and suppressed a laugh. After taking a torrent of English words, Ngotho seemed to tread carefully the fifty violent paces between the two doors, the irreconcilable gap between the classes. As he approached Mrs Njogu, he seemd to sweep a tactful curve off the path, as if to move up to the wall first and then try to back in slowly towards the Master's door and hope Memsahib would make way. For her part, the queen flapped her wings and spread herself luxuriously, as good as saying You will have to kneel and dive in through my legs. Then she stuck out her tongue twice, heaved her breasts, spat milk and honey on to the path and disappeared into the hive. Ngotho followed her.

Kago scratched his big toe and sat down to laugh.

Breakfast for Memsahib was over. Ngotho came out of the house to cut out the painful corn in his toe with the kitchen knife. He could take the risk and it pleased him. But he had to move to the other end of the wall. Mr Njogu was flushing the toilet and he might chance to open the small opaque window and see the otherwise clean kitchen knife glittering in the sun on dirty toe nails.

Breakfast. Couldn't Memsahib trust him with the sugar or milk even after four years? Must she buzz around him as he measured breakfast for two? He had nothing against cornflakes. In fact ever since she became suspicious, he had found himself eating more of her meals whenever she was not in sight, taking also some sugar in his breast pocket. But he had come to hate himself for it and felt it was a coward's way out. Still, what was he to do? Mrs Njogu had become more and more of a stranger and he had even caught himself looking at her from an angle where formerly he had stared her straight in the face. He had wanted to talk to her, to assure her that he was still her trusted servant, but everything had become more entangled and sensitive. She would only say he was criticizing, and if he wasn't happy what was he waiting for? But if he left, where was he to go? Unemployment had turned loose upon the country as it had never done before. Housewives around would receive the news of his impertinence blown high and wide over Mrs Njogu's telephone before he approached them for a job, and set their dogs on him.

Ngotho scratched at his grey hair and knew that respect for age had completely deserted his people. Was this the girl he once knew as Lois back in his home village? She had even been friends with his own daughter. A shy, young thing with pimples and thin legs, she taught at the village school and had been everybody's good example. She preferred to wear cheap skirts than see her aging parents starve for lack of money.

'Be like Lois,' mothers warned their daughters and even spanked them to press the point. What they meant in fact was that their daughters should, like Lois, stay unmarried longer and not simply run off with some young man in a neat tie who refused to pay the dowry. Matters became worse for such girls when suddenly Lois became the heroine of the village. She went to jail.

It was a General Knowledge class. Lois put the problem word squarely on the blackboard. The lady supervisor who went round the schools stood squarely at the other end, looking down the class. Lois swung her stick up and down the class and said, 'What is the Commonwealth, children? Don't be shy, what does this word mean?'

The girls chewed their thumbs.

'Come on!' she shouted and seeing it was hopeless said, 'All right. We shall start from the *beginning*. Who rules England?'

Slowly, the girls turned their heads round and faced the white supervisor. Elizabeth, they knew they should say. But how could Lois bring them to this? England sounded venerable enough. Must they go further now and let the white lady there at the back hear the Queen of England mispronounced, or even uttered by such tender things with the smell of last night's onions on their breath? Who would be the first? They knit their knuckles under the desks, looked into their exercise books and one by one said they didn't know. One or two brave ones threw their heads back again, met with a strange look in the white queen's eye which spelt disaster, immediately swung their eyes on to the blackboard and catching sight of Lois's stick, began to cry.

'It is as if you have never heard of it.' Lois was losing patience. 'All right, I'll give you another start. Last start. What is this country?'

Simultaneously, a flash of hands shot up from under the desks and thirty-four breaths of maize and onions clamoured, 'A colony!'

Slowly, the lady supervisor measured out light taps down the classroom and having eliminated the gap that came between master and servant, stood face-to-face with Lois.

The children chewed at their rubbers.

Then the white queen slapped Lois across the mouth and started for the door. But Lois caught her by the hair, slapped her back once, twice, and spat into her face. Then she gave her a football kick and swept her out with a right.

When at last Lois looked back into the class, she only saw torn exercise books flung on the floor. Thirty-four pairs of legs had fled home through the window, partly to be protected from the white queen's Government which was certain to come, and partly to spread the formidable news of their new queen and heroine.

Queen she certainly was, Ngotho thought as he sat by the wall and backed against it. Cornflakes in bed; expensive skirts; cigarettes. Was this she? Mr Njogu had come straight from the University College in time to secure a shining job occupied for years by a *mzungu*. Then a neat car was seen to park by Lois's house. In due course these visits became more frequent and alarming but no villager was surprised when eventually Njogu succeeded in dragging Lois away from decent society. He said paying the dowry was for people in the mountains.

As luck would have it for Ngotho, Mr and Mrs Knight left and Mr and Mrs Njogu came to occupy the house. He was glad to cook and wash a black man's towels for a change. And, for a short time at any rate, he was indeed happy. Everybody had sworn that they were going to build something together, something challenging and responsible, something that would make a black man respectable in his own country. He had been willing to serve, to keep up the fire that had eventually smoked out the white man. From now on there would be no more revenge, and no more exploitation. Beyond this he didn't expect much for himself; he knew that there would always be masters and servants.

Ngotho scratched himself between the legs and sank against the wall. He stared at the spider that slowly built its web meticulously under the verandah roof. He threw a light stone at it. He only alerted the spider.

Had his heart not throbbed with thousands of others that day as each time he closed his eyes he saw a vision of something exciting, a legacy of responsibilities that demanded a warrior's spirit? Had he not prayed for oneness deep from the heart? But it seemed to him now that a common goal had been lost sight of and he lamented it. He could not help but feel that the warriors had laid down their arrows and had parted different ways to fend for themselves. And, as he thought of their households, he saw only the image of Lois whom he dared call nothing but Memsahib now. She swam big and muscular in his mind.

Ngotho wondered whether this was the compound he used to know. Was this path connecting master and servant the one that had been so straight during Mrs Knight's reign?

Certainly he would never want her back. He had been kicked several times by Mr Knight and had felt what it was like to be hit with a frying pan by Mrs Knight as she reminded him to be grateful. But it had all been so direct, no ceremonies. They didn't like his broad nose. They said so. They thought there were rats under his bed. There were. They teased that he hated everything white and yet his hair was going white on his head like snow, a cool white protector while below the black animal simmered and plotted: wouldn't he want it cut? No, he wouldn't. Occasionally, they would be impressed by a well-turned turkey or chicken and say so over talk of the white man's responsibility in Africa. If they were not in the mood they just dismissed him and told him not to forget the coffee. Ngotho knew that all this was because they were becoming uneasy and frightened, and that perhaps they had to point the gun at all black men now at a time when even the church had taken sides. But whatever the situation in the house, there was nevertheless a frankness about the black-and-white relationship where no ceremonies or apologies were necessary in a world of mutual distrust and hate. And if Mrs Knight scolded him all over the house, it was Mr Knight who eventually seemed to lock the bedroom door and come heavily on top of her and everybody else, although, Ngotho thought, they were all ruled by a woman in England.

Ngotho walked heavily to the young tree planted three years ago by Mrs Njogu and wondered why he should have swept a curve off the path that morning, as memsahib filled the door. He knew it wasn't the first time he had done that. Everything had become crooked, subtle, and he had to watch his step. His monthly vernacular paper said so. He felt cornered. He gripped the young tree by the scruff of the neck and shook it furiously. What the hell was wrong with some men anyway? Had Mr Njogu become a male weakling in a fat queen-bee's hive, slowly being milked dry and sapless, dying? Where was the old warrior who at the end of the battle would go home to his wife and make her moan under his heavy sweat? All he could see now as he shook the tree was a line of neat houses. There the warriors had come to their battle's end and parted, to forget other warriors and to be mothered to sleep without even knowing it, meeting only occasionally to drink beer and sing traditional songs. And where previously the spear lay by the bed-post, Ngotho now only saw a conspiracy of round tablets while a *Handbook of Novel Techniques* lay by the pillow.

He had tried to understand. But as he looked at their pregnant wives he could foresee nothing but a new generation of innocent snobs who would be chauffeured off to school in neat caps hooded over their eyes so as to obstruct vision. There they would learn that the other side of the city was dirty. Ngotho spat right under the tree. Once or twice he would have liked to kick Mr Njogu. He looked all so sensibly handsome and clean as he buzzed after his wife on a broken wing with a spot of jam on his tie, saying he wanted the key to the car.

He had also become very sensitive and self-conscious. Ngotho couldn't complain a little or even make a joke about the taxes without somebody detecting a subtler intention behind that smile, where the servant was supposed to be involved in full-scale plotting. And there was behind the master and the queen now a bigger design, a kind of pattern meticulously fenced above the hive; a subtle web, at the centre of which lurked the spider which protected, watched and jailed. Ngotho knew only too well that the web had been slowly, quietly spun, and a pebble thrown at it would at best alert and fall back impotent to the ground.

He took a look at the other end of the compound. Kago had fallen asleep, while Wambui ran about untied, the rope still lying at the door, in a noose. Kago wore an indifferent grin. Ngotho felt overpowered, trapped, alone. Someday, one could be driven to suicide. He spat in Kago's direction and plucked a twig off one of the branches on the tree. The tree began to bleed. He tightened his grip and shed the reluctant leaves down. Just what had gone wrong with the gods?

The old one had faithfully done his job when that fig tree near Ngotho's village withered away as predicted by the tribal seer.[3] It had been the local news and lately, it was rumoured, some businessman would honour the old god by erecting a hotel on the spot. Ngotho hardly believed in any god at all. The one lived in corrupted blood, the other in corruption itself. But at least while they kept neat themselves they could have honoured the old in a cleaner way. How could this new saviour part the warriors different ways into isolated compartments, to flush their uneasy hotel toilets all over the old one?

Ngotho passed a reverent hand over this wrinkled forehead and up his white hair. He plucked another twig off the dangerous tree. Something was droning above his ear.

'What are you doing to my tree?'

The buzzing had turned into a scream.

'I . . . I wanted to pick my teeth.' Ngotho unwrapped a row of defiant molars.

The queen flapped her wings and landed squarely on the ground. Then she was heaving heavily, staring at him out of small eyes. He tried to back away from her eyes. Beyond her, in the background, he caught sight of Mr Njogu through the bedroom window polishing his spectacles on his pyjama sleeve, trying desperately to focus – clearly – on the situation outside. A flap of the wing and Ngotho felt hit right across the mouth, by the hand that had once hit the white lady. Then the queen wobbled in mid-flight, settled at the door and screamed at Mr Njogu to come out and prove he was a man.

Mr Njogu didn't like what he saw. He threw his glasses away and preferred to see things blurred.

'These women,' he muttered, and waved them away with a neat pyjama sleeve. Then he buried his head under the blanket and snored. It was ten o'clock.

Ngotho stood paralysed. He had never been hit by a woman before, since he left his mother's hut. Involuntarily, he felt his eyes snap shut and his eyelids burn red, violently in the sun. Then out of the spider's web in his mind, policemen, magistrates and third-class undertakers flew in profusion. He opened his eyes, sweating, and the kitchen knife in his hand fell down, stabbing the base of the tree where it vibrated once, twice and fell flat on its side, dead.

Then with a cry, he grabbed it and rushed into the house. But Mr Njogu saw him coming as the knife glittered nearer and clearer in his direction, and leapt out of bed.

Suddenly the horror of what he had done caught Ngotho. He could hear the queen crying hysterically into the telephone, while Mr Njogu locked himself in the toilet. Ngotho looked at the kitchen knife in his hand. He had only succeeded in stabbing Mr Njogu in the thigh and the knife had now turned red on himself. Soon the sticky web would stretch a thread. And he would be caught as he never thought he would when first he felt glad to work for Lois.

NOTES

Afrika nchi yetu[1] – *(Kiswahili) Africa our Land. A patriotic, nationalist song.*

Nyukwa[2] – *A Kikuyu word of abuse.*

Predicted by the tribal seer[3] – *A reference to the well-known prophecy of Mugo wa Kibiru, a famous Kikuyu seer. He foretold the coming of the white man to Kikuyu country but he also predicted that the Europeans would depart when a certain fig tree at Thika near Nairobi withered and died. The tree died in 1963, the year Kenya became an independent nation.*

EXERCISES

1. 'The Spider's Web' opens in a powerfully dramatic and compelling manner. Explain:
   a) Why we can describe the opening as 'powerful' and 'dramatic' and 'compelling'.
   b) How the nightmare is connected with the story's main theme.

2. This story is mainly concerned with the master-servant relationship. How are Ngotho's relationship with the Knights and with the Njogus similar; how are they different?

3. Though 'The Spider's Web' is mainly concerned with the master–servant relationship, it is also about the distorted values of post-Independence Kenyan society. What are the values of the 'new' Kenya which Kibera attacks?

4. Notice how Kibera uses various images and symbols in this story: the coffin, the bee and the title image of the spider's web.
   a) *The coffin image*: Why is this such an appropriate image to describe Ngotho's feelings about his present situation?
   b) *The queen-bee image*: After her confrontation in the classroom with the white lady supervisor, Lois is described as the village's 'new queen and heroine'. Later in the story as Mrs Njogu, Ngotho's employer, she is referred to as the 'queen-bee'. How does this change of image from 'queen' to 'queen-bee' accurately reflect the change that occurs in Lois?
   c) *The spider's web symbol*: As we have noted in the Introduction, a symbol has a suggestive power by being able to work on several levels. This is evident in the symbol of the spider's web.
      i) Read the story closely and then explain how and to what purpose Kibera uses this symbol in the story.
      ii) How can the web image work in a different way, to

suggest another possible human reality, i.e. the web of human relationships and bonds in society?

When you are tackling this question you might want to think about the following points. Firstly, the way ecologists perceive our planet's ecosystem as a web: when any one, even very tiny, part of nature is interfered with, changed or destroyed by man, it has disastrous effects on the whole ecosystem.

Secondly, ponder the implication of the following lines by the seventeenth century English poet John Donne. He emphasizes the oneness of humankind, how all of us are enmeshed in a web of common human needs, sympathies and relationships and how we all share an eventual fate: death.

No man is an island, entire of itself; every man is a piece of the continent . . . any man's death diminishes me, because I am involved in Mankind; and therefore never send to know for whom the bell tolls; it tolls for thee.

General Exercises

1. Read the autobiography of Mugo Gatheru, titled *A Child of Two Worlds*. Compare Gatheru's attitude to his 'dual heritage' (the traditional and the modern) with that of the narrator in 'Who Am I?' in this anthology. Which writer's attitude do you sympathize with more?

2. In several stories in this collection the writers use nature to reflect human feelings and social circumstances. Select three stories and explain how each writer does this.

3. Briefly describe how in *each* of the following stories, the writer uses animal imagery for a specific purpose: 'It's a Dog's Share in Our Kinshasa', 'Tekayo' and 'Incident in the Park'.

4. Re-read 'A Mercedes Funeral' and 'Who Am I?' Compare and contrast the relationship and careers of the narrator and Wahinya in the former with those of the narrator and Gathu in the latter.

5. In a satiric story the author's tone can be sharply or affectionately humorous. Compare the satiric tone in Kimenye's 'The Battle of the Sacred Tree' with the tone in *one* of the following stories: Kibera's 'The Spider's Web', Ngugi's 'The Mercedes Funeral'.

6. Freedom fighters are the subject matter of two stories in this collection, 'Departure at Dawn' and 'A Kind of

Fighting'. On what particular aspects of their lives do Kahiga and Mchombu focus?

7. Instant justice is an issue of concern in East Africa. Read the story 'Incident in the Park' and the poem 'The Kondo of Katwe' by Richard Ntiru which you will find in his collection *Tensions*.
   a) What is the attitude of Meja Mwangi and of Richard Ntiru, in their story and poem respectively, to the victim of instant justice? To the instant justice mobs and the society that breeds them?
   b) How do the accounts in this story and poem differ from reports of instant justice incidents in the local newspapers? (Refer to specific reports to make your comparison.)
   c) Compare Mwangi's treatment of instant justice in 'Incident in the Park' with Kibera's treatment of public executions in 'It's a Dog's Share in our Kinshasa'. What similarities do you notice in both subject matter and style?
   d) What are your own feelings about instant justice? Is it really 'justice'?

8. A major theme in much African writing has been the contrast between the town and the village. The former symbolizes modernism and its attendant evils; the latter stands for the traditional values and way of life. The contrast in most imaginative literature is biased towards village life.

   Referring to relevant stories in this anthology, to other stories, poems, plays and novels you have read, and to your own experience and knowledge, write an essay balancing the merits and disadvantages of both rural and city life.

9. 'The Spider's Web', 'Incident in the Park' and 'A Mercedes Funeral' deal with post-independent Kenyan society.
   a) Collectively, what impressions do these stories give of contemporary Kenyan society?

GENERAL EXERCISES

b) From your reading of other African literary works, would you say the general picture is much the same all over the continent?

In answering both questions illustrate your answer with concrete examples from the stories themselves.

10. Read the description of Nalwoga at work in the first paragraph of 'Her Only Child'. What does the author reveal in this passage about Nalwoga, her feelings about her family and about her life generally?

You will find it rewarding to compare this description of the young housewife at work with similar sections describing work in two other fine African novels.

In chapter seven of *A Grain of Wheat* Ngugi wa Thiong'o describes the carpenter Gikonyo at his daily work and later mending a *panga* handle for Mumbi the young woman he loves. Read both passages (pp. 85–87 and p. 94 in the 1967 Heinemann edition of the novel), then answer the following questions.

a) What do we learn of Gikonyo the man in the detailed description of him busy in his workshop?
b) Why does Gikonyo feel strong, free, peaceful, 'in love with all the earth' when he is mending Mumbi's *panga*?
c) Does daily work, a job well done, have the power to transform our lives even momentarily the way it does Gikonyo's? Is this true of all work or only certain kinds?

In his autobiographical novel *The African Child*, Camara Laye describes a traditional society which values order and ritual. Read chapter two which recounts the work of the author's father, a renowned goldsmith.

d) When Laye's father creates a gold trinket for a customer, it is more like a ceremony than ordinary work. Do you agree with this assessment?
e) Are there some similar ceremonies surrounding certain kinds of work in your community? If there are, describe *one* such ceremony in detail.
f) If you were allowed a choice between two similar items (say two necklaces or leather belts), one hand-crafted, the other factory-made, which one would you prefer? Why?

Further Reading

Below are listed some of the better East African and African collections and anthologies of short stories. An asterisk indicates that the work listed contains other literary material (such as poems, short plays, excerpts from novels) in addition to short stories.

East African collections

Kahiga, Sam *Flight to Juba* (Longman, 1979)
Kariara, Jonathan *The Coming of Power* (OUP, 1986)
Kibera, Leonard and Kahiga, Samuel *Potent Ash* (EAPH, 1968)
Kimenye, Barbara *Kalasanda* (OUP, 1965)
Kimenye, Barbara *Kalasanda Revisited* (OUP, 1966)
Mwaniki, Ngure *The Staircase* (Longman, 1979)
Ngugi wa Thiong'o *Secret Lives* (Heinemann, 1975)
Ogot, Grace *Land Without Thunder* (EAPH, 1968)
Seruma, Eneriko *The Heart Seller* (EAPH, 1971)
Taban lo Liyong *Fixions* (Heinemann, 1969)

African collections

Aidoo, Ama Ata *No Sweetness Here* (Longman, 1988)
Achebe, Chinua *Girls at War* (Heinemann, 1972)
Ekwensi, Cyprian *Lokotown* (Heinemann, 1966)
Guma, Alex La *A Walk in the Night* (Heinemann, 1968)
Honwana, Luis Bernardo *We Killed Mangy-Dog* (Heinemann, 1969)
Idris, Yusuf *The Cheapest Nights* (Heinemann, 1978)

Lessing, Doris *Nine African Stories* (Longman, 1968)
Marechera, Dambudzo *The House of Hunger* (Heinemann, 1978)
Mphahlele, Ezekiel *In Corner B* (EAPH, 1967)
Nicol, Abioseh *The Truly Married Woman* (OUP, 1965)
Salih, Tayeb *The Wedding of Zein* (Heinemann, 1969)

East African and African anthologies

Beier, Ulli (ed.) *Political Spider*, an anthology of stories from *Black Orpheus* (Heinemann, 1969)
*Cook, David (ed.) *Origin East Africa* A Makerere anthology (Heinemann, 1965)
Denny, Neville (ed.) *Pan African Short Stories* (Nelson, 1965)
de Grandsaigne, J. (ed.) *African Short Stories in English* (Macmillan, 1985)
*Green, Robert (ed.) *Just a Moment, God!*, an anthology of verse and prose from East Africa (EALB, no date)
*Hughes, Langston (ed.) *An African Treasury* (Crown Publishers, 1962)
Komey, Ellis Ayitey and Mphahlele, Ezekiel (eds.) *Modern African Stories* (Faber, 1964)
Larson, Charles R. (ed.) *Modern African Stories* (Collins, 1977)
*Mphahlele, Ezekiel (ed.) *African Writing Today* (Penguin, 1967)
*Rive, Richard (ed.) *Modern African Prose* (Heinemann, 1964)
Rive, Richard (ed.) *Quartet: New Voices from South Africa* (Crown Publishers, 1963)

Magazines and journals

Magazines and journals are a very useful source of East African short stories. Unfortunately, most of those listed below have ceased publication but it is possible to find back copies in East African university libraries.

Busara (*Nexus*)
Dhana (*Penpoint*)
Ghala (the annual creative writing issue of *East Africa Journal*)
Joe
Kenya Weekly News
Transition
Umma (*Darlite*)
Viva
Zuka